UNRAVELING

E.W Johnson M.D.

PAGE PUBLISHING, INC.
Conneaut Lake, PA

First originally published by Page Publishing 2020

This book is a work of fiction. The story is merely the construct of a mind gathering fragments of information for six decades on this planet. Any resemblance to actual places or people is coincidental. No harm was intended. If any was perceived, I apologize.

ISBN 978-1-64584-486-0 (pbk)
ISBN 978-1-64701-159-8 (hc)
ISBN 978-1-64584-487-7 (digital)

To Debbie and Mika, who with grace and
great patience tolerated the insanity.
Thank you

INTRODUCTION

THE SCIENTISTS TEACH US THERE ARE four chambers in the heart, and that if these enlarge, they become the precursor to a catastrophic event.

The poets remind us that the human heart is a construct of infinite rooms, each unique in dimension and design; some bathed in vibrant colors and radiant light that overwhelm the eye, others so darkly captive in shadow they defy clarity of vision; some warm and welcome and open to the world; some hidden beyond dim passageways and bolted shut to forever forbid trespass; some an exultant celebration of knowledge and discovery; and some prisons of sadness and grief that offer nothing of salvation beyond the taste of tears. And they set forth the proposition that if the heart does not grow daily, does not enlarge to encompass humanity, the natural world around us, the wonder of the universe, then it is already failing.

If both of these postulates are accepted as concurrent truth, we continue to progress. One without the other condemns us to a barren landscape that leads us no closer to the ultimate plan of creation.

You decide.

1

Dr. Sean Nolan dropped his two daughters off at middle school and arrived at his clinic just before eight thirty. For eighteen years his schedule had always been the same. His number one priority was to make the first of the two pots of coffee that would carry him through the day. His second task was to review all the lab tests and special reports that had come in over the fax machine and to note any follow-up exams that were indicated.

He would only turn on the light in his office while he worked. The rest of the clinic was dark and quiet, the proverbial calm before the storm. It was the only peaceful arc of time he would have until late at night, and he treasured every moment.

At ten to nine every light in the clinic came to life, announcing the arrival of his head nurse, Catherine

Engram. Nicknamed Cat, she had been with him for seventeen years. A local girl, he had hired her fresh out of school, and it was the smartest business decision of his career. She was intelligent, energetic, intuitive, could fix anything, and anticipated his every need. Her talents also included putting up with his fluctuating moods and bearing the waves of anger and frustration that rolled through the clinic if patient care was compromised or delayed.

"Good morning, Cat," Dr. Nolan called out from his office.

"Not so good," she said. "You want to start early?" She nodded toward the door. He knew from her eyes there was a problem. They were always buried under a full schedule of patients two to three weeks out, but there were always add-ons and walk-in emergencies.

"What have we got?" he asked.

"Nosebleed for the last hour," Cat answered. "Now she's throwing up blood."

Dr. Nolan nodded. He grabbed his stethoscope, placing it around his neck, slid a reflex hammer into his left front pocket, a prescription pad into his right front pocket, checked to make certain there were two pens in his shirt, and gave her a smile.

"Okay, let's wag it and shag it! Put her in the surgery room please."

Cat went out to get the patient settled. She had already pulled the chart for him and placed it on the lab counter. Dr. Nolan picked it up and did a quick review, noting her past medical history and list of current medications.

He had known the forty-two-year-old woman for over a decade, and she only came in for legitimate complaints.

She was sitting up on the surgical table when he came into the room, a bloody towel held up to her face.

"You been picking your nose again, Twila?" he asked. He grabbed an otoscope and a wooden tongue blade.

"No," she laughed. "I just woke up with blood all over the pillow."

"Maybe your husband punched you in his sleep. He's an evil man," Dr. Nolan joked. "Now, open your mouth and let me see the back of your throat." With the woman sitting upright, there was no visible fresh blood in the pharynx, a good sign.

Dr. Nolan grabbed a four-by-four gauze bandage, cut it in half, rolled it up tightly, then soaked it in Neosynephrine. He brought the head of the surgical table to thirty degrees.

"This won't feel good, but it will stop the bleeding," he explained. He forcefully shoved the bandage as deep into her nasal cavity as he could, then he had her hold pressure against her nose. The medicine on the gauze would force the blood vessels to constrict.

"This your first bloody nose?" he asked, washing his hands.

"No. One last week," the woman said. "But not this bad."

Cat came back into the room with an ice pack wrapped in cloth. She held this against the patient's forehead.

Dr. Nolan looked at the woman. She was pale with dark circles beneath her eyes. He pulled up the sleeves on her sweater, then both pant legs. There were multiple bruises on her arms and legs.

"You just rest here for a while," Dr. Nolan said. "And I want the nurse to draw some blood. Okay? She's in a good mood this morning, so it should go fine."

He went back to his office. His receptionist and second medical assistant had arrived, and the first patients were already waiting in rooms. Cat followed, and he closed the door behind her.

"What do you want drawn?" Cat asked. She already knew he was worried.

"I need a blood count here, and a chemistry panel to send out. Who brought her in?"

"Her husband," Cat answered. "He's out in the truck smoking. You want him?"

"Not yet," Dr. Nolan said. "I'll be in room one. Knock when you have some numbers."

Cat went back to the surgical suite to draw blood, and Dr. Nolan grabbed the chart for the first scheduled patient. It was one of his log truck drivers, a favorite repeat customer. The man was horribly overweight, suffered from type II diabetes and high blood pressure.

"Sorry we're running late," Dr. Nolan apologized as he entered the room, shaking the man's hand. "So, how have you been, you big fat slob?"

"Doc," the man laughed, "is that any way to talk to your patients?"

"I only talk that way to the big fat slob patients," Dr. Nolan explained. "Your glucose reading is 323, and your

HBA1C is up over eight. What the hell have you been doing?"

The man nodded, held out his hands, and shrugged. "I know. I know," he confessed. "You remember that free sample of medicine you gave me? I ran out."

"When?"

"A month ago," the man admitted.

"You lose my phone number?" Dr. Nolan asked.

"No. I just got busy and I forgot."

"Well, when you get gangrene in your feet and develop heart and kidney failure, you won't be so busy," Dr. Nolan said, looking the man directly in the eyes.

"Jeez, Doc, okay, okay," the man said. "You got any more of those pills?"

"I can always get you medication," Dr. Nolan explained. "But you've got to do your part. I need you to get back on your diet and take your meds every day." He listened to the man's heart, lungs, and checked his legs for any fluid retention. Then he went to the back storage room where they kept samples of drugs acquired from pharmaceutical companies. He brought back enough medication to last for a month.

"I want you back in four weeks," Dr. Nolan told the man. "I'd kind of like to keep you around awhile, so please behave. And in a month, if your numbers aren't better, I'm going to take you out back and shoot you."

The man stood up, laughing again.

"Ain't that illegal?"

"Not in your case," Dr. Nolan explained. "It would be a mercy killing. Now, get out of my clinic." He walked with him to the waiting room door, making certain he was scheduled for a follow-up appointment in one month, then Dr. Nolan went back to the exam room to write his chart notes. He hated computers and refused to adopt any technology that took even one minute away from direct patient care.

He was just finishing his writing when Cat knocked on the door.

"Entre, s'il vous plait," he mumbled. She handed him the lab printout of the woman's blood profile.

"Pretty ugly," Cat said. Her medical knowledge base and years of experience had already made the diagnosis clear.

"Fuck," Dr. Nolan sighed, looking at her cell counts. The patient with the nosebleed was severely anemic, and her white blood cell level was ten times normal. She had advanced leukemia.

"Okay, I'm going home now," he told Cat. "You go tell her."

"Very funny. This is why you get the big money and I get minimum wage," Cat answered.

"When the hell did I raise your pay to minimum wage? It's just one bad piece of news after another this morning." Dr. Nolan shook his head. The attempted humor was failing to offer any redemptive solace. It was the worst duty of his profession, and there was no way to escape it.

"Do you want me to get her husband?" Cat asked.

Dr. Nolan stood up and handed her the chart he had finished.

"Not yet," he said. "I'll explain things to her first. Women are tougher. When she's ready, we can bring him in."

Cat nodded and went to the nurses' station. Dr. Nolan returned to the surgery suite. He gently removed the nasal packing and examined the woman's nose and throat. The bleeding had stopped. He closed the door, then pulled up a stool and sat next to her.

"Have you been tired lately?" he asked, smiling at her.

She knew from his tone of voice that it was not a random question. For weeks she had known something was wrong.

"I get tired easy doing housework, chores," she admitted. "What did the blood test say?"

Dr. Nolan held out his hand and took hers. "Every day we tell people good things and sometimes bad things," he began. "And sometimes terrible, scary things. I'm afraid this is one of the scary things." He could feel her grip tighten around his fingers.

"How scary?" she asked.

"Your blood counts show a type of leukemia," he explained. "An abnormal white cell has taken over your bone marrow, and now there's no room left for the normal cells. That's why you've had the nosebleeds and the bruising."

The woman nodded. She did not cry, but there were tears threatening.

"Is this going to kill me?" she asked him.

"There are treatments that are often curative," Dr. Nolan told her. "But this is going to be a dirty, knock-down fight. There will be chemo and probably a bone marrow transplant. And all of it will be ugly and hard to get through. But I've known you long enough that I believe you can win this fight."

The woman nodded and managed to smile.

"And when does all this start?"

"Now," Dr. Nolan said. "You need a transfusion to boost your blood and platelet levels. We don't need an ambulance. Your husband can drive you to the hospital. And I'm going to call the best cancer specialist I know and have him there to meet you."

"Wow," the woman sighed deeply.

"That's one word for it," Dr. Nolan said. "My word started with the letter 'F'. I'm sorry to have to tell you this. When you're ready, we'll get your husband, and I'll answer any questions you have. Then we have to get you to the hospital. Okay?"

She squeezed his hand again. "Thank you," she said. "I just need a few minutes."

Dr. Nolan stood up and went to the door. "Tell the nurse when you're ready," he said. He went out and found Cat, giving instructions on notifying the emergency room and calling Dr. Browerd at Vancouver Clinic Oncology.

"How did it go?" asked Cat.

Dr. Nolan winced and closed his eyes for a moment. "She thanked me," he said, shaking his head. "Sometimes I hate this job."

"Yeah, I know," Cat agreed. "And now we're way behind."

"What's in room two?" Dr. Nolan asked.

"COPD patient. Bad cough and wheezing for two days," Cat answered.

"Thank God, something easy! Let's get our skates on, people." Dr. Nolan disappeared down the hallway to the second exam room. He ramped up his normal pace and averaged five patients an hour until nearly one in the afternoon, but they were still running late. His daily break time for lunch was no longer possible. After losing a vote taken among the staff, they had pizza delivered and tried to eat in between patients.

Dr. Nolan hated pizza.

"You realize, this isn't really a democracy. This is a dictatorship. And I'm Dick," he told his staff, all gathered around the nurses' station, just near the posted sign that said no food or drinks were allowed in the lab.

"No, you are a dick," Cat corrected him. Amanda, his receptionist, and Evie, the other medical assistant, found this to be a hilarious quip.

"That's why you get minimum wage," he told her. "You're supposed to be my loyal staff. Empathetic. Caring. Nurturing. Subservient. Obedient."

The eyes of the three women grew larger and larger.

"Have you been smoking funny tobacco?" Amanda asked. "Maybe you haven't been keeping up with current events, but those days are long over."

Dr. Nolan pretended to be shocked. "Jesus, when did this happen? You mean my dreams of being the alpha male in a utopian white world are ruined?"

"That's right, buddy," Cat said. "You work for us now. And you can start by giving us all raises."

Dr. Nolan looked at them and smiled. In many ways it was true. They had all been with him for years, and he could not do his work effectively without them.

"Done," he said. "Everyone goes up a dollar an hour starting now. And that means I go down three dollars an hour. At this rate, I'll be out of business in about five years. I hope you're all happy now."

"Very," Cat said, her eyes flashing. They were all devoted to him, even though he was frequently an insufferable ass. And they were all deeply proud of their service to the community.

"Now that I'm bankrupt and have acid indigestion from eating this crappy food, can we get back to work?" he pleaded.

"Slave driver," Amanda muttered, heading back to the front office.

"Ogre," Evie said.

Cat gave him a knowing smile.

"Thank you," she said. Now thirty-eight, she was strikingly attractive with a captivating presence. He had spent more time around her than any woman on earth, and since the death of his wife four years ago, there had been moments of temptation between them. But she was happily married, and he had accepted the reality that his life was equally shared between raising his two daughters and his professional role as the town doctor. There was no room for anything else. But there were moments.

The exam rooms began to fill again, and the constant rotation of patients fell into the usual pattern. At around three o'clock his daughters, Cienna and Aubriel, now 14 and 12, came into the clinic and dropped their book bags in his office. Most weekdays they were stuck there until the clinic closed using the time for homework, and usually complaining about their harsh confinement.

Dr. Nolan kissed them between patients and asked about their day.

"School sucks," Aubriel said. "It's boring. Can we walk up to the drive-in and get French fries?"

Dr. Nolan recognized it was not a perfect system, but there was nowhere else they could spend time. They had an aunt that lived nearby, but she worked until five. He took a ten-dollar bill from his wallet and gave it to Cienna.

"Stay together, and come right back," he instructed her. "Then homework."

"Okay, thanks," the older girl said. At least it would provide a small break.

"You're going to love this," Cat said from the nurses' station. "Jim Belson is on the phone. He says his brother is acting weird. He put a coffee cup on the counter upside down and just kept pouring coffee into it. What do you want me to tell him?"

Dr. Nolan looked at the clock and sighed. It was going to be a late night.

"Tell him to get here as quick as they can."

Cat was back on the phone. Dr. Nolan went up to the front desk to tell them Ed Belson was coming in and to see if one of the later patients could be rescheduled. It was just one of those days.

He finished with two more rooms before Ed and his brother arrived. Over the years he had cared for three generations of the Belson family. They had lived in the area for over a century, settling in Woodhaven just about the time it was founded in 1905. Once a thriving logging community, its location along the I-5 freeway and Columbia River had made it a perfect transition zone for light industry and manufacturing.

Ed Belson was an engineer that had been in charge of a number of multimillion-dollar developments in the Southwest Washington area. He was bright, energetic, and famous for telling stories about local characters.

Cat had gotten him onto the exam table in room one, and his brother was sitting in the corner chair.

"So, what's the story?" Dr. Nolan asked. He shook hands with both men. Ed was quiet and withdrawn, but he was moving all his extremities, and his face was symmetric.

"He started calling me two, three days ago complaining about headaches," Jim started. "And then he would call back and tell me the same thing, over and over. I finally went over to his house, and he did the weird thing with the coffee."

Dr. Nolan nodded, but he was watching Ed. All his responses were in slow motion.

"You have a headache now?" he asked.

Ed nodded and put his hand up to his forehead.

"Any visual changes? Double vision? Dizziness?" Dr. Nolan asked. He had Ed squeeze his hands on the right and left, then checked his reflexes.

"Blurry," Ed answered.

Dr. Nolan took an ophthalmoscope from the drawer.

"Now, I'm going to turn the light out. Then I'm going to examine the back of your eyes. Try to look straight ahead, if you can. This is kind of bright." He looked through both pupils, studying the arteries and optic disc area where the visual nerve fibers entered the retina. The left optic disc was nearly obliterated.

"Okay, good job. Now, I need to go out and make a phone call. Give me a few minutes."

He tilted his head, coming down the hallway, letting Cat know it was time for another private meeting. They were back in his office behind closed doors.

"I need Vancouver Radiology on the phone, whoever's in charge. And I need you to give Ed 100 mg of prednisone now, please."

Cat knew that a dose of steroids so high was not good news. "What are you thinking?" she asked.

"I think he has a tumor in his brain. I just don't know where it is or how big it is. And we don't know if it's a primary lesion or a metastatic lesion."

Cat stared at the floor. She had also known the Belson family most of her life.

"Goddamn it! I wish today was over," she said. She went out to call the hospital, and Dr. Nolan stayed at his desk, waiting.

"Line two," Cat called out.

Dr. Nolan grabbed the phone as if it might escape.

"Hello, who's this?" he asked.

"Dr. Crutchmeir. What's up? That you, Sean?"

Dr. Nolan knew all the staff in the specialty services at Vancouver Memorial Hospital. Even though they were thirty miles away, it was his only option for CTs and MRIs. His clinic dealt with them on a daily basis.

"Yeah, you lazy bastard." Dr. Nolan laughed. "I know all you do all day is look at pictures, but I need a favor. I've got a fairly young man with a probable brain mass. I need you to tell me what we're dealing with."

There was a pause on the line. Dr. Nolan knew the radiologist was looking at the clock and probably an over-booked schedule. It was almost four.

"You have an authorization from his insurance company?" Dr. Crutchmeir asked.

"Fuck, no." Dr. Nolan laughed again. "I don't deal with idiotic referral networks very well. This guy is wealthy, and if he stiffs you, I'll pay the bill myself. I just need answers."

"I'm glad to see your diplomatic skills haven't deteriorated." Dr. Crutchmeir sighed. "Send him down. You want a call?"

"Please," Dr. Nolan said. "I'll stay in the office until I hear from you. And thanks."

"Add it to all the other favors you owe me for. It's a good thing I like you," the radiologist added. And it was true. Dr. Nolan's reputation over the years had been built on a tenacious, no-nonsense approach to putting patients first. It was not about business or rules or regulations or protocol. It was just about people.

"Don't get mushy," Dr. Nolan warned him. "The patient's name is Ed Belson. His brother will bring him in. Half an hour. And no matter what everyone else says about you, I think you're okay."

"Now who's getting mushy? Call you when I can offer some insight." The line went dead.

Dr. Nolan jumped up and went back to room one. Cat had given Mr. Belson the steroids.

"Okay, James. We managed to get an emergency CT at Vancouver. Just pull up to the ER, and they'll get him in as quickly as possible. We don't need to be in the hospital for now. Wait there after the scan and I'll explain what we find. They can't tell you anything."

James was nodding, but he could sense the urgency. "Is this bad?" he asked.

Dr. Nolan forced a smile. He looked at Ed and nodded slowly.

"We've known each other a long time, so I won't bull-shit you. This is bad. We just don't know how bad. The medication will help your symptoms," he explained. "But the CT will tell us where we go next."

"Okay, Doc," James said, helping his brother down from the exam table. "ER. CT. Wait for your call. Got it." Their eyes met for an instant before they left the room. There was no way to minimize the ugly reality.

Dr. Nolan immediately resumed work, seeing two more patients before his daughters returned. They took over his office and desk, leaving him to write chart notes at the nurses' station. It was now almost five.

"We've got a head laceration coming in," Amanda announced from the reception area. Evie gave an audible groan.

"What's the deal?" Dr. Nolan asked. "You got a hot date?"

Evie blushed. Another local, she was the definition of a good girl. Shy and slightly overweight, her social life was not a very deep subject.

"My mom's birthday," she explained. "We were taking her out."

"Jesus, how old is your mom now? A hundred and three, four?" Dr. Nolan asked. Evie's mother was also a patient, and he knew she was just approaching fifty.

Evie laughed. "If I tell her you said that, you'll be in big trouble," she said.

"I'm always in trouble anyway," Dr. Nolan said. "You take off. Cat can set up the surgery room. As soon as the patient shows up, lock the doors, and everyone can go. Cienna can be my assistant."

His older daughter heard her name.

"Do what?" she called out from his office.

"Help sew a guy up," he answered. "You want to scrub in?"

Cienna bounded into the hallway, an enormous smile on her face. She had come to the clinic after hours and on weekends with her father since she was four. The medical emergencies both fascinated and excited her, and she was already making plans to pursue a career in medicine. And Aubriel was the complete opposite. She was the introverted, quiet daughter who read voraciously and spent her free time writing poetry and short stories. The sight of blood made her squeamish.

"I get to glove up?" Cienna asked. It was probably a violation of dozens of rules and regulations, but Dr. Nolan had needed her help on numerous occasions.

"Damn right," he said. "I love to employ people who work for free. And we better start thinking about what to order for dinner. I'm not cooking tonight."

"Pizza!" Aubriel shouted.

"Pizza!" Cienna agreed.

Dr. Nolan held his forehead and leaned forward on the counter.

"Goddamn it," he moaned. "Just kill me now and get it over with."

Cat laughed out loud. "I'll call it in. You want the bake-at-home order?"

Dr. Nolan nodded. "And a Caesar salad," he added. "I can't eat more cardboard."

"Laceration's here," Amanda warned them.

Cat went to the reception area and escorted the young man to the surgery room. He was holding an oily, blood-soaked rag over his right eye. Cat had him lie back on the adjustable table.

Dr. Nolan and Cienna followed close behind.

The rag was removed, exposing a jagged three-inch laceration running at an angle across the man's forehead and into his eyebrow, nearly to the bone. The wound was bleeding heavily.

"Sorry, Doc," the patient said.

"You should be." Dr. Nolan smiled. "Because of you, I have to eat pizza. What the hell hit you?"

"Binder strap broke," the man explained. "Came flying over the truck and smacked me right in the face."

Dr. Nolan was drawing up a syringe of Lidocaine to numb the damaged tissue. "Did it knock you out?" he asked.

"No. Just pissed me off," the man answered.

"Log truck drivers don't have any brains, anyway," Dr. Nolan told him. "So I think you're pretty safe. This is going to sting for a minute." He began to infiltrate the wound edges. When he was finished, he had Cat set up a surgical tray, scrub the laceration site, and open two packs of suture material.

"Okay, you're done," he told her. "And thank you for all your help today. This was a rough one."

"You sure?"

"Easy money," Dr. Nolan said. Cienna was already washing her hands with a sterile brush, eager to get started.

Cat gave him a glance from the doorway.

"Let's hope tomorrow's a better day," she said.

Dr. Nolan nodded his head. "Can't imagine one any worse than today. Now, go home." He watched her leave the room, then went to the sink. He opened two sets of sterile gloves and laid them on the counter. After adjusting the bed position and the surgical light anchored above them on the ceiling, he proudly supervised as his daughter displayed perfect technique putting her gloves on. He positioned her on the opposite side of the table and handed her a stack of wound bandages and a pair of scissors.

"Now," he told the patient, "there should be no pain while we work. If there is, just tell me."

"Okay, Doc. This your kid?"

"My new surgical assistant." Dr. Nolan smiled, glancing at his daughter. "She's earning her dinner. You mind if I do a little teaching while we sew you back together?"

"Nope. Just don't say 'oops.' That would make me nervous."

"Deal," Dr. Nolan laughed. He locked the suture material into the needle driver. "Okay, daughter dear. Usually you repair wounds by always closing the opening by halves. But with a jagged tear, we want to fit the landmarks back together to realign the tissues." He identified two V-shaped gashes just above the eyebrow. The first two stitches closed them perfectly. He slowed his hand motion to let her see the knot pattern that locked each suture in place. Her job was to blot away any excess blood from the wound and cut the stitches as her father worked. In fifteen minutes there was a neatly closed straight line where the gaping wound had been.

Dr. Nolan applied a bandage to the area and lowered the surgical table.

"That's it, man, good as new," he told the patient. "Come back tomorrow and fill out the job injury paperwork. It's too late to worry about it now."

"Hey, Doc, maybe I need some Vicodin for all this pain," the man said, trying to act mortally wounded.

"Nice try," Dr. Nolan laughed. "Go home. Drink some beer and take an Aleve. That's all you get." He led the man back to the main entrance and unlocked the door.

"Thanks, Doc. You're the best," the man said.

"I had a good nurse to help me. See you tomorrow." He watched the man walk to his truck and drive out of the parking lot. He was just relocking the door when the phone rang. He leaned over the check-in counter and picked up the receiver. It was Dr. Crutchmeir.

"You were right. Two and half centimeter mass in the left frontal lobe. The lesion has an enhancing halo around it. Sorry," the radiologist said.

Dr. Nolan closed his eyes for a moment and sighed.

"Thanks for the quick work," he said. "Can you put the man's brother on the phone?"

"Sure, let me switch you back to the waiting area. Talk to you later."

The phone call was transferred, and after a minute, James was on the line.

"Well, not good news," Dr. Nolan began. "There is a tumor, and it appears to be one of the worst types. It's called a glioblastoma multiforme."

"And what does that mean?" James asked.

"Surgery, radiation, and chemotherapy," Dr. Nolan told him.

"And what are his chances?"

"Not very good," Dr. Nolan answered. "I'm sorry."

There was a long silence.

"Man, things can sure change in a day." James sighed. "What do we do now?"

"Go home. Eat. Rest. I'll call the neurologist in the morning, and we need to start him on a medicine called Decadron. That's all we can do for now."

"Okay. Thanks for explaining things," James said. "I'll wait for you to call."

"Try to get some sleep," Dr. Nolan told him. "Things are going to get hectic starting tomorrow."

"Right. Okay. Will you tell Ed all this tomorrow? I can't do it," James said.

"Sure. He'll feel better tomorrow. Come by the clinic in the morning, and I'll answer any questions you have. All right?"

"Good. Good. Okay. Tomorrow then. Thank you again," James said, his voice clouded with both disbelief and anguish.

"Just be there for him," Dr. Nolan said. "That's your job now."

James hung up the phone.

"Man, that was cool!" Cienna said, still exuberant over her role as surgical assistant.

Dr. Nolan hugged her tightly. She had no way of knowing that he had just proffered a death sentence. "I'm proud of you, young lady. You did great," he told her.

"Gross," said Aubriel, wrinkling her face. "Can we go now?"

"Yes, we can finally go. Get your bags." While they went to collect their belongings, Dr. Nolan looked over the day's schedule. They had seen twenty-six patients, and two of them had been potentially terminal illnesses. The day had mostly been positive and constructive, but his mind was overwhelmed by the two patients he could not help.

"Ready. Let's blow this Popsicle stand," Cienna said, still beaming. They went out the back door, already a dark and cold November night. Dinner was collected on the way out of town. The I-5 freeway took them north to the exit near Kalama, then they doubled back on winding country roads to a dead-end street running uphill, ending in a steep driveway to their house.

The home itself was a modest three-bedroom structure, but it rested on a fifty-acre tract of timberland with a sweeping view of the Columbia River and the southern valley all the way to Portland. It was a private, hidden enclave that was visited by deer, elk herds, coyotes, and an occasional bear. And it was peaceful.

Callie, their golden lab, was dancing in the headlights as they drove in, every part of her in animated motion. She half jumped on Dr. Nolan a dozen times, then greeted the girls.

"At least somebody loves me," he lamented, unlocking the door.

"Oh, Dad, we love you," Cienna assured him. "Now you've got dog hair all over your pants."

"How long till we eat?" Aubriel called from the living room, already grabbing up the remote to the T.V.

"Forty minutes," he said, preheating the oven. "Cienna, put this in when the timer goes off. Set it for twenty minutes, but keep checking it till the crust turns brown. I've got to feed the animals."

"Why do I have to do everything?" Cienna demanded.

"Because you're my assistant. Now, just do it, and don't burn down the house," her father said, then jogged up the stairs to the master bedroom. He pulled off his clothes and redressed in barn attire; thick wool socks, jeans, a flannel shirt, and a pullover sweatshirt. Downstairs again, he filled a plastic sandwich bag with six Fig Newtons, slid into the boots by the laundry room door, then headed for the barn. He petted Callie as they walked. Whenever he was home, she was at his side.

As he opened the door to the barn, he was met by an orchestra of baaing and braying. His other family consisted of four miniature donkeys and two Nubian goats named Briggs and Stratton. Feeding time was the highlight of their day. They crowded around him, jostling for position, as he distributed grain in the feeding troughs. Once they were occupied with food, he could clean the floor and restock the mangers with hay.

It was Dr. Nolan's escape. There were no ringing phones, no voices, no questions to answer or decisions to make. He sat down on the edge of one of the steel feeding bins, the donkeys taking turns laying their heads across his lap to get their necks and chests rubbed. They were just bigger than a large dog and were the most gentle creatures imaginable.

"Who wants cookies?" Dr. Nolan asked. They were already nuzzling his pocket, fully aware that he had treats. Each donkey and each goat received their reward, then regrouped to attack the fresh hay supply. He gave each animal a final pet, locked the gate, refilled their water bucket, then headed back to the house.

He kicked off his boots at the doorway, fed Callie and freshened her water, then washed up in the kitchen sink.

"Jeez, you stink," Cienna said, just pulling the pizza out of the oven.

"That's Eau de Mule," her father answered. "And I think they smell wonderful."

"Whatever. What kind of dressing you want on your salad?" she asked. Ever since the death of their mother, she had tried to be more helpful, but her efforts were limited.

"Always Ranch. I'm a rancher, get it?"

Cienna shook her head and gave him a dark look. "Not funny," she told him, getting out plates and silverware. "Abby! Dinner!"

They sat down at the table, but there was always one empty chair. It was a subject that they did not speak about often, but it was always present, just an arm's reach away.

"Good day at school?" their father asked.

"Pretty good," Cienna answered, "but I don't like biology."

"If you want to be a doctor, part of you has to be a scientist too," her father explained. "It's important to know how things work."

"This is flowers and trees. Not very interesting. The animal and human stuff is better," Cienna said.

"I hate it all, except English," Aubriel said.

Dr. Nolan nodded. He tried to avoid lectures and conflict whenever possible. They were actually both good students, and thankfully there had been no serious behavior issues to deal with.

"You seem bummed out," Cienna told him. "Bad day at work?"

His daughters knew almost everyone in town, so he was always careful not to use names when talking about work. But there were days when the darker aspects of his profession followed along with him like a black cloud. And this was one of those days.

"Sad day," he admitted. "I had to tell two fairly young patients that they had cancer."

"We know them?" Cienna asked.

Their father nodded. The rumor network in small towns equaled the speed and efficiency of the internet. He knew that within a few days, the local community would hear some version of the story.

"Are they going to die?" Aubriel asked.

"One yes, the other maybe," he answered. "I don't think I've ever had two people in one day diagnosed with cancer. It pisses me off and makes me sad at the same time."

"Like with Mom," Aubriel said softly, but it wasn't really a question.

"That's right," her father said. "Just like with your mom. It's okay to be angry, confused, sad, hate the whole world for a while. Then we have to get back to the business of living. And sometimes that's the hardest part."

He didn't know what else to say. Dealing with their grief and sense of loss had plagued him for years. His own agony at times was still nearly unbearable, and all he could offer them was to be there every day and to be a stable support.

"What's for dessert?" Aubriel asked. It was a welcomed change in direction.

"Ice cream in the freezer. And I bought Oreos," their father said. He collected their plates and rinsed them.

"I get the bathroom first," Aubriel announced.

"Don't be a bitch, Abby! You get water all over the floor!" Cienna countered.

"Whoa! Whoa! Language, please," Dr. Nolan said. "I need laundry first. Whoever is done with homework first gets the shower. And then you can watch TV till ten." He smiled. Everything was back to normal.

Cienna and Aubriel settled into their standard pattern with only a few minor skirmishes. Over the next three hours, Dr. Nolan ran the dishwasher, did two loads of clothes, vacuumed the dog hair from the living and dining rooms, and helped with random math problems. At about ten he got them into their rooms and kissed them good night, knowing they would be on their computers or listening to music until much later.

He got the coffee ready for the next morning, took Callie out for a final duty call, locked the doors, and retreated upstairs. A quick shower got rid of the residual barn odor. He stood staring at his face in the mirror, noting the dark circles of fatigue under his eyes.

"Just a day in the life," he sighed. He set the alarm. If there were no emergency calls, he might get six hours of sleep before it all started again. There was no longer a beginning or an end to his life. It was all a circle.

He tried to relax and clear his thoughts but kept seeing the faces of the two patients with cancer, the look in their eyes. He rolled over to check the clock, then fixed his gaze on the photograph of his wife on the nightstand. He ached to talk to her, to touch her, to hear her, to feel the warmth of her. He wanted her to know he was trying his best to keep going. And he wanted her to understand that he felt like a complete failure.

2

ONE WEEK LATER, DR. NOLAN EVALUATED a patient in his late thirties with abdominal pain that was worse after eating. His lab work showed only a moderate elevation of his liver enzymes, and an ultrasound was ordered to rule out gallstones. During a break between patients, Cat told him radiology had called and needed to speak with him. He nodded and had her dial the number.

"Line three. Dr. Marshall," Cat said.

"Jesus, now what?" Dr. Nolan asked, picking up the phone.

"Hi, Sean. This fellow you sent down has a liver tumor the size of a golf ball right up against the biliary duct. I'm surprised he's not jaundiced. You guys have bad water up there?"

"Bad something," Dr. Nolan said. His mind was filing through a dozen questions. The patient had no risk factors that would lead to liver cancer. He was not a drinker or a smoker, and his work did not expose him to any known carcinogens.

"What do you want to do?" Dr. Marshall asked.

"You have time to CT him from his head to his pelvis?" Dr. Nolan asked.

"Can do. We can't give him any results. You want him back in your office?"

"Oh, sure. I'm getting good at telling patients they have life-threatening diseases."

"You do seem to be on a roll lately," Dr. Marshall admitted. "I'll fax the CT report as soon as it's typed."

"Thanks," Dr. Nolan said. "I wish I could say it was nice talking to you."

"Yeah. I get that a lot. Later, Sean."

Dr. Nolan stared out the window. Three patients with advanced cancer in one week. For a small town, that was an extraordinary number. The statistical probabilities were like winning the lottery.

"Hey, Cat! Can you come here for a minute?"

Cat came to the doorway, and he motioned for her to sit down.

"We've got another cancer patient," he told her. "Mr. Watkins didn't have gallstones. He's got a goddamn liver mass."

Cat frowned. She had gone through school with Jared Watkins and graduated in the same class. She knew his wife and their three children. "Does he know yet?"

"No. He's coming back after they do a full CT scan. I get the pleasure of telling him he's in big trouble," Dr. Nolan said. He took a legal pad from his desk and handed it to her.

"What's this for?" she asked.

"Your penmanship is a little better than mine," he admitted. "I want a list of all the patients with cancer in the past few years. Start with the three we have now and work backwards. We've had two smokers with lung cancer, three or four old guys with prostate cancer, two breast cancer patients last spring, and the teenage boy with leukemia last summer. The Martin boy. But I know I'm forgetting some. See what you and Evie can come up with."

Cat looked at him and shook her head. "You want Megan on the list?" Megan was his wife, another breast cancer victim.

"Yes, Megan, too," he said. "Maybe Amanda can run some kind of computer search based on cancer codes? Whatever you can think of. This is bugging the hell out of me."

Cat already had nine names written down. "Okay. Let me see what we come up with. You all right?"

"It's a little challenging to be upbeat and jovial when my patients are dying," he admitted.

"I know the feeling," Cat said. It had affected everyone in the office.

"We could run off to Tahiti," Dr. Nolan suggested. "You think your husband would mind?"

She looked at him with just the trace of a smile. "Probably," she said. "And your daughters might not like it either."

He nodded. It was that damned reality thing again. "Oh, well, back to work," he said.

Cat took the list of names with her and went to talk to Amanda in the front office. The chart belonging to Jared Watkins was on Dr. Nolan's desk. He put his right hand on it, knowing that later in the day he would have to deal with the human side of what they had found instead of the paper version. He hated it.

At the completion of his specialty training in internal medicine, Dr. Nolan had accepted a position with one of the larger HMOs in the Portland area. The salary and benefits were both extremely generous, but the rules and restrictive nature of how he was allowed to treat patients were suffocating. Evaluating even the most simple medical complaints became an obstacle course of referral forms and delays, often taking weeks to obtain test results that could have been done in hours. He could not justify the system to his patients or himself.

It had seemed an act of insanity to his peers when he purchased the solo practice of a retiring physician in Woodhaven. He would make far less money, would have no benefits, and would have to manage his own business. But from the first day he worked in his own clinic, it felt like home. And taking care of patients and their needs became the only priority. He did not work for a corporation. He only worked for them. The patients were his boss.

But the one thing he had never considered was that becoming part of the community meant he was joining a family. The upside was the personal connection of knowing his patients; their work, their families, the contributing factors that affected their lives, their hopes and dreams. And that was also the downside. Every loss was an intimate wound.

He buzzed Amanda on the intercom.

"Woodhaven Medical Clinic," she answered politely, then realized her mistake. "Sorry. It's a habit. Sometimes I answer at home the same way. What's up?"

Dr. Nolan laughed. "You sounded very professional. When my phone rings, I yell, 'What the hell do you want?' It's a much more direct approach."

"Hmmm, maybe I'll try that," Amanda said. "Now, what the hell do you want?"

"Smart ass," Dr. Nolan said. "See if you can find a number for the National Cancer Registrar. It's in DC or Virginia, if that's any help."

"Okay. I'll look it up in my spare time."

"You don't have any spare time," Dr. Nolan reminded her. Amanda also had two young daughters at home. Between work, school, and sports, her life was as hectic as his own.

"That's right," she agreed. "Then I'll just do it anyway."

"Good answer. Thanks." He checked his watch, noting it was already two thirty on the East Coast.

On another gloomy day, their last patient before lunch reluctantly provided a degree of comic relief. It was an eighty-year-old Scandinavian named Lars Helglund. He was barely able to walk, only taking small steps as he came down the hall with help from his wife. Lars rarely came to the clinic, much more content to let nature take her course or rely on home remedies. The fact that he had shown up meant everything else had failed.

"What's going on, Lars?" Dr. Nolan asked, shaking hands with the couple near the nurses' station.

"Oh, well, I have a butt pain," the elderly man explained, still with a heavy accent from the old country. "I can't sit. I can't walk. I can't do nothing."

"Let's go to the surgery room," Dr. Nolan said. He took Lars by the other arm and guided him along. Helga, the man's wife, was just shy of eighty, only about five feet tall, but still strong and active on their farm. Together they got Lars situated on the surgical table, rolling him to one side. Mrs. Helglund sat in a chair along the wall.

"Let's see what we've got," Dr. Nolan said softly. With Cat's help, they managed to inch his trousers and under-wear down, exposing a large abscess on his left buttock. The red, inflamed area was tense with pressure and mea-sured nearly four centimeters across.

"Wow," Cat sighed. She went to set up a surgical tray, already knowing what would be needed.

Mrs. Helglund leaned forward for a closer look.

"Oh my god, what is that!" she exclaimed, also with a thick accent.

"That's a Norwegian brain tumor," Dr. Nolan told her, and the old woman began to laugh, and her laughter grew in volume and pitch like rolling thunder. She was slapping her legs and rocking back and forth in her chair, laughing so hard that tears were streaming down her face.

"That's not so funny," her husband protested, but even he was laughing.

"Oh yes, oh yes, that's what it is," the old lady assured him. "And it's a big one!"

Cat was laughing as well, but tried not to make any sound. Only Dr. Nolan remained stoic and in control.

"I have seen cases like this before, and they're often fatal. Luckily, I think we've caught this just in the nick of time," he told the patient. "And speaking of nicks, you're going to feel one just about now." He swabbed the dome of the abscess and began injecting a numbing medicine.

"Aye, aye, aye, aye. That burns," Mr. Helglund moaned. Mercifully, the Lidocaine worked quickly.

"Will there be permanent brain damage?" Mrs. Helglund asked, starting to laugh again.

"We must all hope and pray for the best," Dr. Nolan said solemnly. He went to the opposite side of the surgery table, indicating to Cat and Mrs. Helglund to move out of the way. With one swift scalpel plunge, he opened the abscess pocket. Pus literally exploded from the wound, with the initial spray splattering the wall. Then it slowed to a thick wave of green, foul-smelling liquid, the consistency of syrup.

"Thar she blows!" said Dr. Nolan. He began squeezing the surrounding tissues to empty the wound pocket, then used blunt scissors to explore the cavity for any residual fluid. Satisfied, he had Cat flush the site with a diluted

Betadine solution, then packed the area with medicated gauze.

"My work is done," Dr. Nolan announced. He bowed to Mrs. Helglund, who politely offered him a round of applause. Her cheeks were still rosy red, and her eyes were sparkling with joy.

Dr. Nolan helped the old man sit up and readjust his clothing.

"God, that feels better already," Mr. Helglund sighed with relief.

"I'll bet it does," Dr. Nolan said. He wrote out a prescription for antibiotics. "Start taking one of these every eight hours. And come back tomorrow so we can check your wound."

"Can I work?" the old man asked. Dr. Nolan smiled at him. He was a tough old bird that never took a day off for any reason.

"Do whatever you feel like doing," Dr. Nolan answered. He knew the old man would do whatever he pleased, no matter what advice he offered.

"We've got potatoes to dig," Mr. Helglund said. "You want some?"

Dr. Nolan knew it was the man's way of thanking him and his staff.

"That would be great. Just don't get too rambunctious," he warned the man.

"Okay. Tomorrow. See you tomorrow." The old couple went out. Mr. Helglund was walking with his normal stride, and his wife was still smiling.

Cat was spraying the wall and floor with a strong disinfectant. The odor in the room was nearly unbearable.

"You're horrible," she said.

"But in kind of a sweet way, don't you think?" Dr. Nolan offered.

"No! Look at the chair," Cat said. "You had Mrs. Helglund laughing so hard she peed her pants."

There indeed was a large wet spot on the cushion of the chair. Dr. Nolan almost laughed, but knew it would not be a wise response.

"Now I have to clean the room and the furniture," Cat lamented. The temptation to push the boundaries of the moment tugged at him, but Cat's mood would not allow it.

"Okay. I'm going to lunch," he said. "Sorry for the extra work."

"Enjoy your lunch. You ruined mine," Cat said. He quietly left the room, got his coat, and snuck out the back door. After a quick drive home, a tuna sandwich that he shared with Callie, he was back in the clinic before one thirty. Amanda left a phone number on his desk.

"National Cancer Registrar," a woman's voice said.

"Hello. This is Dr. Sean Nolan out in Washington. Not DC. The state," he explained. "Do you have a research department or a statistics division?"

"Do you know the extension?"

"No. I'm sorry. I'm just trying to get information on how many cancer reports there are in this area."

"Hold please." He listened to music for two minutes, then had to explain his request all over again.

"Hold please." More music.

"This is Marcus. How may I help?" Dr. Nolan repeated his request a third time.

"You want all cancer reports for Woodhaven? We can't do that. Only counties," the man explained.

"That would be great," Dr. Nolan said.

"How far back?"

"As far as you can go," Dr. Nolan answered.

"That would be 1974," the man sighed. "And that would be a lot. Can you be more specific?"

Dr. Nolan tapped his pen on the desk.

"Take out prostate cancer. Every man gets prostate cancer if he lives long enough. And take out basal cell or squamous cell skin cancer. Will that help?"

He could hear computer keys being activated.

"Some," the man said. "You're still talking about tons of data. What county?"

"Cowlitz. C-O-W-L-I-T-Z," Dr. Nolan spelled it out. "Southwest Washington."

There was a long pause.

"It's late," the man apologized. "And this will take some time. Give me a fax number and your DEA number please."

Dr. Nolan read off the numbers.

"If there's a fee, I'll be happy to pay," Dr. Nolan told him.

"No. No charge. Hopefully, I can run this and get it to you tomorrow. Is this some kind of research project?"

"It is," Dr. Nolan answered. "We seem to be having an epidemic of cancer cases."

"We see weird patterns all over the country sometimes," the man said. "Let me know if you need anything else."

"Thank you. You've been very helpful, and I appreciate it," Dr. Nolan told him. He wrote down the man's name and number on his calendar. Now it was time for the living. He stuck his head out of the door and caught Evie's attention.

"Is it safe to come out?" he whispered.

"She's drawing blood in room two. The coast is clear." She laughed.

He pretended to make a dash for room one, giving Evie an exaggerated sigh of relief when he made it. If he stayed hidden in exam rooms and kept his mouth shut, he might just make it through the day.

3

When Dr. Nolan arrived at his clinic the next morning, his office floor was covered in copy paper that had overflowed from the fax machine. The information screen indicated there were over one hundred pages to go. After two failed attempts, he managed to reload the machine, and it dutifully began to print out another stack of names along with their diagnosis.

At the completion of the data transfer, he had over six hundred pages of cancer victims spanning nearly five decades. But the base figures were only the starting point. He would have to devise some way of narrowing the search to Woodhaven and the surrounding area before it would have any real value.

As usual, Cat was the first of his staff to clock in, but Amanda was only a few minutes behind her. Dr. Nolan called them into his office and pointed toward the mountain of paper neatly arranged on his desk.

"These are all cancer victims in Cowlitz County since 1974," he explained. "I need just people from Woodhaven and the rural area. You guys are the computer whizzes. Is there a way we can use zip codes or something to narrow this down?"

Cat and Amanda were staring at the tower of copy paper.

"But that data's not in our system," Amanda informed him. "We can't even institute a search."

Dr. Nolan frowned.

"I can access the medical examiners' files," Cat said. "It's all public information. But it will be one case at a time. If the zip codes don't match, we take them off the list."

"Good. Can you guys do that?" Dr. Nolan asked. Cat took the first page from the stack. It contained thirty names.

"Sure," she sighed. "If we both do this full-time, we should be done in about two weeks."

Dr. Nolan sat down and nodded. It was a daunting request.

"This is important," he said. "Would either of you put in extra hours to work on this? I know it's asking a lot, but I need answers."

The two women looked at each other and exchanged a shake of their heads.

"It'll cost you," Cat said. "But we'll split this up and get started. If Evie will help with patients, I can do some of this during the day."

"Perfect. And I'll cover all your time," Dr. Nolan said.

"Time and a half," Cat said.

"Jesus, I just gave you a raise." Dr. Nolan laughed.

"That was for normal stuff," Cat answered. "This isn't normal."

And she was right. This was above and beyond.

"How about double time?" Dr. Nolan suggested. "Will that ease the pain?"

Cat and Amanda smiled, each taking half the papers from his desk.

"That's a good start," Cat said. "And that list of our patients with cancer. We're already at sixty-two over the last four years."

Dr. Nolan seemed surprised by the number. Taking care of six thousand patients a year, it had become much too easy to erase the bad outcomes from his memory. Or perhaps it had become a necessary safety measure to keep moving forward.

"Okay. Good. Thank you both," he said. "I appreciate your help with this."

It was going to be a slow, time-consuming labor, but at least it was a beginning. He watched Cat and Amanda leave, deeply aware of their value to his practice and even more grateful for their loyalty to him.

The morning passed quickly, and before going home for lunch, Dr. Nolan stopped by the small building that served as City Hall and the police station. Everyone who worked there was a patient.

"Whoa, Doc, is this a house call?" one of the secretaries asked.

"Not medical," he smiled. "I was wondering if you had a large map of the city I could copy? And maybe the upriver area."

"We've got the big Pittman map of the county," she said. "I could downsize that to just this area."

"Great. That would be perfect," Dr. Nolan said.

The woman used the large copy machine for blueprints and managed to produce a three-foot map of Woodhaven and the surrounding hill country and farmland.

"This work?" she asked, laying it on the counter. "What are you looking for?"

Dr. Nolan surveyed the chart and smiled.

"This is a work of art," he told her. "I just wanted a bird's-eye view of the whole area. The town is growing so fast." He had no intention of telling her the real reason.

"Boy, that's for sure," she agreed. "New homes. New businesses. The high school is already talking about adding buildings."

"And more patients." Dr. Nolan smiled. He took the map from her. "Thank you for helping."

"Anytime, Doc," she said. "You have flu shots?"

"Every flavor you can imagine. Just stop by. No appointment necessary," he said.

She answered a ringing phone and waved as he went out.

Dr. Nolan headed home, then turned into Walmart at the last second. He purchased a large corkboard and an assortment of brightly colored pins. He was going to turn his new map into a color-coded display. Fully armed, he loaded up his car, checked on his animals at home, then enlisted Cienna and Aubriel to assist him when work was done.

He nailed the corkboard to his office wall, then taped the map in place at the corners.

"Okay, blue is for breast cancer, green for GI, red for blood cancers, black for brain, yellow for lung, and white for melanoma." He scribbled the key on a sticky note and placed it on the wall next to the map. Cienna looked at his handwriting and laughed.

"Maybe we should type this," she suggested.

"You sound like my nurses," Dr. Nolan said. He had the list of his own patients that had been diagnosed with cancer over the past four years. One by one he gave the color and general location, and his daughters took turns placing them on the map. Some of the hill addresses were difficult to find, but in twenty minutes, he had a plot of his first real data. When their mother's name came up, Dr. Nolan took a blue pin from Cienna and stuck it in the area north of town where their home was. He did not say anything, but both girls understood.

"So, what do we see?" Dr. Nolan asked, stepping back as far as his office space would allow.

"Most of the pins are right in town," Aubriel noted.

"So! That's because most of the people live in town," Cienna said sarcastically.

"Yes, but that's important," Dr. Nolan explained. "What else?"

"The yellow ones are mostly up in the hills," Aubriel said.

"Right. Good," their father said. "Old loggers and ranchers who smoked a lot. Good call."

"Most of the green and red ones are in the Bottoms," Cienna commented. "And three black ones too."

"Very good," Dr. Nolan complimented her. He stepped closer to the map. She was right. Most of the leukemia, breast and GI cancers were located between the town and the Columbia River in a flood zone nicknamed the Bottoms. It was a low-lying area bordered by the Lewis River to the south and the Columbia River on the west. In years with heavy rains and a large snowmelt from the Cascade Mountains, it was vulnerable to flooding. The worst of it came in 1948 when over twenty feet of water killed dozens of people and thousands of cattle.

Following that catastrophic event, Federal and State agencies worked together to build a dike system that proved amazingly effective. Thousands of acres of fertile soil were reclaimed and made safe, and a new generation of farmers and ranchers had taken root. Then, as the population soared, little by little, some land on the Bottoms was reclassified as commercial, and large and small businesses began to displace the farmers.

"What now?" Cienna asked. They were both enjoying the time spent helping their father.

Dr. Nolan looked at his watch. It was almost six thirty.

"Dinner. And we're late again," he said.

"Mickey D's!" Aubriel shouted.

Dr. Nolan made a face of disgust.

"Okay. But no more fast food for a week," he proclaimed. "I know you hate my cooking, but we can't eat like this."

"Whatever you say, Father dear." Cienna giggled. They had heard the same lecture a hundred times.

"I'm serious," he said, trying to sound serious. "I'm making spaghetti sauce tonight."

"But then you make us eat it three nights in a row," Aubriel whined.

"That's because it's good," their father said. "And I know how to make it."

Now both girls laughed. Their father's lack of culinary skills was a running joke.

Dr. Nolan pulled on his coat, took one last look at the map on the wall, then ushered them out to the car. He would never admit it, but McDonald's actually sounded good.

4

OVER THE NEXT TWO WEEKS, WORKING nights and weekends, Cat and Amanda streamlined the data from the
National Cancer Registrar down to just the patients in
the Woodhaven area. And each night, Dr. Nolan and his
daughters updated the map. There were now over five
hundred pins of various colors noting types of cancer and
where the people lived. And the vast majority were located
in the Bottoms.

The sheer number was at first a shock to Dr. Nolan.
Then it dawned on him that they were not all his patients.
Some families in the area had Kaiser coverage, some sought
care elsewhere, and some just never went to the doctor at
all. There was no conceivable way that anyone would have
noticed the increased cancer rate.

And it was not an aberration of just one category of malignancies. There was a notable increase in cancer rates for leukemia, breast cancer, and primary liver tumors, and a smaller statistical elevation for brain cancer. Even more disturbing was the age factor. Many of the patients affected were younger than expected based on nationwide averages.

Every time he entered his office, his eyes were drawn to the map. He could not stop thinking about it, and he could not stop looking at it. Even his dreams had been plagued in recent days. It had become a monolithic torment.

"Amanda! Can you track down whoever runs the city water system?" he yelled from his office, not bothering to use the phone system. His irritation was becoming more obvious to his staff, and even he was aware of it. He went to evaluate the next patient and was just finishing when Amanda knocked on the door.

"Line two. Tim Phillips," she said.

"Thank you," he said. "I promise not to yell for at least ten minutes."

He went back to his office, closed the door, glanced at the map, then picked up the phone. Tim Phillips had been a patient for over ten years.

"Tim, sorry to bother you, but where does the city get its water?"

"Reservoir above the Merwin Dam," Mr. Phillips answered. "The system was put in about fifteen years ago."

"Where before that?" Dr. Nolan asked.

"Came directly out of the river to a treatment facility. Why you asking?"

"Oh, nothing specific," Dr. Nolan said. "And how often is it tested?"

"Twice a week," Mr. Phillips said. "Is there a problem?"

"No. No. Just someone out in the Bottoms with an intestinal bug," Dr. Nolan lied.

"A lot of those folks still use well water, Doc. That way they avoid the water bills."

Dr. Nolan himself drew water from a well on his own property. "That's probably it," he said. "But could I get a printout of your last few test results? It would be interesting to look at."

"Sure. No problem. I'll drop them by. I've been meaning to schedule a physical anyway," Mr. Phillips said.

"That would be great," Dr. Nolan answered. "I always look forward to seeing you naked."

The other man was laughing. "You know why I like you, Doc! You don't have big hands. See you later."

Dr. Nolan was smiling when he hung up, but it did not last. City water was probably not an issue, but he wrote *well water* on a notepad and taped it next to the map with a question mark. Next he buzzed Amanda on the phone.

"Yes?"

"See? No yelling," he reminded her. "Now I need someone at the EPA please. Anybody but the janitor."

"I'll try," Amanda sighed.

Two more patients were dealt with before he was summoned back to the phone.

"Hello. Dr. Sean Nolan in Washington State. Who would I talk to about any known dump sites or environment hazards?" he asked.

"That would be archives. Please hold," the woman said, not waiting for a response. He wrote a complete chart note before a human being was back on the line.

"Yes?"

"Hello. Thank you. This is Dr. Sean Nolan in Southwest Washington. I'm trying to find out if there are any past or present toxic dump sites in this area?"

There was a pause before the man answered. "Do you have a specific complaint?"

"No. Totally nonspecific," Dr. Nolan admitted. "I have no idea what I'm looking for. A needle in a haystack probably. I just have a high number of cancer patients and a lot of questions."

"You'll need to fill out a request form on our website. Typical response time is two to three weeks," the man said.

Dr. Nolan sighed. His patience level did not extend to those boundaries. "You can't just look in your computer and tell me if there are any known sites in this area?"

"Not without the official request. Sorry. Get us the paperwork and we'll do our best to answer your questions."

Dr. Nolan thanked him curtly and slammed the phone down. Not only was the delay maddening, but it meant he had to spend time on his laptop. He wasn't certain which of those was the greater torture.

Amanda knocked on the open door. "Eileen called and asked if she could be seen as a walk-in?"

"Sure," Dr. Nolan answered. "She say why?"

"Nope. Personal," Amanda answered with a shrug of her shoulders.

Eileen Carson was his sister-in-law. Two years older than his wife, she had married a local berry farmer and had been a pillar of the community all her adult life. With three children of her own off to college or graduated, she had stepped in after Megan's death to help with his girls. She was a frequent babysitter and a constant source of emotional support. He had nicknamed her Saint Eileen.

But why did she need to see him? The farm had Kaiser insurance, and other than a rare sore throat or cough that could be dealt with over the phone, she never sought care from his clinic.

"Pencil her in last," Dr. Nolan said. "My girls will want to see her too."

He turned back to his desk and keyed in the EPA website. The request form was three pages long.

"Cat! I need a nurse!" he yelled, then remembered he had promised to stop shouting.

"You've got patients, you know?" Cat admonished him as she entered.

"I've got to fill out this goddamn form, and it's longer than a football field," he whined. "Can you get started on this? Then I'll fill in anything missing. I'll give you nine thousand dollars if you do it."

"No, you won't," Cat said. His allergy to computer work was legendary. "You're too cheap. Let me have a look." He vacated his chair, and she sat down, scanning the three pages.

"You're an angel of mercy," he said.

"No. I'm an enabler," Cat corrected him. "Go see patients. I'll fill in everything but the reasons for your request. That part you do."

Dr. Nolan smiled. He was off the hook again. By late afternoon the form was completed and sent off for consideration. Now came the wait.

Finishing with the last scheduled patient, Dr. Nolan could hear laughter and animated voices from his office. His daughters and their Aunt Eileen were catching up on family gossip. The latest farm disaster was that Uncle Mike had hit a drainage ditch in his new John Deere and broken the front axle, along with one of his front teeth.

"What's he more upset about? The tractor or his tooth?" Dr. Nolan asked.

"The tractor, naturally." Eileen laughed. "The tooth is a cheap fix. The John Deere will be thousands."

Eileen Carson was a pleasant-looking woman with an ever-present smile. Mildly overweight, her work schedule as a bookkeeper, coupled with farm duties, carried with it a seven-day-a-week job. Now nearing fifty, the lines of age and fatigue were beginning to show around her eyes.

"Maybe he's so old now he needs glasses?" Cienna joked, and they all laughed.

"I'll tell him you said that," Aunt Eileen warned.

Dr. Nolan caught her eye. "I've got to steal your aunt for a few minutes, ladies. Get back to homework." He motioned Eileen to the farthest room down the hall where their voices could not be heard. He had her sit on the exam table while he washed his hands.

"So, to what do I owe the pleasure of your company?" he asked.

"I found something," she said, looking down at the floor. "I check myself every month or two, and this wasn't there before."

Dr. Nolan forced himself to not show any emotion, but he was already concerned. "I have to bring a nurse in. Is that okay?" he asked. "Cat doesn't talk about patients."

Eileen nodded. "No. It's fine," she said. "I understand."

Dr. Nolan went into the hall far enough to catch Cat's attention and waved. She understood the implied necessity. Once she was in the room, Dr. Nolan had Eileen remove her blouse and bra. He laid her back on the table and had her place her left hand behind her head. Using the tips of three fingers, he slowly but firmly palpated the breast tissue and the lymph nodes in her axillae. Then he examined the right side. In the upper, outer quadrant was a firm nodule about one centimeter in diameter. No lymph nodes were enlarged.

"Is that painful?" he asked.

"No. Not at all," she replied.

He helped her sit up. "Put your top on and quit showing off," he quipped, handing her clothing back. Once she was dressed, he nodded to Cat and she left them alone.

"Well?" Eileen asked.

Dr. Nolan looked her in the eye. For a brief instant, he considered minimizing his findings or offering alternative possibilities, but he already knew the truth. And country people didn't appreciate anything less.

"You probably have an early breast cancer," he told her. "The good news is that none of your lymph nodes are enlarged. You need a CT and a biopsy as quickly as possible."

The color faded from her face. Eileen nodded at the news, but there were no tears. Those would come later in private. "I thought so," was all she said.

Dr. Nolan gave her a long hug. She had been there for his family during every phase of Megan's illness. Now the situation was reversing itself.

"You want to use Kaiser for that?" he asked. "It's going to get expensive fast, and they have good people. It's just the bureaucracy that slows things up. It will take them weeks to do what I can get done in two days."

Eileen nodded her head. "Can you call my doctor at Kaiser and tell them what you found?"

"I can," Dr. Nolan said. "And I can probably light a fire under their ass. Actually sounds like fun."

Eileen managed to smile. "I watched Megan go through this," she said. "Is it still the same?"

"CT. Biopsy. Lumpectomy. Radiation. Chemo," Dr. Nolan explained. "But now we save eighty-five percent of patients. That's a gigantic improvement."

Eileen sat for a moment, trying to sift through her thoughts. "Isn't there some gene that causes breast cancer? Do I need to worry about my daughters?" she asked. They were twenty-four and twenty-one.

Dr. Nolan nodded. "BRCA gene," he said. "But I tested Megan, and she was negative. You have no family history of this and no risk factors. This is like lightning hitting the same place twice. Or maybe more than twice."

"What do you mean?" Eileen asked, puzzled by his remark.

Dr. Nolan shrugged. "Just something I've been working on," he said, not wanting to offer any details. "It might help if you and Mike could give me a list of pesticides and chemicals you use the most. And your water. Where does it come from?"

"The river now," she answered. "We have our own purification system."

"And before?"

"Well water," she said.

He thought for moment. If there was a good place to start, it was with his own extended family. "Is the old well still in use?" he asked.

She shook her head. "Capped off years ago," she said. "But it's still there. Why?"

"I'd like to get water and soil samples from your farm. But it has to be a secret. I don't want any town talk to get started."

Eileen stared at him. "You think something could have caused this? Megan and me?" she asked.

Dr. Nolan was suddenly struck by his own mistake. He had placed Megan's pin in the map based on where their home was. But she had grown up on the Bottoms. He felt his cheeks flush.

"It's possible," he said. "All I know for certain is that the cancer rate is higher here than it should be. I'm just looking for answers."

"Okay. Let me talk to Mike," she said.

"And I'll call Kaiser," Dr. Nolan assured her. "I need your doctor's name and your insurance ID number. Expect a call early tomorrow." He gave her another hug.

"You won't say anything to the girls?"

"Not one word," he said. "If any information gets out, it will have to come from you."

Eileen smiled and tucked her blouse into her slacks. She took a deep breath and went back to his office to visit more with her nieces. She acted as if nothing out of the ordinary had just taken place, and it was a very convincing performance.

Dr. Nolan took the chart back up to the front desk and gave it to Amanda.

"No fee slip and no chart note," he told her. He did not want the risk of any breach in privacy. He would call her doctor first thing in the morning before his staff arrived.

"Okay, party's over," he said, clapping his hands. "We've got spaghetti waiting, and Aunt Eileen has to go plow the north forty."

His daughters hugged their aunt and headed for the back door. Dr. Nolan walked Eileen to the front entrance, watched his nurses leave, then locked up. He went back to his office and stared at the map. He took the blue pin from where it rested, held it in the palm of his hand for a moment, then placed it where Megan and Eileen had spent their childhood.

5

THE PERSONAL CALL TO EILEEN'S ASSIGNED physician at Kaiser went much smoother than Dr. Nolan had feared. No doctor wanted to be told how to treat their patient, so it was delicate ground to walk on. He identified himself, explained his findings, and made it very clear that this was family. It was an implied urgency.

The physician was a woman just two years out of training. She was warm, genuine, engaged, and left no doubt the problem would be handled quickly. He thanked her for listening and was delighted when Eileen called his clinic not twenty minutes later.

"Boy, you lit a fire, all right. You must have used a blowtorch," she told him. "I have an appointment at eleven and a CT this afternoon. Thank you, Sean."

He was both pleased and relieved. "I liked her," he said. "I think you're in good hands. She's young enough that she hasn't been corrupted by the system yet. But keep me updated. I want to know what the plan is."

"I will," Eileen promised. "Oh, and that other thing. I talked with Mike. Whatever you need to do it's fine with us. But weekends would be better. Fewer workers around."

"Good. Good," Dr. Nolan said. "Now I've got to figure out what I do with water and soil samples when I get them."

"Okay. I've got to run," Eileen said. "I'll call you later."

Dr. Nolan hung up just as Cat came into his office to retrieve a piece of equipment.

"Hey, Cat. Now that you're done horsing around with all that research on cancer patients, I've got another job for you," he smiled.

Cat gave him the dreaded look. "And when my husband divorces me, are you going to put my daughter through college?"

"Your daughter wants to be a barrel racer," he reminded her. "Besides, this is an easy one. If I get water and soil samples, where the hell can I get them tested? I don't want it to be local."

"Ask Google," Cat said. "Or Siri."

"Who are they?" Dr. Nolan asked, half seriously.

"Never mind," Cat sighed. "I'll see what I can find at lunch. Anything else? You want me to change the oil in your car?"

"That's tomorrow," Dr. Nolan said.

The look was deepening in intensity.

"Sometimes," she warned.

He nodded and pointed to the map. "You're the only one I can trust to do this," he told her. "There can't even be a whisper. Not to Amanda. Not to Evie. No one."

She understood, but sometimes the needling got a little too sharp. "We're all tired," she said. "You know how many extra hours we've put in. It's a lot."

He did know. And the consuming search for some kind of rational explanation was taking a toll.

"I'm grateful for everything you've done," he said. "Just not so good at telling you. How about lunch on me for the rest of the week?"

Cat smiled just enough to ease his guilt. "Anything we want?"

"Anything legal," he answered.

"You just bought a reprieve," she said. "And I'll find out about your samples. But you might consider a personal assistant. This is turning into a full-time job."

She left his office in a better mood, already making a mental list of nearby restaurants.

Dr. Nolan considered what she had said. He could actually use an assistant. But then the trust issue ended his deliberations. There was no one other than Cat that held his confidence. It was a partnership that had matured and strengthened over many years.

The rest of the week passed with just the routine of seeing patients. There were no terminal cases or suspected ones, and the easy flow of caring for common, everyday issues was a welcome relief. It was an emotional oasis for everyone in the clinic.

By noon on Friday, Cat had located a commercial lab in Portland that dealt with hazardous and toxic materials. That was the good news. The not-so-good news was the cost and the time frame.

"Four weeks! Are you kidding me!" Dr. Nolan exploded.

"There's more," Cat said. "If you collect the samples, they can't validate their authenticity. You'll get results, but they won't be certified."

Dr. Nolan nodded. At least that part made sense to him. For the findings to be officially recognized, there would have to be a chain of evidence, proof of their source. But that meant bringing in outsiders, and he was not yet willing to take that step.

"Okay. I get that," he acknowledged.

"And…you'll love this," Cat began. "Each sample will cost between three and four hundred dollars." She waited for his reaction, surprised when he just stared at his desk.

Dr. Nolan was doing math. If he pursued the testing of samples from the old floodplain, it could easily run into the thousands in a very short time period. He made a comfortable living, but he was not wealthy. Most of his IRA had vanished in the financial collapse.

"Well, what the hell," he said. "I'm not going to let this slide. Thanks, Cat. Anything back from the EPA?"

"Nothing yet," Cat told him. "You want me to call them?"

"No. Next week," Dr. Nolan said. "You've done enough."

Cat went back to her nursing duties. For the first time in weeks, she would have a normal Saturday and Sunday, with no distractions. It was almost surreal.

Dr. Nolan finished with the last patients, then went to the supply room and filled a bag with sterile sample bottles. His results might not be official, but he certainly knew how to protect them from any accidental contamination. His staff would have the weekend free, but he had other plans.

He and his daughters were just about to leave when the phone rang again. It was their Aunt Eileen. Her CT scan had been positive for a calcified mass in the right breast, and she had undergone a biopsy yesterday morning.

"How are you doing?" Dr. Nolan asked, not using her name.

"A little sore," Eileen said. Her voice was tired. "They just called with the results. You were right."

Dr. Nolan closed his eyes for a moment. He did not want to be right. "You okay? I could come over," he offered.

"No. It's just…you know. A little overwhelming right now. I haven't even told Mike. I think it's best if we just spend some time letting this settle in."

"I understand. Maybe we can drop by tomorrow," Dr. Nolan said. "But I'll leave that up to you."

"That would be good," Eileen answered. "We just need a little time."

Dr. Nolan put down the phone gently, even though his first instinct was to throw it against the wall. He took a deep breath.

"Who was that?" Cienna asked, sensing he was upset.

"Santa Claus." Her father forced a smile. "He wanted to know if you'd been naughty or nice."

"Right," she said. "That hasn't worked since we were little."

Dr. Nolan looked at them both, remembering them as children at Christmas time. It was often a shock to him to see how grown-up they were now.

"Just business," he said. "Let's go home."

He wanted to take a blue pin from the bottom of the corkboard and place it on the map, but it would have to wait until his daughters were not there as witnesses. It would be right next to their mother's.

6

SATURDAY MORNING WAS COLD AND OVERCAST, but there was no rain. Dr. Nolan made breakfast for his girls and finished his barn chores before calling Eileen. She was more rested and back to her cheerful self.

"Sure. Come down," she said. "We're just taking care of farm duties."

"You need anything?" he asked, leaving the question as open as possible.

"No. I'm good," she said. "You and Mike can go do something, and I'll talk to the girls."

He did not envy her that assignment, but he was also glad that he was not the bearer of bad news.

"Okay. About an hour," he told her. His daughters were grateful for the escape. They dressed in record time and then fought over who would sit in the front seat with their father. It was a daily ritual.

"One of you on the way down, the other on the way back," he said, smiling. "Same as always."

They weaved their way out of the hills and drove south to Woodhaven. Dr. Nolan stopped at a local bakery and picked up a dozen doughnuts on the way. Uncle Mike did not drink or smoke, but he did have a sweet tooth.

Both Mike and Eileen were in the old farmhouse when they arrived. It was a creaky, drafty two-story structure built in the thirties, but it had been the family home serving three generations. They were financially well-off and could afford to build a mansion if they chose, but there was no need. It was where they belonged.

"Doc, is that medicine?" Uncle Mike smiled, eyeing the pastry box.

"Best kind," Dr. Nolan said. "And it's free."

Mike took the box and immediately grabbed a chocolate-covered cake doughnut. His front tooth was still missing from the tractor mishap. At fifty, a lifetime of farm work had left him with bad knees and hips, and he moved stiffly, like someone much older.

"Jesus, Mikey, you look more like a Republican every day," Dr. Nolan joked. "You're fat, white, and you've got no teeth."

"Oh, don't start. Don't start, Doc." Mike laughed. "I just believe in hard work and earning your keep. No free handouts."

"Then give me back my goddamn doughnuts," Dr. Nolan said. Their favorite pastime was arguing political issues, but never to the point of acrimony.

"I'll give you the box back when it's empty," Mike offered.

The girls grabbed the doughnuts and headed for the kitchen. Aunt Eileen was lining up coffee cups.

"I want some," Cienna said.

"Me too," Aubriel added. It was a life pleasure their father had allowed them in their early years.

"I made enough for everybody," Eileen answered them. They all took seats around the large oak dining table.

"Doesn't that tooth hurt, Mikey?" Dr. Nolan asked.

"Damn right! Have to tip to one side to drink anything hot or cold. Can't fix it till next week," he said.

"You're lucky you didn't break your neck. Did it knock any sense into you?"

"Nope." Mike laughed. "I'm still farming." It was a tough business. He and Eileen managed over three hundred acres of strawberry and raspberry fields, and workers, legal and otherwise, were becoming harder to find each year.

"And what have you girls been up to?" Eileen asked.

"Just school," Cienna said. "No softball or soccer until spring."

"And you, Aubriel? You still writing?"

The younger girl nodded. "Mostly poetry," she said.

Eileen filled them in on what their older cousins were doing, then lamented that none of them had produced a grandchild yet.

"You're too young to be a grandma," Cienna told her.

Eileen was genuinely amused by her statement. "If only that were true," she said. "Besides, I want to spoil them while I can."

Her words were a sober reminder of why she wanted time alone with her two nieces. She caught Dr. Nolan's eye.

"Girls, Uncle Mike and I have an errand to run," he began. "Why don't you help your aunt for a while?"

"We're going to make cinnamon rolls so that Uncle Mike can have them with his doughnuts." Eileen laughed. "You two ready?"

Cienna and Aubriel were thrilled. At home he could rarely get them to help do anything, but anywhere else they became eager volunteers. It was a mystery he could never solve.

"Lead on, Mikey," Dr. Nolan said. The two men grabbed coats and gloves, and Dr. Nolan got the sample bottles from his car.

"You have a shovel?"

"Doc, I got any tool you can name," Mike told him. "Let's take the four-wheeler. Too muddy for the truck."

They loaded up and drove out through the rows of staked raspberries. The farm stretched for over a mile and a half north to south. A well-worn service road dotted with deep puddles finally led them to the old pump house.

"This hasn't been used in years," Mike told him. "I don't know if the pump will fire up or not. We may be hanging a tin cup down the pipe on a piece of string."

He took a large pipe wrench from the toolbox on the four-wheeler and strained to loosen the well cap. It wouldn't budge.

"Time for physics, Doc," he said. Mike rummaged around until he found a three-foot section of smaller pipe that fit over the wrench handle. "Now come here and help pull on this. More torque."

The two men pulled together, and the cap came loose.

"Pretty good for a dumb-ass farmer," Dr. Nolan complimented him.

"That was the easy part," Mike said. "Now, go flip that breaker switch inside the shed and pray this thing doesn't blow up."

Dr. Nolan did as instructed, closing his eyes when he clicked the breaker to the on position. There was no explosion, just the low hum of the pump motor. Mike tried to open the flow valve on the side of the well casing. A few taps with the wrench coerced it into compliance. A jet of filthy rust-colored water shot out nearly ten feet, then slowly began to clear.

"No lead pipes, right?" Dr. Nolan asked, taking one of the sample bottles from his pocket.

Mike turned the valve down to a trickle.

"No lead. All steel," he said.

Dr. Nolan filled the small container and tightened the cap. "Perfect. Now, I'd like to get a soil sample every half mile along your property. Is that okay?"

Mike shut off the electrical switch and replaced the wellhead. "You're the doctor." Mike smiled.

They drove out to the corner fence and took turns digging down about two feet in the rich earth. One by one they labeled specimens from the four different locations. Even in the cold air they were sweating.

"Jesus, this is like real work," Dr. Nolan said, his exhaled breath a heavy vapor.

Mike laughed. "Now you know why my knees and hips snap and pop like Rice Krispies." He scooted up and sat sideways on the four-wheeler. For a moment he looked up at the clouds, then stared at the ground. He was no longer smiling. His shoulders shook from one deep sob, then he held himself in check, refusing to show any tears. He took a series of deep breaths, clenching his fists.

"It's okay, Mikey," Dr. Nolan said. "I know everything you're feeling. I've been here before."

Mike nodded his head, but a full minute passed before he could speak. "Those guys at the hospital with their white coats," he said. "I don't know them. I don't like them. And I don't trust them. I just need to understand this in plain English."

Dr. Nolan knew exactly what he meant. "Eileen's cancer is early, and it hasn't spread," he told Mike. "The odds are very good that this can be cured."

Mike looked at him for the first time. "Are they going to cut her up?" he asked. There was fear in his eyes.

"No. They will not," Dr. Nolan said firmly. "They just take out a small area. Not like the old days. Then there will be radiation and medical therapy, but even that's much easier to take than it used to be."

Mike's breathing was back to normal. "So, you don't think this will kill her?" he asked.

"No, I don't," Dr. Nolan said. "I think this is a big, fucking, pain-in-the-ass nuisance, and that she's going to be just fine."

"Then that's good enough for me," Mike said, obviously relieved. "You done playing in the dirt?"

"For now. Who owns the next farm over?" Dr. Nolan asked, looking to the north.

"That's Lenny Darden. Darden Farms," Mike said. "He's got fifteen hundred acres now. Berries. Grass seed. Corn. Big operation."

Lenny Darden had been in his clinic before, but not on a regular basis.

"You know him very well?"

"Enough not to like him," Mike answered. "He's an asshole with money."

Dr. Nolan smiled. Mike was rarely so enthusiastic with insults.

"I think I smell cinnamon rolls," Dr. Nolan said, sniffing the air. "What do you say we head back? But I'm driving. You can't afford to lose any more teeth."

"You trust me to sit behind you on that machine?" Mike joked.

"I do," Dr. Nolan answered, climbing on the four-wheeler. "I've got long johns on."

Mike laughed and scooted up behind him. "I don't want any pictures of us on Facebook. You better drive fast."

Dr. Nolan opened the throttle and followed their tracks back toward the farmhouse, but did his best to hit every mudhole. By the time they arrived, both men were covered with globs of thick muck. And they were both laughing. Eileen caught sight of them through the kitchen window. She met them at the door and threw each of them a towel.

"Not yet, boys! Coats off! Shoes off! And wash up with that hose over there!" she ordered.

"Jesus, that's cold water," Mike said.

"Do it, or I'll do it for you!"

Both men took turns gingerly trying to remove as much mud as possible. Finally satisfied, she allowed them into the kitchen. The smell of vanilla, yeast, and cinnamon was intoxicating.

"Jeez, did you have an accident?" Cienna asked, staring at her father and uncle.

"The accident was I let your dad drive," Mike explained.

Dr. Nolan just smiled, but he took note that Eileen and his daughters had reddened eyes. He knew they had shared a good cry. And he knew that Mike had been able to exorcise some of the demons of fear that had tormented him. All in all it had been a good day.

They ate fresh cinnamon rolls out of the oven, drank more coffee, and spoke of nothing that neared a serious boundary. When plans were finalized to have dinner the next weekend, Dr. Nolan and his daughters said goodbye and headed for the car.

"Maybe you should let Cienna drive, Doc!" Mike yelled from the porch. "Might be safer."

"Very humorless," answered Dr. Nolan. He waved going down the driveway, but instead of turning toward the freeway, he went left. A mile or so down the road, he saw the sign marking the entrance to Darden Farm. He drove in slowly, then saw Lenny Darden near one of the large barns.

"Jesus Christ, Doc, you're a mess," the older man said.

"Oh, yeah, four-wheeling with Mike," he explained. "Hey, I'm sorry to bother you, but I was wondering if I could get a water and soil sample from your property?"

Mr. Darden frowned. He was in his seventies, grossly overweight, with short cropped gray hair.

"Why? There some kind of problem?" he asked.

"No. No problem. I'm just helping with a study on pesticides and herbicides," Dr. Nolan fibbed.

The older man looked at the ground and spit tobacco juice. "Don't think so," he said. "Don't want no trouble. Who's doing this study?"

"Oh, it's an NIH thing. You know. All the stuff about Round Up on the news," Dr. Nolan fibbed again.

The man spit a second time. "No thanks," he said. "Not on my land. Anything else?"

"No. Just that," Dr. Nolan apologized. "Sorry to bother you." He got back in the car, turned around, and drove to the main road.

"Who was that?" asked Cienna.

"An asshole with money," her father answered.

7

ON MONDAY MORNING DR. NOLAN SENT the soil and water samples to the environmental testing lab. He made a red star on his calendar, noting it would be mid-December before any results would be available. Even one week of not knowing was a nagging irritation. A month would be agonizing.

He tried his best to restrict his energies to immediate patient care, but on every pilgrimage into his office, he came face-to-face with the map and its brightly colored pins. He did not see them as symbols. They were human beings with faces and names, and he had cared for many of them.

On Thursday, Eileen underwent a lumpectomy and lymph node resection. She was only required to spend one night in the hospital, and Friday at lunch, he drove over to check on her. She was already back to work in the kitchen, trying to follow her normal routine left-handed. Her right arm was in a sling.

"Unscrewing a lid with one hand is a challenge," she joked. She had devised a system of sitting in a chair with the container pinched between her knees, trying her best to loosen the lid.

"You might want to use a hammer," Dr. Nolan suggested.

"I've thought about it." Eileen laughed. He took the jar of sauce and opened it.

"Can't you get one of your kids to help for a few days?" he asked.

"Haven't told them yet," she said. "They're all coming over tonight. Now I've got some good news to go with the bad."

Dr. Nolan's interest was immediate. "You hear from the surgeon?" he asked.

Eileen smiled. She poured coffee, and Dr. Nolan carried the cups to the table.

"Thirty minutes ago. All of the lymph nodes are negative," she informed him.

It was the best news possible. The size of the mass and the fact that it had not spread were both key factors in her survival.

"See? I told you. Just a walk in the park." Dr. Nolan smiled.

"Kind of a scary park," Eileen told him. "I'm going to take a leave of absence from the office during the treatments, though. I'll probably die from boredom."

Dr. Nolan nodded. It was a good idea to unburden her schedule and concentrate on the upcoming therapy, but it also led him to another thought.

"This thing I've been working on, the high levels of cancer patients. Cat and Amanda have been helping as much as they can, but there's too much to do. Cat made a joke about a personal assistant, but maybe when you feel like it, you could do some digging for me?"

Her response was instantaneous. "When do I start?" she asked. "I've kind of got a stake in this too, you know?"

Dr. Nolan regarded her with pure admiration. One day after surgery she was eagerly applying for a new job.

"Not so fast," he cautioned. "Maybe next week. You still have the office upstairs?"

"Yep. It's a little dusty and cluttered since the kids left home, but it's usable. And I can bring my computer from the office," she offered.

"Perfect," he said. "But there's one big prerequisite to be my assistant. Except for Cat, you're the only person I trust with my life. No one, not even Mike, can know about this. There can't be one hint about what I'm really looking for."

Eileen nodded. She had a vague understanding of his concerns, but had never really thought of the serious consequences they could unleash. If there truly was a problem, then someone was to blame. She thought about her sister and the other patients that might have been victimized. It also occurred to her for the first time that her own children could be at risk.

"You have my word," she said. "How have you been handling this so far?"

Dr. Nolan laughed half-heartedly.

"I came up with a story about testing for pesticides as part of an NIH study," he explained. "As long as no one asks any questions, that will work for now. And since you know everyone in town and all the farmers, you can help getting their consent to get more samples."

Eileen was already making a mental list of close contacts and family friends. He explained it would be three weeks until the report came back on their property.

"You're not going to wait, are you?" she asked.

Dr. Nolan shook his head. "I can't," he admitted. "But I'm still trying to figure out how to go about this. We need a lot of data from multiple sites to try and draw a picture."

"I can talk to our nearest neighbors," Eileen said. "They're all good people. At least it's a start."

"Okay. Good. But just phone work for the time being. That you can do with one hand. See if anyone will let me take samples this weekend."

"You got it, boss. I'll call you tonight."

He stood up and gave her a gentle hug. "And great news about the biopsy," he said again. "Just a bump in life's highway."

Eileen rolled her eyes. "My right booby feels like more than a bump, thank you. But thanks for being here, Sean. I know this isn't easy for you either." She walked him to the door.

"You just made it a whole lot easier," he told her. "And if you get any ideas on how to approach this, I'd appreciate it. Taking care of sick people is a lot more simple and straightforward. I didn't get any training in detective work."

"Then we'll figure it out together," Eileen smiled. "Just like the cancer. One day at a time."

8

Lenny Darden pulled up to City Hall and parked his truck in the handicapped zone. Two secretaries were at their desks when he entered.

"Can I help you, Mr. Darden?" one of them asked.

"Need to see the mayor," he said.

"Do you have an appointment?"

"Don't need one," he said. "Just tell him I'm here."

The woman's cheeks reddened, but she did not respond. She went to the mayor's office, knocked, and disappeared behind the frosted glass door. In half a minute she was back.

"He'll see you, Mr. Darden," she said, opening the locked partition of the security counter.

Mr. Darden did not thank her. He brushed past the woman and entered the mayor's office without knocking, then slammed the door. He sat down heavily across from Byron Tillis, a balding man in his mid sixties. He had been elected to the part-time, low-paying position of mayor just one year ago.

"Mr. Darden, how can I be of service?" the mayor asked, shaking hands across the desk.

"You can get the fucking town doctor to mind his own business for starters," Mr. Darden said.

Byron Tillis could feel the anger in the room but had no idea what the other man was talking about.

"I'm missing something here," the mayor confessed. He was intimidated by the Darden name and their position in the local community. "What does Dr. Nolan have to do with this?"

"Came on my land to get water and soil samples," Mr. Darden explained. "Looking for bug spray or something. He's got no business on my farm."

"Did you let him?" the mayor asked.

"Fuck no! Told him to get off my property," the older man said. "With all that's going on right now, I don't need any bad publicity or people in my business."

The mayor nodded. There were ongoing negotiations with the city and county to rezone a large section of the Darden Farm from agricultural use to commercial property. The change in designation would increase the land value by millions to the Darden family and would create a tax bonanza for the city. There had been the anticipated battles over infrastructure and traffic issues, but the plan, with help from the mayor and city council, was moving ahead smoothly.

"I don't know anything about his," the mayor told him.

"You don't know shit about much, Byron," Mr. Darden said. "It's something about Round Up and those lymphoma reports. I don't even care. Half of my employees are illegal anyway. They don't make trouble."

"Okay. Okay," the mayor said, trying to get Mr. Darden to lower his voice.

"I don't know what I can do," the mayor told him. "I could talk to him, I suppose."

Mr. Darden leaned forward in his chair. "You better do something, goddamn it! Don't forget, you've got an iron in the fire too. If this zoning deal goes through, you get a nice little bonus check for all your help. If it doesn't, we all get nothing."

Byron Tillis was sweating. He took a Kleenex from the box on his desk and wiped his forehead and upper lip. "Let me see what I can find out," the mayor said. "Maybe somebody at county knows what's going on."

"Earn your money," Mr. Darden said. "Either you do something or I will."

"Jesus, take it easy. Give me till next week," the mayor pleaded. "This is probably nothing."

"Probably doesn't pay the bills," Mr. Darden told him. "I've worked my whole life to build this business, and I don't want some newspaper story fucking it up."

"I hear you. Just give me some time," the mayor said again.

Lenny Darden stood up and pointed to his watch. "You've got till next Friday," he warned. "I want answers." He marched out of the office and past the two women staring at him without making eye contact. They had heard the heated exchange of words but could not make out what they were yelling about. One of the women thumbed her nose at Mr. Darden's back.

"Fat toad," she said.

"That's an insult to the toad," the other woman said, and they both laughed.

The mayor stuck his head out of his office. It was nearly five on a Friday. No one at county would bother to answer the phone.

"First thing Monday," the mayor said, "I need to talk to the agriculture extension office. First thing." He went back to his desk and reached for another tissue.

9

EILEEN HAD BEEN BUSY. SHE HAD already spoken to three local families with smaller farms that were agreeable to the testing. With young children, they were all concerned with pesticide use and possible health risks, so the cover story turned out to be an effective tactic. And being fully engaged in her new duties was like therapy. It kept other thoughts at bay.

Dr. Nolan left his daughters at home while he collected the samples. All but one of the families were patients, and all were helpful and open to his research. Two of the farms had active wells, and the last one required another uncapping ceremony. The soil samples were sweaty work but easily accomplished. He thanked everyone involved for their assistance, then requested that they not discuss his visit until the results came back from the lab. He knew full well that the pledge of secrecy would not hold, but still wanted to minimize it.

He dropped the labeled specimens at his clinic, then took the map down from the wall. It would have a new residence in Eileen's office, and he would not have to see it fifty times a day. More importantly, no patients would accidentally catch sight of it and ask questions.

He was just loading the corkboard when an SUV pulled up next to him in the parking lot.

"Hey, Doc, you lose your cell phone?" the young man asked with a smile.

"Damn. When did you get home?" Dr. Nolan asked. He had taken care of the young man since he was nine years old. Now twenty-eight, he had served one tour of duty in Iraq and two in Afghanistan, and then transitioned over to private contractor work with Blackwater. He was a handsome, personable fellow with a keen intelligence. Dr. Nolan was always trying to encourage him to get back in school, but he was addicted to the adrenaline rush that came with active duty deployment. And the money was an additional draw. His yearly income exceeded Dr. Nolan's.

"Last week," the young man answered. "You got time to look at my toe?"

"As long as I don't have to kiss it to make it better, kid." Dr. Nolan laughed. "I'll go unlock the door."

The young man's name was Jed Marcus, but Dr. Nolan had always called him 'kid'. He also took care of his mother and tried to soothe her worries every time he went overseas.

"You still have all your body parts?" Dr. Nolan asked, directing the young man to the surgery room.

"All in one piece, Doc," Jed assured him. "This was an easy trip. Mainly I just drove politicians around in armored cars."

"How long you home for?" Dr. Nolan asked.

"Six weeks," Jed answered, pulling off his left boot. The medial great nail had grown under the skin and caused an infection.

"If I stick a needle in your toe and numb you up, it will hurt just as bad as cutting it out. Your call, kid."

"Oh, just cut it," Jed told him.

Dr. Nolan left for a moment and returned with an ice pack. "Hold that on there for a few minutes," he told Jed. "I bet your mom is glad you're home. Any chance you'll stay this time?"

"They already gave me three options." Jed laughed. "I can go shoot Somali pirates, guard an oil rig in South America, or go back to Afghanistan."

"So...?"

"Probably back to Afghanistan," Jed answered. "I don't want to shoot anyone if I don't have to. And in South America, you have no backup. If something goes wrong, you're on your own."

"How about you stay home and use your school benefits?" Dr. Nolan suggested. It was the same conversation they had shared before.

"Oh, someday, Doc," Jed told him. "I think every time is the last time, then I get antsy. You know. I'm like the guy in *The 'Hurt Locker.'* I just don't seem to fit in."

Dr. Nolan nodded his understanding. It was a well-established component of PTSD. The young men and women serving prolonged duty tours found it nearly impossible to assimilate back into a normal lifestyle. They were plagued by high levels of anxiety, insomnia, and frequent night terrors. Their nervous systems had been reprogrammed to an elevated set point. They were much more prone to self-medicate with alcohol and drugs, and even more tragically, the suicide rate among veterans was nearing epidemic levels.

Dr. Nolan scrubbed the young man's toe with a Betadine solution, then searched through his sterile instruments for a pair of straight-edged scissors.

"What are you doing to keep occupied?" Dr. Nolan asked him.

"Oh, helping Mom around the farm, some small repair jobs," Jed explained.

"You know, your mother goes crazy every time you ship out," Dr. Nolan told him. "Hell, even I worry about you, kid."

"I know," Jed acknowledged the fact. "We had one of our guys blown up in an outdoor café. Believe me, I think about it. I just can't do the college thing yet."

Dr. Nolan had him lie back on the surgical table. "Okay, tough guy," he warned. "This is going to hurt you more than it is me. Try to hold still." He began to work the scissors beneath the nailbed, slowly moving deeper until he neared the growth plate zone. With a single snip he removed about one-third of the toenail. It had grown downward into the tissue bed nearly a half inch.

"That it? Burned like hell." Jed sighed, examining his foot.

Dr. Nolan scrubbed the area again. There was only a small amount of bleeding. He covered the infected tissue with an antibacterial ointment and wrapped the toe in a simple Band-Aid.

"Put this on twice a day for a week," he told Jed, tossing him the tube of medication. Now he would be in trouble with his nurses again. He was forever giving away free samples and leaving their own supplies depleted.

"Thanks, Doc," Jed said. "You saved me a trip to the ER. What've you been up to?" He was busy retying his boot.

Dr. Nolan was washing his hands. It was premature, but having Jed back home could prove to be an asset.

"Same old stuff," he said. "But I am working on a little side project. You available for some part-time work?"

Jed smiled. "What are we talking about?" he asked.

Dr. Nolan sat down again. He did not want to offer any specific information. "Let's just call it a community health issue," Dr. Nolan explained. "I've been trying to quietly do some testing on the Bottoms, and some people aren't very cooperative. Not too many so far, but I may need some samples without permission."

Jed was smiling more by the minute. "So, you're talking about a little covert activity, is that it? Off the radar?"

Dr. Nolan nodded. "Would that be something you'd consider?"

"That's easy, Doc," the young man said. "Hell, for five hundred dollars, I know people that can permanently solve problems with no questions asked."

"Jesus, kid, it's nothing that extreme," Dr. Nolan assured him, suddenly uncomfortable. "I'm just talking about water and soil testing."

Jed laughed. "Whatever you need, just call," the young man said. He wrote his cell phone number on a notepad and gave it to Dr. Nolan. "Anytime."

Dr. Nolan took it and tucked it into a hidden fold in his wallet. He did not know if it would be needed, but he was happy to have the option available.

"Okay. Great. Remember, twice a day with the medicine," Dr. Nolan reminded him. He walked him out to his truck. "And say hi to your mom."

"Okay, Doc. Thanks. Send me a bill," Jed said. He saluted as he drove away.

Dr. Nolan checked his watch. Although he had lived and worked in the area for nearly twenty years, his knowledge of the topography was limited. He got in his car and drove west, crossing the main tracks of the Burlington Northern Santa Fe railroad into the Bottoms. He first drove around the perimeter of the dike access road, all the way to the Columbia and up the other side. Then he toured each of the crossroads that ran east to west. The reclaimed floodplain was much larger than he had thought, perhaps two miles deep and four miles wide. There was already a heavy industrial zone built up around the rail line and freeway, but the bulk of the land was home to hundreds of farmers, both large and small. And he had only managed to collect samples from four of them.

He pulled into a small park area at the bank of the river, watching as a large cargo ship navigated the channel toward Portland. Woodhaven had always been touted as a perfect port location for sea shipping, but for some reason it had never happened. The area was pretty much as it had been for a century.

The challenge that was facing him seemed larger by the moment. He had a new assistant just beginning cancer treatment, his already overburdened clinic staff, and a potential part-time problem solver. It did not even qualify as a motley crew. The motivation was there, but the implementation was a daunting task.

He headed home to his daughters and the looming argument over what to make for dinner. The gallon of spaghetti sauce had been exhausted, and he had been too occupied to make the weekly shopping trip to the local market. He had narrowed the option list down to French toast and bacon as he arrived home, then reconsidered.

"You guys get spruced up and we'll go to that new restaurant in Kalama. The one on the river," he told Cienna and Aubriel. The proposal was met with approval.

"Cool. Where were you?" Cienna asked.

"Got ambushed at the clinic," he told her. "Ingrown toenail."

"You always say death and taxes are the two things you can count on," she reminded him. "The third thing is that you always get ambushed on the weekend."

He smiled and headed upstairs to change. It was true. There was never a weekend without multiple phone calls and emergency trips to the clinic. So, now it was death, taxes, and emergencies. He sighed deeply, then suddenly realized Cienna had just handed him a key. It was taxes. If they could get the most recent taxable property map for the Woodhaven area, they could plot out all the current land-owners with addresses, names, and phone numbers.

Now the job no longer seemed impossible.

10

"A TAX MAP," DR. NOLAN SAID. He had called Eileen first thing Monday morning. "Either the city or county will have all the updated material we need. It's public information. We can use it to check off sample sources for different areas."

Eileen listened enthusiastically. She was already running low on neighbors to call.

"That could work," she agreed. "I've got radiation treatments every day this week, but my mornings are free. I'll go to the courthouse tomorrow in Longview and see what I can get."

"Not an emergency," Dr. Nolan told her. "Only if you feel like it. None of this is going to happen fast."

"I know. But it's kind of exciting in a way," Eileen confessed. "Like working on a puzzle."

"This puzzle has a shitload of pieces, and some of them are missing right now," Dr. Nolan told her.

"Then we'll just have to work harder to find them," Eileen answered. "And I've got two more farm owners that will let you do testing. You know them."

"Good job," Dr. Nolan said. "Probably next weekend. It's already dark when I get out of here."

"Like you said, it's a marathon, not a sprint," Eileen repeated. "I'll call when I get the tax records."

"Good luck," he said, hanging up the phone. He was constantly amazed by her positive attitude. She made him feel better.

The morning patient load was an avalanche of respiratory infections and influenza cases. Some could be helped with medication, and others just needed reassurance that death was not imminent. Sometimes it seemed that a fair part of his day was merely babysitting, quieting fears that minor symptoms were not the messenger of some life-threatening disaster. But it was all part of the job. He loved to teach, to explain to patients what was happening and why. And he was equally famous for his questionable art projects trying to depict medical causality.

Just at noon, Amanda told him the mayor's office had called and wanted to schedule a meeting. Dr. Nolan frowned. He lived outside the city limits and could not even vote in local elections. He had no interest in political intrigue.

"Every time I hear from the city, it's about donating to some cause of the week. Tell the little dweeb he can stop by here any day at noon and I'll talk to him. I don't want him showing up later in the day when my daughters are here."

"I'll probably rephrase your answer." She smiled. "But I'll let him know."

Dr. Nolan dismissed the brief exchange from his thoughts. He literally had no curiosity about why the mayor would be seeking his counsel. It was actually a surprise to him when the man showed up in his waiting room the next day.

"Seriously?" he asked Amanda when she told him. "His Dweebyness is actually sitting out there waiting to talk to me?"

"Afraid so," Amanda said. "And he knows you're still here, so you can't sneak out the back door."

Dr. Nolan grabbed his coffee cup and headed for the breakroom.

"Have him come in and sit down. I need a drink," Dr. Nolan said, then whispered, "and hide the checkbook."

Amanda laughed and went to fetch the mayor. He was seated in the guest chair when Dr. Nolan returned to his office.

"Mayor Tillis. How's your prostate?" Dr. Nolan asked. He greeted the older man, noting his hand was cold and sweaty.

"I think it's okay," the mayor answered.

"As long as you're here, you want me to check it?" Dr. Nolan offered. He could see the man was already uncomfortable, and he wanted to worsen the experience. It might dissuade him from future visits.

"I think I'll pass on that," the mayor said, forcing an awkward smile.

"So, what can I do for you? Rotary Club? Little League?"

"No. Nothing like that," the mayor said, shifting in his chair. "It's just...there's been a complaint from a local business. Not really a complaint. More of a concern that was brought to our attention."

"Jesus! Only one?" Dr. Nolan laughed. "I must be slipping." He was enjoying himself at the other man's expense. Mayor Tillis fidgeted in his chair again.

"We have to take these things seriously," he said. "There was a report that you were trying to force people into testing for pesticides. Some kind of study. But when I called the county, they didn't know anything about it."

Dr. Nolan regarded the mayor for a long moment. There were beads of perspiration on his forehead.

"Let me take a wild guess here," Dr. Nolan said. "Mr. Lenny Darden was whining about my request for water and soil samples?"

Mayor Tillis swallowed hard. "We don't discuss names," he answered. "It's just a publicity thing. We don't want any stories that make Woodhaven look bad. This area is growing, and there's no reason to scare people."

"I'm not trying to scare anyone," Dr. Nolan answered. "My job is to keep people safe. I would think that would be your job too."

"Of course," Mayor Tillis said. "But this study. Why doesn't county know about it?"

Dr. Nolan chose his words carefully. He wanted to avoid constructing an outright lie. "It's more of a voluntary effort to gather data," he began. "You've read or heard about the lymphoma cases associated with Round Up? I'm just trying to make certain we don't have a problem here. All voluntary. No one is being forced to do anything. Why is that such a worry for Mr. Darden?"

Sweat trickled down the mayor's temple. He had no choice other than to wipe it away with his coat sleeve.

"Oh, there's no worry. He's just very private when it comes to his business, that's all," the mayor said. "Have you tested other properties? Other farms?"

"Some," Dr. Nolan answered. "It turns out that a few of our local farmers actually want answers. It's a matter of public health. The pesticides go from the soil to the water, and from the water to people. Kind of a big deal, don't you think?"

The mayor shook his head, but without conviction. "What have you found so far?" he asked.

"Nothing at all," Dr. Nolan said truthfully. "So far, there seems to be no problem." He did not explain that the first samples had not yet yielded a report.

"Well, that's good news," the mayor said. "That will put everyone at ease. Good. Good. I'm glad we talked." He stood up to leave.

"Now you can go call Mr. Darden and tell him not to worry," Dr. Nolan said. "And tell him he can kiss my ass."

The mayor did not answer. He left the clinic and headed up the street toward City Hall.

Up to this point, Dr. Nolan had not given any thought to Lenny Darden. He had just written off his curt reception the other day to rude behavior and nothing more. But this was an interesting change in climate. Why was Mr. Darden upset enough to involve the local political forces? Why did his visit to the Darden Farm pose any threat?

It was another nagging question now added to an already crowded list. Dr. Nolan thought for a moment, then dialed Amanda at the front desk. "Who's the largest employer in the area that would do background checks?" he asked her.

The query caught Amanda off guard. "Jeez, let's see. The hospital? The banks? City workers? The airport?" she said, trying to narrow the possibilities.

"The airport! Perfect," Dr. Nolan told her. "TSA is a contractor for security services. You would think they'd do a pretty good job of screening employees. See if you can find out who does their background checks."

"You do realize it's lunchtime," Amanda reminded him.

"That's for normal people, and we're not normal," Dr. Nolan said. "Just get me a phone contact, and I'll make the call."

Amanda sighed but was already on her computer. In half a minute she had found the business office for TSA at Portland International Airport.

"Okay. Thanks," Dr. Nolan said. "Go to lunch. Just lock the front door so no one wanders in."

He waited until Amanda and his nurses left the clinic, then went to the front office to find Lenny Darden's chart. Back in his office he dialed the number she had given him.

"TSA Portland," a woman's voice answered.

"Hello? This is Dr. Sean Nolan up in Woodhaven. We have a fellow applying for a job opening in our clinic, and we need to check his work history. Who do you people use for security clearances?"

There was only a brief pause. "Exigence," the woman answered. "They're out of LA, but they handle all our personnel requirements. Do you need their number?"

"Please," Dr. Nolan answered. He wrote down the information and thanked the woman for being so helpful. He then dialed the home office for Exigence, repeating the same story. He was then referred to another department that actually conducted the screening process.

"How far back do you want us to look?" the man asked. Since Lenny Darden was in his seventies, the end of high school seemed a good place to begin.

"You have a date of birth? Social Security number? Address?"

"All right here on his application form," Dr. Nolan fibbed, reading off the required information from Mr. Darden's medical file.

"And you have a signed release of information form?" the man asked.

"Oh, sure, right here," Dr. Nolan responded. "Give me a fax number and I'll send it over." Satisfied, the man took his billing information and told him there would be a return call within the week.

"Great," Dr. Nolan said. "Have to be careful with all these federal privacy laws. Thank you for your help."

He hung up the phone, then went to Amanda's office. After searching through a dozen drawers, he finally located an employment application and filled it out himself. For some silly reason, he forged Lenny Darden's signature left-handed. It made the crime seem less overt.

With that completed, he stood staring at the control panel on the fax machine. He had never bothered to learn how to use it.

"What are you doing?" Cat asked. She had come back from lunch and entered through the rear door. Dr. Nolan was startled.

"Uh, I need to send this to California," he said.

Cat looked at him as if viewing a Neanderthal exhibit at the museum. "You're helpless," she mused.

"But not hopeless," he countered.

"Give me the paper and the number," she said.

A sheepish grin appeared on his face. "This is a highly unusual document that I don't want anyone to know about," Dr. Nolan began. "Is there any way you can send this without actually looking at it?"

"It's a job application," Cat said, glancing at the paper he held. "What are you up to?"

"Hmmmmm. One word that might fit is skullduggery," he admitted.

"Or lying?" she asked.

"Let's say misleading," he admitted. "But for a good cause. I would just prefer that you can honestly say you never saw this."

Cat nodded her head slowly. She took a blank piece of copy paper and handed it to him.

"Cover your page with this, and I'll send them both," she said. "And maybe you should watch how I do this. You just type in the number and press 'send'." The papers disappeared into the machine, then reappeared with a confirmation notice. Cat handed him the contraband material.

"I'll shred these," Dr. Nolan said. "I know how to do that."

"Any other crimes you want me to help with?" Cat asked sarcastically.

Dr. Nolan smiled at her. "No more today," he said. "I'm trying to limit felonies to one a day. I'm going to grab a sandwich. It's too late to go home. Thanks."

Cat gave him the look and left the office. He did not offer any additional account of what he was up to, and she did not ask. Minimizing his staff's exposure to any sensitive information was the safest way to proceed. If there were any questions posed, there would be no answer.

The rest of the week passed quickly, and on late Friday, a report arrived from the EPA. Their database was only reliable to the early 1970s, but a review of their records showed no known toxic spills or dump sites, and the only active investigation was in Longview, some fifteen miles to the north. A major port for processing and shipping timber, preservative chemicals, and creosote had contaminated some small area near the river.

While the information had value, it was not definitive. It only encapsulated a narrow time frame, and it only dealt with what was known, not what was hidden. Dr. Nolan was relieved by the fact that no major problems had ever been reported in the Woodhaven area, but it did nothing to explain the number of cancer patients.

When the clinic closed, he and his daughters drove to Eileen's home. They stopped on the way, Cienna and Aubriel arguing over what flowers to buy, then made a house call to check on their aunt. She was no longer wearing her sling but could only use her right arm and hand for simple tasks. She was delighted with her bouquet.

"How thoughtful." She smiled. Cienna and Aubriel took turns hugging her.

"You look great," Dr. Nolan said.

"Feel great," she said. "This radiation thing is easy. I'm only there for a few minutes. I spend most of my time driving. You want to stay for dinner? Fried chicken, mashed potatoes, and gravy."

"Oh, please, can we, Dad?" Cienna begged.

"Please, please, pretty please," Aubriel chimed in, clasping her hands in mock prayer.

"My cooking that bad?" Dr. Nolan asked, already knowing the answer. "Okay, but only if you help. You peel potatoes. I need to talk to your aunt."

His daughters gleefully headed for the kitchen. Up in the second-floor office, Dr. Nolan closed the door.

"Don't BS me," he warned. "You really feel okay?"

Eileen nodded and smiled. "No BS," she assured him. "So far, this has been a breeze. I know the chemo won't be, but that's later."

"I just worry that you want to do too much. That's all," he said. He filled her in on the EPA documents.

"Well, that's good," she said, then motioned toward the large oak desk. "I got the tax map from the county clerk. I've already called another fourteen people with farms or homes. All of them are happy to help you get samples. And I'm marking off all the test sites with red pen as we take them off the list."

Dr. Nolan could see the four sites already visited. "Jesus, that's sixteen already," he smiled. Both Saturday and Sunday would now be spent in frigid weather collecting specimens.

"Mike wants to help," she said. "That will speed things up."

Dr. Nolan was pleased by the offer. He knew Mike would keep this confidential. He studied the map more closely. Even after the weekend, the ratio of tested and untested locations appeared to be twenty to one.

"Big job," he sighed.

"Not as big as two weeks ago," Eileen said. "How long before you hear back from the lab?"

"Two more weeks. Then a few days later some of the others will follow," he said.

"And I'll be starting chemotherapy. We need to get as much done as we can now," Eileen told him.

Dr. Nolan nodded. He was staring out of the window, with nothing visible but darkness.

"I had a dream about Megan last night," he said. "The girls were small again. They were in the yard playing, and Megan was just watching them, with the most beautiful smile on her face. She never spoke a word. Just stood there smiling."

"She is still here, Sean," Eileen said. "And that's her job now. Watching over her girls. I truly believe that."

Dr. Nolan sighed, but there were no tears. "I hope she's watching out for all of us," he said.

11

LENNY DARDEN WAS AT THE FEED store when he heard the man at the counter mention that Dr. Nolan had collected samples from his farm. The clerk was mildly interested, but it was news to him. He didn't know anything about it.

Mr. Darden left without filling his order. He drove home, went to his study, and rifled through the top drawer of his desk. He pulled a faded business card into the light, squinted at the numbers, then dialed the phone.

"Dukayne Chemical Corporation," the woman said. "How may I direct your call?"

"Legal department," Mr. Darden barked. He was breathing hard.

"Legal," another woman said. "How can I help?"

"You got any old-timers still working there?" he demanded. "This is Lenny Darden. I don't want to talk to any fucking kids just out of school. Find someone with some fucking gray hair and tell them to call me back!" He slammed the receiver into its cradle and waited.

The return call came in twenty minutes.

"Mr. Darden? This is Doug Saunders. It's been a long time," the man said. "I was hoping you were dead by now."

"I'll bet that's one of the few honest things you've ever said," Mr. Darden responded. He made no effort to hide his contempt. "I've got the town doctor snooping around here getting soil and water samples. I was waiting to see if this would blow over, but it's not. And I don't like it!"

Doug Saunders was one of the senior lawyers at Dukayne Chemicals. He did not actively practice law any longer but served more in an advisory position. He had been with the company since the late 1960's. Mr. Darden's file was open on his desk.

"The very last thing you do not want to do is overreact right now, Mr. Darden," he said slowly and very clearly. "This is a time to assess our position and consider options, nothing more. Any unnecessary attention would not be wise."

"There's already attention, goddamn it! That's what I'm telling you."

"I understand your concern," Mr. Saunders told him. "But you should know better than anyone that there are quieter, more civilized ways of dealing with problems like this. Give me a few days to get someone down there."

"And what? Have a fucking board meeting and pass out cookies? This is my life here!"

Mr. Saunders was tempted to respond in kind, but took a deep breath. "Patience, Mr. Darden. Someone will be in touch next week," he said. "Until then, you do nothing."

"Or what? You going to take away my allowance?" Mr. Darden said sarcastically.

Doug Saunders tightened his grip on the phone. "Let me be clear," he said. "If there is any premature activity on your part, some people might perceive you as the problem."

Lenny Darden did not slam the phone down. He put it gently in place and sat staring at his desk.

12

Saturday was the very definition of miserable. With the temperature balanced precariously above the freezing point, the entire day was a shifting tug-of-war between snow flurries and icy showers. Collecting water samples was fairly straightforward. But digging in heavy mud and attempting to claim soil samples from water-filled holes was a nightmare.

Dressed in three layers of warm clothing and a rain coat, Dr. Nolan had not been able to feel his hands for hours. His waterproof boots had failed their warranty, and his hat brim kept directing frigid drops of rain down the back of his neck. Between target sites, he sat in his car for a few minutes with the heat on full. If the wages of sin was hellfire, it was beginning to sound like a viable option.

He scanned the angry gray cloud cover for any sign of appeasement, but it was hopeless. Mike Carson had taken half of the addresses for today, and that was his only salvation. With two more farms to visit, he put his car into gear and moved farther west along the Bottoms.

His next-to-last stop was the Reynolds homestead. It was a forty-acre nursery that supplied trees and landscaping shrubbery to local retailers. The entire Reynolds family were patients, and Dr. Nolan had also taken care of the patriarch of the clan until his passing some six years earlier.

He parked, then half jogged up to the front door.

"Jesus, Doc, you look like a drowned rat." Mr. Reynolds laughed, ushering him into the kitchen. "You want some coffee?"

"Anything hot," Dr. Nolan said. He peeled off his hat and outer coat.

"Sit. Sit. Thaw out for a while," Mr. Reynolds said. "Eileen said you would be coming by. Something about chemical sprays?"

Dr. Nolan nodded, wrapping both of his hands around the coffee cup.

"Every day we keep finding out about new side effects from all these chemicals," he began. "Now it turns out even sunblock is hazardous. I'm trying to find out if we have any local problems."

"I think that's great," Mr. Reynolds said. "After Eileen called, I got to wondering if maybe my dad got exposed to something. We're always spraying something around here. We try to be safe, follow the guidelines, but half the time the damn wind blows it back in your face."

"Jesus, that's right," Dr. Nolan said. "Your father had some kind of rare gallbladder cancer. I'd forgotten. He went to the ER with abdominal pain and never came home." Because he had not been involved with the case, it had completely escaped his memory.

"It was fast," Mr. Reynolds explained. "He was here working, and three days later he was gone. I just remember them saying it was a very rare disease."

It was indeed, Dr. Nolan thought. One of the marker pins in his map represented the senior Mr. Reynolds.

"I'm sorry about your dad," he said. "Every time he came to the clinic, I had to listen to him brag about your athletic achievements. You were hot stuff in football and baseball, right?"

Mr. Reynolds smiled, remembering. "Long time ago," he said. "When Dad died, I had to step in and take over the farm. It all worked out."

Dr. Nolan recalled that there had been scholarship offers and a world of other possible futures for the young man, but that door had closed.

"He was proud of you then, and he'd be even more so now," Dr. Nolan told him. "You still taking care of your mom?"

Mr. Reynolds leaned forward and lowered his voice. "She's still hanging in there," he said. "But yesterday we found the remote control in the freezer. She traded it for an ice cream bar."

Dr. Nolan laughed and nodded. "We call that Old Timers' Disease," he told the young man. "If you live long enough, you start to get a little whacky."

Mr. Reynolds stood up and put his cup in the sink. "This weather isn't going to let up," he said. "Suit up and I'll help with what you need."

Dr. Nolan finished the last of his coffee, then reclaimed his rain gear.

"What you asked about your dad? If he might have been affected by some contaminant. I think it's possible," Dr. Nolan admitted. "I can't help him, but maybe we can keep you and your family safe."

"That's good enough for me, Doc," Mr. Reynolds said, then he laughed. "You ready to freeze your balls off?"

"Not a problem," Dr. Nolan assured him. "That happened two hours ago."

13

ON MONDAY MORNING THERE WAS AN urgent meeting scheduled at Dukayne Chemical Corporation. It did not involve the board of trustees, but was confined to regency members only, a small and select group of older officers of the firm that dealt with the most sensitive and confidential business matters. There were to be no notes or written records.

Doug Saunders sat at the head of the table. The majority stockholder and the CEO were not in attendance.

"We have a potential exposure issue that could evolve into a public relations disaster," he began. "An old factory site in Southwest Washington could come back to haunt us. The location was abandoned some forty-five years ago and sold off to another business, but there are still fingerprints."

"So, what's the problem today?" one of the members asked.

"Local doctor on some kind of crusade. We don't really know why or what he's looking for," Mr. Saunders explained. "We just know he's looking."

"Has there been any contact?" another man asked.

Mr. Saunders shook his head. "Too early," he said. "I just found out about this on Friday. But we need to be ahead of this. We need to construct a set of contingency options that are acceptable."

"What is the best-case scenario?" another man asked.

"Best case, if something comes out, we deny any knowledge of the matter, pay a fine, clean up the mess, and go back to normal business," Mr. Saunders told them.

There was a long silence in the room, everyone waiting for the next question.

"And worst case?" someone finally asked.

"If it comes to light that this was a known problem that was ignored, there would be enormous financial losses and possible criminal accountability. Neither of those are acceptable outcomes."

Now there was a longer silence. Each member of the group was held captive by their own thoughts.

"Is this local physician a reasonable man?" a voice asked.

Doug Saunders folded his hands on the table. "You mean, is he corruptible? I don't know the answer to that," he said. "But I do think that is one avenue to explore."

"Is there a paper trail that could prove existing knowl-edge of this?" another man asked.

"Nothing at all," Mr. Saunders assured them. That had been dealt with decades ago. "But we do have a local family that settled a lawsuit against the company back in the day. The terms of the agreement were sealed, but there's no telling how many people actually know about it."

"Have we heard from them?"

Mr. Saunders shook his head in the affirmative. "That's how I became aware of the problem," he explained. "The old bastard we paid off years ago knows that if this comes out now, it will ruin him as well. Let's just say he's a little unsettled by the prospect."

Again there was a break in the conversation.

"Is he asking for more money?" one man finally spoke.

"No. He's already been bought," Mr. Saunders said. "Money isn't the issue. He's terrified his life could be destroyed. It's just about self-preservation."

"So, what do you suggest? Do we wait? Do we risk being proactive?"

Mr. Saunders regarded each man in turn. "I propose we send one of our younger lawyers down to assess things on the ground. We need to know the players. And we need to know immediately if a story is developing. I can't stress enough how consequential this might be."

The board members were in agreement. They adjourned with a follow-up meeting scheduled the next week.

Doug Saunders went back to his office. His first call was to the legal department. The son of a major stockholder was an aggressive, personable young attorney on staff, eager to please and more desirous to move up the corporate ladder. He had been on the payroll for three years and could be relied on to conduct himself accordingly. The background information granted him would only be of a limited nature, but enough so he could serve his purpose.

While he waited to give the young man his assignment, he made a second call on his cell phone. He had to scroll back nearly two years on his caller index to locate the number. There was an answer on the third ring.

"Are you available in the next few weeks?" he asked.

"Yes."

"Same fee schedule?"

"Add five," the woman answered. "Inflation."

"I'll call if I need you," Mr. Saunders told her. The woman hung up without answering.

14

MYRON LENTZ WAS AN INTERNATIONAL LAW expert in his
third year with Dukayne Chemical Corporation. At twenty-seven, most of his time had been devoted to crafting legal
agreements between his US-based employer and members
of the European Union. He was comfortable in an office
setting or a boardroom, but the less structured task he had
now been given was foreign territory.

He had been told by Doug Saunders that his job consisted of two separate paths. The first was to define the
characters at play and establish the status of their activities.
The second was more ominous. He would be the public
face for the company in the event damage control became
the priority. The only background material given to him
was that there had been a chemical spill at an old ware-

house site and that a sealed lawsuit had been collecting dust since the late 1960's. Nothing else.

He had privately wondered why Mr. Saunders had not used a professional investigator, but the fastest way to gain favor at the company was not to question decisions. If you were given an assigned role, the primary course of action was to accept graciously and comply.

His plane landed in Portland on a Thursday evening, the cold rain blowing sideways from the force of an east wind tearing through the Columbia Gorge. He picked up his rental car and used the navigation system to plot a course north on I-5 to the small town of Salmon Creek. A suite at the La Quinta Inn had been reserved in his name. After checking into his room, his smartphone located a nearby sushi restaurant. His three-piece business suit seemed wildly out of place, but in his rush to fly out, he had neglected to select less formal attire.

Finally back in his room, he reread the files he had been given on a Mr. Lenny Darden and a Dr. Sean Nolan. Permission had been given to speak with Mr. Darden, but he was not to establish direct communications with the town doctor. His immediate charge was to observe and report.

First thing in the morning he would try to find more protective clothing. Outside the window now was the beginning of a light snowfall. He remembered an old joke about the Pacific Northwest: If you don't like the weather, just wait ten minutes.

It wasn't a joke.

15

FRIDAY AFTERNOON WAS HIGHLIGHTED BY THE arrival of Lenny Darden's dubious security clearance. By luck it was Cat who saw it come over the fax machine. She quickly grabbed it and placed it facedown on Dr. Nolan's desk. When he came out of an exam room, she gave him a subtle nod. There was not time to review it, but he was able to hide it in a desk drawer before his daughters arrived. They both had a penchant for exploring things left out in the open.

When the last patient had left the clinic, he bribed Cienna and Aubriel to get hamburgers and fries from the nearby drive-in. It was enough time to review the report in private. Alone in his office, he sat down and slowly read the three-page analysis. Born in 1943, Lenny Darden was a third-generation local boy. Average student. Two years of peacetime Army service after high school. Took over the small, twenty-acre berry farm in 1964. Married his high school classmate the same year. Two children, a daughter and a son. The girl had died at age two from an unknown cause. The son, now fifty-one, had earned a degree in architectural design and worked for a large firm in San Francisco. There was no hint of any financial or legal problems in his past.

It was the last page that proved intriguing to Dr. Nolan. In 1968, Mr. Darden began to buy out one neighbor after another. Some properties were as small as five acres, and others were measured by the hundreds of acres. He leveled existing homes, only preserving a large barn here and there if they could prove useful to the farm. By 1972 he had accumulated over fifteen hundred acres of prime farmland on the Bottoms and expanded from berries into a dozen other crops. Weyerhaeuser was the largest landowner in the county, but it was all in timber. Mr. Darden owned the largest working farm in the area.

Dr. Nolan knew what current land prices were. Just in the past decade they had more than doubled. Simple math indicated that Lenny Darden had managed to construct a multimillion-dollar business enterprise. But the question was how? Had there been an inheritance, some wealthy relative or partner in the mix? Had he won the lottery?

"You want to eat here or go home?" Cienna asked, holding up the food order.

"Oh, god, here," her father said. He put the papers away. "At least when it's hot, the acid indigestion is less severe." He fished out the onions on his burger.

"I like their food," Aubriel said. It was not a surprise. She had yet to meet a fruit or vegetable that pleased her palate. Dr. Nolan felt like a miracle worker if he could coax her into drinking V-8 juice on rare occasions. He actually saw her eat an apple once and pretended to faint.

He looked at his two girls and smiled. A hidden part of him always wished he could be a better parent to them, but they were doing all right. Not perfect. But weighted by the scale of what they had been through in their young lives, he was grateful and pleased.

"Any big weekend plans I need to know about?" he asked.

"Just a book report," Aubriel answered. It was her area of comfort and not viewed as an act of torture.

"Can I stay over at Jessica Harden's tomorrow?" Cienna asked. "You know her parents."

Dr. Nolan nodded. "I'll talk to them," he said. "There won't be any boys around, right?"

"Oh, jeez, Dad," Cienna protested. "You realize I'm almost fifteen. We're just going to the movies."

Dr. Nolan was not so old that his memory had failed. He had gone to the movies, too.

"Yes, dear," he told Cienna with a serious tone. "You know I hate violence, but remember, in this county, it's not a felony to shoot teenage boys. Only a misdemeanor. In fact, I think they just fine you or something."

Aubriel was laughing.

"Not funny," Cienna responded. "Next year I can take drivers ed. Then what?"

"I buy more ammunition," Dr. Nolan told her. "Or a bazooka."

"Boys are creepy," Aubriel said.

"See! That's why I like you best," Dr. Nolan told his younger daughter. "You have a much more mature outlook."

Cienna threw a French fry at him. "She's a brat, and you're a brat!" she informed them both. "Now, can we go home?"

They had finished eating.

"We can go," Dr. Nolan said, putting on his coat. "I've got work to do. After I feed the animals, I've got to clean my rifle."

Cienna pushed him from behind, but they were all laughing as they left the building. It had been a good half hour of private time.

The next morning, after speaking with Mrs. Harden and reviewing ground rules, he dropped Cienna off and took Aubriel with him to Eileen's house. She had lined up another twenty-four testing sites to visit, and once again, Uncle Mike had willingly volunteered to help. It would bring their total sample list to forty-two, and there were still no results back from the lab. It was the first week of December.

Mike and Eileen were in the kitchen with fresh coffee and banana bread. Aubriel hugged her aunt and sat down, a plate already waiting for her.

"You do realize that's actually good for you," her father warned. "It has real bananas hidden inside."

Aubriel made a face but kept eating.

"At least it's not raining today," Mike offered. He smiled, his broken tooth newly replaced.

"I thought you were getting a gold tooth with a diamond in it," Dr. Nolan joked. "Like the Rappers."

"For what this cost, it should have been gold," Mike answered. "You've got to be a millionaire just to go to the damn dentist!"

Dr. Nolan shook his head. "Speaking of millionaires," he said, "what do you know about Mr. Darden? I just found out he had a daughter that passed away in infancy."

"Before my time, Doc," Mike said. "He's got the same number of friends as I have enemies, which is zero. He keeps to himself, and that's good news for everybody else."

"Any idea how he managed to buy up so much land?" Dr. Nolan asked.

"I knew one old family that sold out to him and moved into a city house," Mike remembered. "He just kept upping his offer until they couldn't say no. But that was before I was even born. Sorry."

"No. No. It all helps," Dr. Nolan assured him. He sat thinking for a while.

"You wouldn't know where his well was located? Before he switched over to river water for irrigation," he finally asked.

Mike shook his head.

"But there would be records," Eileen said. "Every well and septic system has to be permitted and tested."

Dr. Nolan gave her a knowing smile. "If you feel like it, maybe you could do a little computer work with Aubriel while Mike and I go play?" he suggested.

"We can try," Eileen said, patting Aubriel on the arm. "It'll be like a treasure hunt." She gave Dr. Nolan and her husband a list of addresses. "Better get to it while the sun is shining."

The two men headed out, both collecting samples along the same road leading to the river, but on opposite sides. At every stop they were greeted openly and without hesitation. Word was slowly getting out about the pretext of their work, and to date no one had refused their visit except for Mr. Darden.

Dr. Nolan was so focused on finding house numbers that he didn't notice the gray Jeep that was following him. At every stop, the Jeep would pull over to the side of the road and wait, only moving again when Dr. Nolan drove to the next location. But somebody noticed. In a small, close community, strangers lit up the scenery like a neon sign.

Myron Lentz was making entries of addresses in a ledger when the town sheriff pulled in behind his rental car and switched on his roof lights. The sheriff radioed in for a license plate check before approaching the driver side window.

"Howdy," the sheriff greeted him. "You having car trouble?" Bob Dent was sixty and a little overweight, but he had an affable personality and a combined thirty years of military and civil police experience. He was a common-sense, no-frills official that had the full support of the community.

"Oh, no, no," Myron Lentz answered. He tried to recall the cover story he was supposed to use. "I'm here on business. Scouting real estate for future development."

"You seem to be scouting in slow motion," the sheriff said. "Got a call that you've been parked out here for hours. You have any ID?"

Myron Lentz handed over his driver's license. "I don't know the area very well," Mr. Lentz explained. "I've been checking site maps on my computer. Pretty time-consuming." He was starting to sweat.

The sheriff handed him back his paperwork. "Who do you represent, Mr. Lentz?"

Myron Lentz shifted in his seat, trying to find a comfortable position. "My clients wish to remain confidential for now," he lied. "They don't want word getting out that they're looking for property in this area."

"You better get a new map," the sheriff said. "This is all agriculture and private homes. All the commercial land is back about a mile or so, up by the railroad tracks. Probably best you go up that way."

Myron Lentz nodded. "Okay. Thanks for your help," he said. He slowly made a U-turn and drove east, back toward the industrial zone.

The sheriff walked down the road to the next driveway, just as Dr. Nolan was finishing.

"Hello, Doc," he said, extending his hand. They had known each other for fifteen years. The sheriff looked in the back of the car at all the labeled sample containers. "I heard rumors that you and Mike were back at it. Any news yet?"

"No, not yet. Maybe next week," Dr. Nolan answered. He knew, of all the people in town, it would be nearly impossible to keep any secrets from Sheriff Dent.

"You piss anybody off lately?" the sheriff asked.

"Don't think so, but it's early." Dr. Nolan smiled. "We're only testing farms by invitation. Somebody unhappy?"

The sheriff scratched his neck and nodded toward the road. "I think someone was following you this morning. I ran him off for now, but his story was pretty weak. I've got his name and address. Keep your eyes open for a gray Jeep with a rental tag on the back bumper."

"No shit?!" Dr. Nolan laughed out loud. It seemed like something out of a movie. "Go find the guy and tell him he can ride with me. Save him some gas money."

The sheriff smiled, but it was not a totally benign situation. "I don't like strangers that are bad liars," he said. "Just keep your eyes open, that's all. Might not amount to anything, but maybe you poked a stick in a bees' nest. You take care."

Dr. Nolan felt his smile losing traction. He nodded, but the idea that someone was worried enough to follow him was unnerving.

"Thanks, Bob. Lay off the doughnuts," Dr. Nolan called after him. The sheriff did not turn around but gave him the finger as he disappeared up the driveway.

Dr. Nolan drove to the edge of the street and sat there, looking in both directions, over and over. There were no cars, no trucks, nothing. He shrugged off a chill and headed to his next stop, but every few seconds he checked his rear-view mirror. It was an odd feeling.

Three miles to the northeast, Myron Lentz had located the home belonging to Lenny Darden. He knocked on the door and was greeted by Mrs. Darden. She was small, almost painfully timid, and did not make eye contact.

"Check the barn," she said, already closing the door.

Myron Lentz went down the stairs and made his way across the large, open parking area to the first barn. He had purchased jeans, a wool shirt, and a heavy outdoor jacket, but was still wearing designer shoes. The mud was deep enough that it reached his ankles.

The first barn was empty. He found Lenny Darden in the second building, trying to replace a broken hydraulic line on one of his tractors. A large propane heater kept the work area bearable. Myron Lentz stood as close to it as possible without bursting into flames.

"Who the fuck are you?" Mr. Darden asked, eyeing the younger man from head to toe. He chuckled when he saw the mud-caked shoes.

"Mr. Darden. I'm Myron Lentz. Mr. Saunders suggested I stop by and speak with you."

"You a goddamn lawyer too? You look like one," Mr. Darden said. He spit tobacco juice.

"Yes, I am an attorney. I was asked to come here and make an assessment of where things stand. If there's any publicity…"

"Publicity!" Mr. Darden tossed his wrench on the ground. "They send some Jew boy lawyer down here to handle publicity? How about my fifty-million-dollar land deal? That concern you at all?"

Myron Lentz backed away a few steps. He had no idea what the other man was talking about. "I don't know all the details of what you're referring to," he admitted. "I'm trying to find out what Dr. Nolan knows, and to keep the company informed."

"And what is the good doctor up to? I'd like to know that, too!" Mr. Darden said. "Fucking asshole can't mind his own business!"

Myron Lentz backed up another step. "He's out visiting farms on the other end of the dike area. Getting more samples, I think. Your local sheriff ran me off. But I don't think he has any information yet."

"That's probably true. You don't think. But I'll tell you what I think. If Dr. Nolan keeps fucking around, he's going to eventually find something. And you and that cocksucker boss of yours want to do an assessment! That's not good enough."

Myron Lentz had dealt with a fairly wide range of difficult and demanding clients, but Mr. Darden was coarse, irrational, and barely able to control himself.

"Mr. Saunders was hoping you would feel better with someone from the company on site. Any added attention at this point will only make things worse."

Mr. Darden wiped his oil-soaked hands on a rag. "Remind your boss I don't work for him. I work for me and my family. I'm not going to sit around when they're being threatened. You got that?"

Myron Lentz nodded. "Give me forty-eight hours, Mr. Darden. That's all I'm asking," he said.

"My time clock is already running," Mr. Darden said. "And I ain't Santa Claus. I'm not here to hand out presents. Like I said, I don't work for you or your company." He tossed the filthy towel to the younger man. "You can use that to wipe off your pretty shoes on the way out."

Myron Lentz understood their meeting was over. He nodded, turned, and went back to his car. With some effort, he was able to remove the heavy mud from his feet, but the shoes were ruined, and as the car warmed up, he realized it wasn't just mud. The thick aroma was a mixture of cow manure and diesel. By the time he reached his hotel, he could feel the first stages of a migraine headache.

He took a Vicodin and a hot shower, then wore his bathroom slippers to a nearby department store. The options were not extensive, but he managed to buy a pair of insulated work boots that would offer some protection from the elements. With his headache in slow retreat, he picked up Thai food, ate in his room, then called Mr. Saunders on his home phone.

"Myron. All settled in?" Mr. Saunders asked.

Myron Lentz looked at his surroundings. It was not exactly what he was used to in his normal travels.

"I'm good," he said. "I spent a lovely morning watching Dr. Nolan collecting more environmental samples. Then I met Mr. Darden this afternoon."

"And…?"

"I don't think Dr. Nolan knows anything," he said. "As far as I could see, it's just him and one other man visiting farms. It's just too quiet. Too low-key."

"Well, that's comforting. At least for now," Mr. Saunders added. "And Darden? Is he keeping a low profile?"

Myron Lentz took a deep breath before he answered. "He's a low IQ, vulgar, bigoted pig," he said. "He tries to act tough, but it's not just anger driving him. He's in panic mode. I don't think he heard one thing I said."

Doug Saunders sat back in his chair. The chess match he was playing was nearing end-game status. There were only a few pieces left on the board, and their possible moves were limited. There were basically only two choices: act or react.

"Do you believe he can be reasoned with?" he asked the younger man.

"No, I don't," Myron Lentz answered. "He's a caveman looking for a club. He was ranting about some big land deal. How this was going to ruin him. I got the feeling there's more going on here than what I was told."

Doug Saunders smiled slightly. He had personally chosen the young lawyer because he was smart, efficient, and followed instructions. For the immediate situation, he was the perfect front man.

"There are some aspects of this that were not made clear," Mr. Saunders admitted. "But that was done to protect you. They are not facts that would influence your role. What are your plans tomorrow?"

"I'm going to meet with the mayor in the morning," Myron Lentz explained. "I managed to run into the local sheriff today, so I'm using the same real estate development cover. I'll see if anyone seems nervous."

"Good. You might think about getting a haircut, too," Mr. Saunders suggested. "Small-town barbers can be a valuable source of gossip."

Myron Lentz took note of the suggestion. He was still extremely uncomfortable, but some aspects of his assignment were new and strangely exciting.

"Okay. I'll update you tomorrow," he said. "You still want me to call your home after business hours?"

"That's best," Mr. Saunders said. "The fewer people that know about this, the better. Good job, Myron."

The young lawyer hung up the phone. He fluffed up his pillows, layed back, and searched for the cable channel streaming business news. The Dow Jones and NASDAQ had been on fire, and his stocks were soaring.

16

Turning toward his clinic on Monday morning, Dr. Nolan noticed the gray Jeep Cherokee parked outside City Hall with the engine running. There was a man behind the wheel, but the tinted glass made it impossible to see his face. Dr. Nolan circled around the block, slowed long enough to see the rental decal on the bumper, then went to his office.

He thought about calling Sheriff Dent, but to what purpose? If someone was actually taking an interest in local business, that in itself was not illegal. Just interesting. He put on coffee and waited for Cat to arrive. The door had not closed behind her before he started on his list.

"I need you to search death certificates back in '62, '63, and 1964. Lenny Darden had a daughter who died during that time period. I don't have a first name, but she was only two or three. Then I need to know if Eileen found out anything about the original well on the Darden Farm. Not the big farm now, but the old farm." He stopped to take a breath.

"Can I hang my coat up first?" Cat asked him, her eyebrows raised.

"Oh, sorry. Sure. You want coffee?" Dr. Nolan asked.

"And a Xanax," Cat said. "Maybe you should take one."

He realized his urgency was becoming unbearable. "I'm sorry," he said again. "But now I'm being followed. The sheriff caught some guy keeping tabs on me out on the Bottoms, and just now I saw the same Jeep parked at City Hall."

Cat leaned against the wall in the nurses' station. "Jesus, Sean, this is creepy," she said, clearly concerned. "You don't think there's any real danger, do you?"

Dr. Nolan shrugged. "The sheriff questioned him, but he thought the guy was lying his head off. But at least they know about him. I guess that's good."

"Well," Cat said, "if anyone driving a Jeep comes in, I'll shoot them. I've got my 9 mill Beretta in my purse." She rarely went anywhere alone without it.

"Shit, half our patients drive Jeeps." Dr. Nolan laughed. "You can't shoot that many people."

Cat laughed too. "Okay," she admitted. "I'll only shoot strangers driving Jeeps. Now give me that list again, but slowly this time. Maybe then I can make sense out of what you want."

He brought her coffee, then repeated his catalogue of requests, just as the first patient was arriving. He disappeared into an exam room, and Cat settled in at her computer. It took an hour, but a death certificate for an Amy Elizabeth Darden was registered in February of 1964. Cat left it on the screen and waved him over between patients.

He squinted at the nearly illegible handwritten document. The girl had died at the age of three, and the cause was listed as AML, acute myeloid leukemia. Dr. Nolan muttered something under his breath.

"What?" Cat asked.

"That's exceedingly rare," he repeated, keeping his voice down. "Wrong age group. But it all fits into a bigger picture."

"What bigger picture?" Cat asked, but Dr. Nolan was already elsewhere in his thoughts.

"Eileen? Did you talk to her yet?"

Cat sighed, trying to remember the message. "She said she found what you wanted and that she would print it out and bring it by on the way to her treatment."

Dr. Nolan nodded. He was staring at the wall. Eileen's radiation schedule required her to be at the hospital by 1:00 p.m.

"The 'kid'," Dr. Nolan almost whispered. "You know Jed. Jed Marcus. I've got his cell phone number. See if he can be here at noon."

Cat was not pleased to be handed another errand, but she could sense something had changed. Dr. Nolan was almost trancelike. "You okay?" she asked.

He did not look at her, but continued to stare straight ahead.

"When you were little and a thunderstorm came, you know how you see the lightning, and then you wait, and you count, and you almost hold your breath until the thunderclap?"

"Sure," Cat said. "We all did that."

"That's what this is now," he told her. "We're just counting the seconds."

Before she could ask for an explanation, he got up and went to see the next patient. She was worried about him, but could not accurately read his emotions. He almost seemed sad. She called Jed Marcus as he had asked, and just before noon, Eileen dropped off an old survey map of the Darden homestead. The original well site was clearly marked, as was the water flow rate and the drilling depth.

Dr. Nolan was at his desk studying the chart when Amanda interrupted.

"Jed Marcus is out here. Said you called."

"Great. Have him come in. And at least make a pretense of not eavesdropping," he told her. Dr. Nolan pulled a second chair close to his desk, then closed the door when Jed was in the office. Dr. Nolan shook his hand.

"My toe is back to normal," the young man informed him, sitting down.

"That's good, kid, you may need it," Dr. Nolan said. "You interested in a little moonlighting, so to speak?"

Jed smiled. He could already tell this was not a routine social call. "What do you have in mind?"

Dr. Nolan explained he had been collecting water and soil samples from the Bottoms and that Lenny Darden had refused permission. He made it clear it was an aggressive rejection, and that now he was being followed. There was no mention of the real reason he was so determined to obtain them.

"So, you want me to trespass on this guy's land and get water from the old well and some bottles of dirt?" Jed repeated.

"Pretty much. And you make five hundred dollars toward your college fund," Dr. Nolan said.

Jed laughed at the implied use of the money. He looked at the map again, noting where the wellhead was in relation to the house.

"Simple job, Doc. This guy have dogs?" Jed asked.

"At least one," Dr. Nolan said. "And you need some way to get the water. The well is around forty feet deep."

Jed nodded and smiled. "You got any Ativan?" he asked. "While the dog takes a nap, I can use a hand pump to get your sample. We carry them to get fuel when there's no gas station around."

"I can write a script for the Ativan," Dr. Nolan told him. "But I need this done in a hurry."

Jed pulled up the weather report on his cell phone. There was barely a sliver of moon.

"Tonight fast enough? This sounds like fun," he said. "And what about the guy following you? You want me to discourage him?"

Dr. Nolan laughed nervously, a little uncertain of how the young man might define "discourage."

"Not just yet," he said. "Besides, Cat already offered to shoot him free of charge."

"I bet she would too." Jed nodded.

Dr. Nolan caught his gaze and held it. "You okay with this? I don't want anyone to get hurt, especially you."

Jed folded the map and tucked it into his coat pocket. "Two-hour job," he said. "But I could use a driver. I don't want to park my truck out in plain sight. You up for some excitement?"

Dr. Nolan had not considered acting as an accomplice, but he could see the necessity of having two sets of eyes and hands. He would ask Eileen if his girls could stay at her house for the night.

"I guess that makes me your wheelman," Dr. Nolan told him. "What do you need me to bring?"

"You supply the sleeping pill and the sample bottles," Jed explained. "I've got to make a quick trip to Home Depot. Let's say we meet here at about 1:00 a.m."

Dr. Nolan nodded. "Thanks, kid," he said. "But don't tell your mom. She'd skin me alive."

"Both of us." Jed laughed. "See you later."

Dr. Nolan finished the afternoon but was horribly distracted. He had Cat run to the pharmacy to fill a prescription for the dog tranquilizer, packed a bag with sterile sample bottles, collected his daughters, and went straight home. He fed the animals, fed the dog, fed his girls, then explained they needed to stay at their aunt's for the night.

"You got a date?" Cienna asked. He was never away from them, and this was a change that caused some anxiety.

"Yes. I have a date," he admitted. "But it's with a young man."

"Oh, oh." Aubriel laughed, her face red.

"No, smart ass," her father said. "I'm helping him with getting into college." It was not entirely a fabricated story. He had them come sit with him on the sofa, then placed an arm around each girl, and hugged them tightly.

"You ever think about dating?" Cienna asked.

"Yes. No," he answered. "I've already got too many women in my life. Why make it worse?"

Aubriel elbowed him in the ribs. They just sat for a moment.

"You think about Mom?" Cienna finally asked.

"Every day," he said.

"We do too."

He sighed and hugged them even tighter. "She'd like that," he said.

$\overline{17}$

JED MARCUS PULLED INTO THE CLINIC parking lot at 12:50 a.m. He was wearing camouflage fatigues with a knit cap, and carried a bulky Knapsack and a plastic bag from Safeway. He got into the passenger seat of Dr. Nolan's car.

"You bring snacks?" Dr. Nolan asked, noting the shopping bag.

"Meat for the dog," Jed explained. "You got the pills?"

Dr. Nolan handed him the medicine bottle containing two Alprazolam. He used the grip handle of a small screwdriver to crush them into a coarse powder, then made a patty of hamburger and folded the medicine inside. Then he rolled his sleeping potion into a ball.

"We ready?" Dr. Nolan asked. He was eager to get started, nervous energy heightening every sensation.

"Head down there." Jed nodded. "I've got night vision, a shovel, a hand pump, a pipe wrench, tubing, and a semi-automatic Glock. We're all set."

Dr. Nolan turned down the main street and crossed the tracks into the Bottoms. There was no other traffic on the roads, and they reached the outer fence line of the Darden Farm in just a few minutes. Jed motioned for him to pull over. He took a small, two-way radio out of his pocket and handed it to Dr. Nolan.

"No talking," Jed instructed him. "If there is any problem on either end, just key the mike button three times. When I'm coming out, I'll key it five times. And you can't be more than half a mile away. Clear?"

"Clear," Dr. Nolan said. "But where's the part where I get to drive fast?"

Jed smiled and shook his head. "With luck, no one will ever know we were here," he said. "You only get to drive fast if we get caught."

"Okay, kid, and please be careful," Dr. Nolan answered.

Jed got out of the car and moved to the tree line running along the fence, then watched as Dr. Nolan slowly drove off to the north. Kneeling, he smeared his face with a nonreflective paint and put on his night-vision goggles. He tossed his bag over the barbed wire barrier, grabbed on to a sturdy tree limb, and swung over the fence. He was officially on enemy territory.

The outdoor light from the farmhouse and the barns made it seem like full daylight. It was a simple task to navigate through the trees and shrubbery. About fifty feet from the side of Mr. Darden's home, he crouched down behind the trunk of a maple tree.

From the front pocket of his pack he took out the medicine-laced hamburger and a dog whistle. To this point he had not seen the guard animal. He gave a low-effort puff of air on the device and waited. With no response, he then turned up the volume with his next attempt.

The old black lab came running down from the porch, barking and turning in all directions, not certain where the high-pitched sound had come from. Jed waited until the dog moved in the opposite direction, then rolled the ball of meat past him. The animal barked some more, but the scent of the bait was winning out over duty. After a few tentative sniffs, he downed the offering, then started barking again.

A second porch light came on, and Jed heard the front door slam.

"Goddamn it! Shut up!" yelled Mr. Darden. He was scanning the yard and parking area with the beam of a flashlight. Once, twice, three times he slowly illuminated the perimeter around the house but saw nothing out of the ordinary. The dog retreated to the porch with her tail down.

Satisfied, Mr. Darden slammed the door again as he disappeared inside, then switched off the light. Jed checked his watch, then sat with his back against the tree, waiting patiently for half an hour. Then he tried the whistle again, and then again. There was no answer.

He stood up, stretched, then made his way out past the second barn. One soil sample was taken from that area, and a second about one hundred yards out into an open field. Done, he retraced his path toward the homestead, but made his way to the rear of the barns where their map had shown the location of the old well. It was partially covered with blackberry vines, but exactly where it was supposed to be.

Wearing thick gloves, Jed cut away the bushes to expose the rusted pipe. He sprayed a generous coating of WD-40 on the cap and threads, adjusted the pipe wrench, and began pulling with all his weight. Young and in excellent shape, he could not get it to budge.

He had anticipated such an argument. A small propane torch was the next item out of his pack. He ignited the blue flame and heated the rusted cap until it was more favorably inclined, then kicked the wrench handle with his boot. The cap released its grip.

Once off, Jed threaded a thin black hose down the open casing, secured it to the hand pump, and began cranking the handle. There was a flow of water in less than a minute. Dark and thick with sediment at first, another minute allowed him to fill one of the sample containers with clear fluid.

He replaced the cap, packed up his work tools, and tried to rearrange the weeds and vines back over the wellhead. It was not perfect, but it was the best he could manage. Without making a sound, he made his way back along the outer fringe of the mowed lawn to the area of fence where he had entered. It was now two thirty. He took out the walkie-talkie and keyed the mike button five times.

Dr. Nolan had driven in slow circles around the Bottoms so many times he almost felt dizzy. He had tried to park at a dozen sites, but felt so conspicuous after just a few minutes that he would pull back onto the road and keep moving. The few times that he passed another car, he was convinced they were watching him, taking notes of his every action. His shirt was soaked with sweat.

When the two-way radio began its signal pattern, his heart rate doubled. Each crackling squeal was separated by what seemed like minutes. At the third keyed stroke, he held his breath, then exhaled when the fourth and last sequence were transmitted. He turned once again onto the road that passed the Darden Farm, then stopped at the original drop site.

Jed checked for other cars, lowered his bag over the top of the fence, then did an acrobatic summersault over the barrier, landing squarely on his feet. He took off his night-vision headgear and grabbed the door handle. It was locked.

"Oh, shit! Sorry," Dr. Nolan apologized, releasing the safety latch. Jed threw his pack in the rear seat and climbed in, a broad smile on his face.

"Doc, we can't make a quick getaway if you lock me out of the car," he laughed. "That's not how this works."

"This is my first heist," Dr. Nolan admitted. "Now, do I drive fast?"

"No, just regular speed," Jed told him. "Like I said, simple. Routine."

Dr. Nolan put the car in drive and headed back to the clinic.

"Simple for you, maybe," he said. "I'm exhausted. Everything went okay?"

"Well was stubborn, but you have your samples. You said it takes a month to get them back?"

"To test everything, yes," Dr. Nolan said. "If you're testing for something specific, it's a lot faster."

"And do you know what you're looking for?" the young man asked.

"Not a fucking clue," Dr. Nolan admitted. "Just something."

They had arrived at the clinic. Jed pulled the sample bottles from his pack and laid them on the seat.

"Been fun, Doc," he said.

"Come by tomorrow and I'll write you a check," Dr. Nolan said.

Jed leaned down and looked at him, still smiling. "Keep your money, Doc. This was just plain fun. I'm glad I could help." He closed the door, climbed into his truck, and was gone before Dr. Nolan could respond. He sat back in his seat and let out a long breath. Whenever he was becoming pessimistic about people or the state of the world, there were always acts of kindness or selfless homage that restored his hopes. He was deeply grateful for the young man's help.

Dr. Nolan looked at his watch. If he was lucky, he could manage to secure three hours of sleep before returning to work. It would be enough, but his level of fatigue was growing exponentially. At some point there needed to be a resting point.

He headed home, climbing into bed just after 4:00 a.m. He let Callie sleep on the floor beside him.

Two hours later, Lenny Darden walked out of his house just as the sun was beginning to reclaim the sky-line. His dog usually greeted him, but this morning she was fast asleep, snoring loudly with each breath. He gave her a shove with his foot, but she barely lifted her head.

He buttoned up his coat against the cold air and headed for the barn, still trying to get his tractor back in service. At the door he noticed a series of boot prints in the half-dry mud that were sharp and undisturbed. He followed them around the side of the building to the rear, all the way to the old well. The overgrown brush showed evidence of recent activity. There were cut vines, and the grass had been trampled flat. He touched the well cap, then smelled the oily residue it left on his hands.

He clenched his jaw until the muscles ached.

18

THE MEETING BETWEEN MYRON LENTZ AND Mayor Tillis
had been cordial and reassuring. As he had done with the
sheriff, the young lawyer represented himself as the agent
for a large corporation seeking to expand their operations
into the area. He intimated that it would bring a number
of high-paying jobs into the community. When pressed
for details, Mr. Lentz would only say that it was related to
high-tech manufacturing.

"Your location on the rail line and the river would be
perfect for us," he told the mayor. "Not to mention the
freeway access north and south."

Mayor Tillis was elated. Any promise of enriching the
tax base was eagerly embraced.

"I can't speak for the whole city council," he said, "but
we might be able to negotiate some tax benefits to help get

things started. And we would certainly speed up permits and inspections along the way. Anything to help."

Myron Lentz nodded and pretended to take notes. "This does seem like an ideal site," he told the mayor. "No problems with power supplies or available water?"

"None at all," the mayor assured him. "Those are the two things you can count on in the Pacific Northwest—water and hydropower. We even have our own local power plant up the Lewis River."

Myron Lentz wrote down more invisible information. "So, no major obstacles that you can think of? Nothing that would hold up a large project like this?"

"Nothing at all," Mayor Tillis answered. "The growth in the area is phenomenal. Started in Portland, then Vancouver, and now it's pushing up this way. Every week there's something new."

Myron Lentz put his notepad into his briefcase and stood up. He shook hands with the mayor. "This is all good news," he said. "We'll be in touch with you in the very near future."

"Do you have a card?" the mayor asked.

Myron Lentz smiled at him. "I'll write down my office number and my cell phone number," he said. "But no company name for now. This is just a preliminary contact."

"I understand completely," Mayor Tillis said. "Let me know if we can help with anything." He walked the young man out and held the door for him.

Myron Lentz drove through town until he found a barbershop. He stayed in his car until there were two people ahead of him, then went in and sat down to wait. He listened to stories about fishing, timber prices, the high school football team, and a bad wreck on the river highway. It was all just normal talk.

When it was his turn, the barber looked at him with an amused expression. "You don't look like you need much of a haircut," he commented.

"Just neaten it up." Myron Lentz smiled. "I like to stay ahead of the game."

The barber placed a cover over him and fastened it at the neck. "You here on business?" he asked.

"Yes. Just scouting new business sites," Myron Lentz answered. "Seems like a nice, quiet little town."

"It is," the barber agreed. "Nothing much ever happens around here."

"Perfect," said Myron Lentz. He was smiling at himself in the mirror. "That's just perfect."

19

DR. NOLAN MANAGED TO SURVIVE THE morning clinic schedule on Tuesday by sheer willpower. He was physically and emotionally drained. Cat helped him ship out the newly obtained samples from the Darden Farm by UPS, but at noon, it was not food that offered any interest. He went home, put his feet up on the ottoman, and fell asleep for ninety minutes.

Even though it had barely been three weeks since the beginning of his search, the investigation had assumed control of his life. Every waking moment was devoted to finding answers, and half of his dreams were populated by the apparition of those who had been made ill or died. Those were not his responsibility. But if there was a reason, a cause, then not finding it would be his fault.

When the workday mercifully ended, he and his daughters headed straight home. Dr. Nolan was determined to force a more normal schedule and retire early. After surveying the dinner options in the freezer, he placed a Stouffers Lasagna in the oven and set the timer.

"When this goes off, just set it on the top of the stove," he told Cienna. "I'll be back in half an hour."

With Callie at his side, he stopped to fill the water trough, then made his way to the barn. But tonight there were no welcoming calls. He switched on the inner lights and waited for his eyes to focus. The miniature donkeys and goats were tightly huddled in the far corner of their pen, nervously shifting positions and trying to compress themselves into an even more compact company.

He had only seen them behave this way when there were wild dogs or coyotes nearby, and usually Callie would sound the alarm. Tonight, at least since he had been home, there had been no hint of any unusual visitors.

"Whoa. Easy," Dr. Nolan soothed them, unlocking the gate to their enclosure. "What's everybody so upset about?" He came forward slowly, holding out the plastic bag filled with Fig Newtons. It was the one panacea that never failed. One by one, the animals came to him. It was then he realized they were not all there.

Sasha, the first donkey he had purchased as a baby, was not with the others. As herd animals, his wards were never apart from one another, and her absence was an immediate serious concern. Only illness or injury would have caused her to separate from her friends.

Dr. Nolan quickly filled the grain bucket and set out hay, then grabbed a flashlight from a shelf near the door. He went out into the open pasture area and began to call to her.

"Sasha, where are you, girl? Are you hurt? Talk to me, girl." His eyes squinted through the beam of the light. Then, near the corner of the fences, he found her hanging from a low branch in an old cottonwood tree. He ran, half stumbling in the tall grass, but he already knew it was too late.

Someone had knotted a rope around her neck, thrown it over the supporting branch, then hoisted her up so only her back feet could touch the ground. The torn-up earth where she had tried to save herself was testimony to her last moments. She had died in agony and terror.

"Oh, no, no, no, no..." he cried. "Please, God. No." He threw the flashlight down. Then hugging her, he cut the rope and lowered her to the ground. He sat down and pulled her head across his lap, rubbing her along the neck.

"My baby, my baby," he sighed. He was rocked by one wave of tears after another, his eyes burning. He kept imagining what she had suffered in the final moments before death. And it had been his responsibility to protect her and keep her safe from harm.

"I'm so sorry," he told her. "I didn't keep my promise. I'm so sorry."

He cried for many long minutes until there were no more tears, and then slowly, the anger began to build. His most gentle and loving animal had been murdered in the most loathsome and inhumane way imaginable. And there was no doubt in his mind who was responsible.

He sat holding Sasha until he heard Cienna calling his name over and over from the house. He dreaded telling his daughters what had happened, but it affected their lives as much as his. He gently laid Sasha's head on the grass, stood, and went back to the house.

"What's wrong?" Cienna asked the moment she saw his face and reddened eyes. He had her get Aubriel from her room, sat them at the kitchen table, and explained what he had found.

"Who would do that?" Cienna began to cry. While neither of his girls helped much with the farm duties, they knew and loved all the animals.

"Someone filled with hate," their father said. He let them have their tears, then consoled them as best he could.

"What happens now?" Aubriel asked him.

Dr. Nolan thought for a moment. Since their home was outside the city limits, he would have to call the county sheriff. When they finished, he would have to dig a grave. He explained what needed to be done and asked them to stay and finish their homework and baths without him yelling and begging them each step of the way. And he knew dinner was a low priority, but urged them to eat something.

He dialed 911 and gave a brief report to the dispatcher. An officer would be there within an hour. Then he went upstairs and unlocked his gun cabinet. He kept a .227 rifle with a scope on hand to persuade intruders they should vacate his property. He loaded five shells into the receiver, slid the bolt, and chambered a live round, then double-checked the safety.

He was just about to go back outside when another sobering thought occurred to him. Anyone capable of such a hideous act was no longer governed by the rules of humanity. They had moved beyond such restraints. And what might they do next?

He looked through his wallet, relieved he had saved the cell phone number for Jed Marcus.

"Jesus, Doc, another night job?" The young man laughed. Dr. Nolan told him what had happened.

"I need to know my girls are safe," he said. "Are you free for a little security work?"

"Absolutely," Jed answered. "Let me pack some clothes. You mind if I bring some extra manpower? One of my buddies is on home leave right now too."

"I'd appreciate it," Dr. Nolan said. "And, Jed, bring whatever you feel might be necessary. There are no more rules when it comes to my family."

"Understood," Jed acknowledged. "Give me your address. I should be there in about an hour."

Dr. Nolan hung up and kissed both of his daughters on the forehead. He forced a smile.

"The sheriff will be here soon. Tell him to follow the lights out by the barn. And lock up when I leave."

He took the rifle with him, collected a pick and shovel from the garage, then loaded everything into the front bucket of his John Deere tractor. He fired up the engine, turned on the headlights, then drove to the large gate leading to the pasture. With the darkness held at bay, he chose a spot near the dead animal and began to dig.

His anger steadily mounting, he used the tractor as if it was a weapon. The soil was soft from heavy rains. Pushing the throttle to full, he cut through the sod, ripping it away with each forward run, then bit deeper and deeper into the earth. As the pit grew, his angle of attack became ever steeper. At four feet, his machine was nearly vertical, barely able to back out of the hole.

He parked his tractor so the lights would illuminate the work area. Climbing off, he slid down the wet dirt into the grave, then used the pick and shovel to sculpt the edges and corners. Soaking with sweat in the cold air, he knelt, filled both hands with damp soil, and smeared it over his face and forehead. He breathed in the musky, thick odor of it, and then tasted it, wanting to remember.

"Hello. Mr. Nolan. You out here?" a voice called. "Deputy Rosen from county."

"Down here," Dr. Nolan said. He saw the flashlight beam come nearer.

"You all right?" the deputy asked.

Dr. Nolan stood and looked up at him, only his eyes visible in his earthen mask.

"No," he said in a muffled voice. "No, I'm not. But I could use a hand."

The deputy leaned over and helped pull him up from the excavated pit.

"What happened to your face?" the deputy asked.

"Took a fall," Dr. Nolan explained. He pointed to the body of the miniature donkey. The deputy bent down on one knee, examined the rope tied around the animals throat, then aimed his light up to the tree limb that had held her.

"That's pretty fucking sick," he sighed, and it was a genuine disgust. "This is how future murderers begin their careers, killing defenseless animals. Unruly kids. You have any idea? Any problem with local teenagers?"

Dr. Nolan did not answer. He shook his head to say no. There was no point telling the deputy sheriff what he suspected.

"Can't get prints from rope," Deputy Rosen explained. "Unless someone saw something, there isn't much I can do except file a report. Then, if something else like this happens, we might be able to establish a pattern."

"Can I bury her?" Dr. Nolan asked.

"Let me take some pictures. I've got a camera in the car." He left for just a minute, then returned with a digital camera. He took a dozen photographs of the scene from various angles, checking his viewing screen to make certain they showed every detail.

"I'm very sorry about this," he said. "You're the doctor in Woodhaven, right?"

"I am," Dr. Nolan said.

"In our jobs, sometimes, I don't know. You see things no one should have to see. Things that just don't make sense. Things that make you feel sick."

Dr. Nolan knew what the younger man was trying to say. Any profession that dealt with the darker side of life knew the feeling, and the weight of it could be crushing.

He was grateful that Deputy Rosen still had his empathy intact.

"I'm glad they sent you," Dr. Nolan told him. "You have everything you need?"

The deputy nodded. "You want me to help?" he asked.

"No, thanks. Too painful," Dr. Nolan said. "This is my job."

Deputy Rosen nodded again. He handed his card to Dr. Nolan. "Anything comes up, call me," he said. "Whoever did this doesn't belong on this planet anymore."

"That we agree on," Dr. Nolan said. "And thank you again."

The deputy took one last look at the lifeless animal, half waved, then headed back to his patrol car.

Dr. Nolan repositioned the tractor so the loader was just at the back of the dead animal. As he was starting to push and pull her into the bucket, Jed Marcus appeared. He was carrying an assault rifle and had his pistol in a holster beneath his left arm. Without a word, he knelt down and began to help.

With her body secure, Dr. Nolan moved her to the gravesite and slowly lowered the bucket, then tipped the blade gently downward until she slid into place. Then he began the process of covering her until there was no visible trace left. Only the scarred earth remained as a marker.

Jed made a quick inspection of the hanging tree, then placed the pick and shovel back in the tractor. He handed Dr. Nolan his rifle, then followed him out of the pasture, locking the gate behind them.

Dr. Nolan parked near the driveway and stepped down, shaking the young man's hand.

"Sorry, Doc," he said. "You think this is our buddy from last night?"

"Yes. He was sending me a message," Dr. Nolan explained. "A big 'or else.'"

"It's still early," Jed told him. "I could pay my respects if you want."

The suggestion was tempting as an immediate reaction, but not a long-term solution. There was no proof, no evidence, no reasonable explanation for anything yet.

"Thanks, but no thanks," Dr. Nolan said. "I just need to make sure my daughters are safe. I know it's a lot to ask, but can you and your friend cover guard duty at night? At least for a while?"

"I've got over a month of free time, Doc," Jed told him. "It would be a pleasure to keep an eye on things. But if someone tries to come on your property after dark, I won't be as charitable as you. That a problem?"

"Not after this," Dr. Nolan answered. "Let's go inside. You've met my daughters at the clinic. I want to explain that you'll be staying with us for a while. The couch okay?"

"Beats a foxhole." Jed laughed. He followed Dr. Nolan into the kitchen.

"Holy shit!" Cienna said. "Is that a machine gun?" She was staring at the AR-15.

"Kind of." Jed smiled. "It's actually a semiautomatic with a few, let's say, special modifications. But very effective for close-range use." He was proud of his work.

"I just hired Jed as your new babysitter," Dr. Nolan announced. "He's going to stay here at night until things settle down."

"God, you look horrible," Aubriel told her father. "Did you bury Sasha?"

Dr. Nolan nodded. "She gets to stay here forever now," he said, but could not go on. He had thought the tears had ended, but they were not very far away.

"You want something to eat?" Cienna asked, her maternal instincts stirring. Neither girl knew how to make him feel better.

"No, thanks. Just a shower and sleep." Dr. Nolan smiled, but with a forced affect. "Cienna, it would help if you got sheets and a blanket out for Mr. Marcus. And, Jed, pantry and refrigerator are all yours. If you need anything special, just make a list."

"It's all good, Doc," he said. "I won't be sleeping much tonight. You guys just try to get back on schedule."

That was a tall order, but at least they all felt better having him there. Dr. Nolan thanked him again, then, still covered in dirt, very gingerly gave his daughters a hug.

"We're perfectly safe," he assured them. "I know how horrible this is, but it's over, done. Nothing else is going to happen."

"But why?" Cienna asked him.

"I don't know," their father said. "But I'm damn well going to find out."

20

Sheriff Dent was waiting in the parking lot when Dr. Nolan arrived at work on Wednesday. He had heard the police report from last night, and then had called county for a more detailed account.

"This is bad business, Sean. You taking any precautions?" he asked.

Dr. Nolan nodded. "Come in and I'll get coffee going. I've got Jed Marcus and one of his co-workers on guard duty," Dr. Nolan told him.

"That's good," the sheriff said, following him in through the back door. "This just escalated to a whole new level. Jed's a good hand. He'll know how to handle security."

"I'm lucky he's home," Dr. Nolan said. "I wish the damn kid would quit going back overseas though."

"It's in his blood now," Sheriff Dent said. He sat down on one of the chairs in the small breakroom. He had experienced active military duty and fully understood the draw, the camaraderie, the heightened sense of tension.

"Kid's too smart to make that his life." Dr. Nolan sighed, pouring two cups of coffee.

"Keep working on him, Doc. Between you and his mom, he doesn't stand a chance. He'll come around. But let's talk about you right now. You got any idea who did this?"

Dr. Nolan met his gaze. "Pretty sure," he answered. "But I can't prove anything. Within a few days, there might be some new information, but right this minute, I have nothing to stand on."

"You want to share a name with me?" the sheriff asked.

Dr. Nolan stared out the window. Even without evidence, there was no doubt Lenny Darden was somehow involved. "So far, Darden Farm is the only place that refused to let me take samples," Dr. Nolan told him. "Kind of curious. With such a large business, you'd think they would want to know about a potential problem."

The sheriff nodded, then finished his coffee. He stood and stretched his back.

"That old man's a hard nut," he remarked. "He doesn't have many friends, but I'll keep an ear open. You call me direct if anything else happens. Hear?"

Dr. Nolan smiled and shook his hand. Small towns did come with benefits. He thanked the sheriff and walked him to the door, just as Cat was entering.

"What the hell?" she demanded, looking at both men, her eyes dark. "Half of Woodhaven knows some version of the story already. What happened?"

Dr. Nolan gave her only the facts, but went no further. He knew that the rumor mill would be working overtime, and did not want the truth to lose out to fiction.

"There's going to be questions all day from every patient," he told her. "Everyone gets the same answer. Yes, a miniature donkey was killed on my property, but that's all. Nothing else. Same goes for Evie and Amanda."

Cat nodded, but her anger was palpable. She had brought her daughter to Dr. Nolan's ranch on more than one occasion to see his animals. She knew them.

"Cienna and Abby. They okay?" she asked.

"Upset. A little scared," Dr. Nolan said. "But I've got Jed watching the place now. There won't be any more trouble."

There was a photograph of Dr. Nolan at home with his menagerie on the entry wall. She looked up at it and shook her head. "This happened because of the testing?"

"Probably," Dr. Nolan admitted. "Someone is very nervous or very scared. The sheriff is going to have his deputies drive by more often during the day. Just a little show of special attention."

"You okay?" Cat asked, searching his face.

"Not really," he told her. "I can't even believe this is real, and it makes me sick. They killed one of my babies. And worse, for the first time in my life, I wanted revenge on a visceral level. I wanted to murder someone."

Cat nodded her understanding. After all these years, Dr. Nolan accepted her as family, and in some ways, she had become his closest confidante. She also knew that he was in pain.

"That's not true," she said.

"What do you mean?"

"You've threatened to kill me hundreds of times," she reminded him, forcing him to smile.

"That was pretend homicide," he explained. "Besides, then I'd have to train a new nurse. That's too much extra work."

"Plus, no sane person would want my job," she assured him. "Too much overtime."

"Which reminds me," Dr. Nolan said. "Can you call the environment lab and see if they can speed up our results?"

Cat laughed out loud. "See what I mean?" she said. "You ready for today?"

He nodded, grateful for her expertise in redirecting his focus. "Let's go to work," he told her. "And thanks for being here."

She gave a quick smile, then went to check in the first patient of the day. When there was finally a moment of calm, she called the lab. But no, they could not expedite the testing. The report would be available on Friday. Disappointed, she relayed the answer to Dr. Nolan. He sighed, hung his head for a moment, and then went to the next exam room. Work was his only escape.

By noon, most of the town had heard about the tragic events of the previous evening. By nightfall, half the county had heard. There had even been a call from the local newspaper requesting an interview. Dr. Nolan's response had been succinct and not suitable for publication.

It was an emotionally draining day for all of them. In virtually every room, he had to relive the night before. He accepted their condolences and knew they were heartfelt and sincere, but it accentuated the loss and delayed the grieving. His entire staff was grateful when the day ended.

"Better day tomorrow," Cat promised, putting on her coat.

"Couldn't possibly be worse," Dr. Nolan said.

"You need an extra gun at your house?" Cat asked. "My husband texted me and offered to help."

"No. Thanks. It's all covered. Tell him I appreciate it," Dr. Nolan said.

He had asked Eileen to pick up his girls from school. After a quick exchange, he and his daughters drove home in silence. They passed Jed Marcus at the entry gate, and he gave them a smile and a thumbs-up signal.

"I'm making hamburgers and fries," Dr. Nolan told them. "I need easy tonight."

"That's cool," Cienna answered. "You want help in the barn?" She rarely offered to assist with chores, and Aubriel never did. He was touched by her thoughtfulness.

"Thanks, but not tonight," he explained. "I need to spend a little more time with my other kids. They're scared, too."

Cienna hugged him. "Give them extra treats tonight," she suggested.

"That will help," he said, but his voice was sad. "And I'll try to explain to them that only a few members of the human race are capable of such horrendous cruelty. I hope they understand."

Cienna hugged him even tighter. "Good," she said. "Then maybe you can explain it to me."

21

Myron Lentz had spent another morning in Woodhaven. He had visited a Starbucks, a local café, and the sporting goods store, always staying in close proximity to the locals, listening to whatever bits of conversation drifted his way. It was nearly eleven when he heard the first clear reference to something horrible that happened at Dr. Nolan's ranch.

He sat in his car weighing his options. It would seem overbearing to visit the mayor again, and the local police would probably not be eager to share information with an outsider. And he certainly did not need another haircut. It seemed best to go to the source.

He drove to the older part of town to Dr. Nolan's clinic. There were still five other cars in the parking lot. He took a deep breath and entered the building, smiling at the young woman at the reception desk.

"Hello. I'm sorry to just walk in like this, but I'm from out of town," he began. "I woke up this morning with a bad cough, and I can't afford to get sick. Is there any way I could see the doctor?"

Amanda was a pro. She looked past him and counted bodies in the waiting room.

"Any fevers? Chills? Sore throat?" she asked.

"No. I don't think so," Myron Lentz answered.

"Coughing up yellow or green phlegm? Is it hard to breathe?"

Mr. Lentz felt it was advisable to provide a symptom. He made the gesture of a slight cough. "Yes. Yes," he answered.

"Okay," Amanda said. She handed him a clipboard and information form, along with a ballpoint pen with a large, hideous plastic flower on the end of it. "Have a seat and fill this out. Should be about half an hour."

Myron Lentz thanked her, then took a seat between two elderly women, one with a walker, and the other so heavily covered in perfume his eyes began stinging.

"I'll tell you this," one woman said. "If they catch the guy, they should just hang him from a tree. Serve him right. That's what I say."

"Not today," the other woman answered. "Now you go to jail with a color TV and free college. I'd be better off in jail!"

"You'd get your medicine free, that's for sure," the first woman said.

"Excuse me," Myron Lentz said. "Did something happen? I couldn't help hearing what you said."

The woman with the walker smiled at him. "You didn't hear? It's terrible," she said, delighted to retell the story. She offered the few facts that were known, then launched into a lecture about crime and punishment.

Myron Lentz nodded his head and listened, but he was not smiling. When the woman paused to catch her breath, he told her he had to get some paperwork from his car. He put the blank billing sheet on a small table and escaped outdoors, the perfume fog following him. He got in his car and drove back to his hotel, but did not wait until after hours to call his boss.

"Myron, can this wait?" Mr. Saunders asked.

"No," was the answer.

Doug Saunders was in a meeting. He excused himself and found a nearby conference room that was vacant. He stood looking out the window.

"Okay, I can talk now. What's so important?"

He listened intently as the young lawyer explained what had happened. The quiet, low-key approach had just been shattered. He closed his eyes and pressed his forehead against the cold glass.

"Okay. I want you out of there. Tonight," Mr. Saunders said. "You did your best, but Mr. Darden is no longer your problem, Myron. Pack up and come home."

"I'm sorry, sir. I tried to reason with him," Myron explained. "He wouldn't even give me the forty-eight hours I asked for."

"I understand," Mr. Saunders said. "It's difficult to reason with a moron. Come by next week and give me a full report. Have a safe trip."

"Thank you, sir," Myron Lentz said. He hung up and began to pack.

Doug Saunders sat down in an overstuffed leather chair. This time he only had to search back on his phone register a week. He dialed the number.

"Yes," the woman answered.

"I'd like you to fly into Seattle," he said. "Check in with Avis. A company car will be waiting. Drive south to Olympia and get a room. That puts you about an hour out of town."

"We're not green yet?" she asked.

"Not quite," he said. "But lights change with the flick of a switch. Time frame?"

"Tomorrow is workable," she said.

"Okay. Keep your phone charged up."

"Always do," she assured him. "I'll be waiting."

22

Thursday was blissfully mundane. But the tension level was mounting by the minute. For nearly a month there had been no answers to any of his questions. Some eighty-three sample packages had been sent to the lab, and not one had returned. Dr. Nolan refused to even mention the pending results.

Every patient was still asking about the incident on his ranch, but the shock of it had moderated. It had already become a routine part of every patient's visit, and he was growing numb from the retelling. It was old news now.

Jed and his friend were still standing night watch on his property. They took turns patrolling and napping on the sofa. But their presence was still necessary. Without the protective barrier they created, there would have been no peace of mind.

Thursday evening, Dr. Nolan took his daughters out for Mexican food before going home. He had not been shopping for a week and could not even think of making dinner. Every household responsibility was falling into disarray. After taking care of the animals, he managed two loads of laundry and a quick vacuum excursion of the living room. For the first time as a single parent, he entertained the idea of a paid housekeeper.

With his daughters in bed, he took Callie out for a walk and turned in early, trying to force sleep. But once again, the night was a broken series of fitful naps and vivid dreams, and in the morning he felt more tired than the night before. A shower and coffee were his only salvation. But it was finally Friday.

He checked the fax machine at the clinic before even taking off his coat, but there was nothing. When Cat came in, he immediately had her phone the lab.

"Dr. Nolan here. Any word yet?" he asked.

"Nothing so far. We'll call when we get them," the voice assured him. There was no physical way to push the system into a higher gear. Dr. Nolan knew that all too well, but it was a provocation that only grew. After finishing with each patient, he would once again check the fax tray, then look to Cat for any hint of deliverance, but all she could offer was a shake of her head. At noon, there was still no contact.

"Goddamn it! Cat, get them back on the phone!" he yelled, kicking the door of his office closed. When line two began blinking on his console, he did not wait for an official announcement.

"Hello. Is this the lab? Dr. Nolan again. I need those reports, now," he said.

"Please hold," was the answer. The call was transferred.

"Dr. Nolan? We still haven't received any paperwork. But stay on the line. I'll call the home office and try to get a verbal report."

"Jesus Christ, please. Anything." Dr. Nolan was almost pleading. He closed his eyes, waited through one, then a second Christmas carol cheerfully offered over the receiver. There had not been one free moment to even entertain the thought of Christmas, or presents, or the promise of a joyous holiday season. It seemed all so ridiculously out of context.

"Dr. Nolan. Thank you for waiting," the lab tech said. "I have the phone account only. The official printout will be here shortly. This is pretty remarkable."

"You're killing me," Dr. Nolan said, scooting closer to his desk. He had a pen ready in his right hand.

"Let's see. Let's see," the tech mumbled. He was reading the submitted samples by their designated sites. "You had well water from an abandoned source. That tested positive for PCBs at a level five hundred times above normal. Let's see. And then there were soil samples from the nearby area that were also contaminated, but at lower concentrations."

Dr. Nolan was busy writing down the information. His belief was always that some toxin would be found, but he had never imagined it would be a chemical banned over forty years ago. He could feel his heartbeat pounding.

"Jesus," he sighed. "Not what I expected."

"There's more," the lab tech offered. "The soil from the northwest corner of the property showed some PCB presence, but it also had high levels of benzene. You figure that out. Sounds like you're standing knee-deep in a toxic cesspool."

Dr. Nolan could not even offer a response. There was now the first evidence of a dangerous, lethal chemical in the ecosystem of the Bottoms, but it was not a single entity; it was two. And they had no apparent connection to each other.

"So, there was no benzene in the well water?" he repeated.

"Trace levels, but all below current safety points," the lab tech answered. "I'll get the official transcript to you within a few minutes."

"Okay, wait. Just wait a minute." Dr. Nolan was considering options. "Now that we know what we're looking for, is it possible to tailor the other samples to just these two agents? Will that speed things up?"

"By light-years," the tech answered. "We could run all of them within days."

"Perfect. Fucking perfect. There are over eighty samples. Just give me levels and locations for PCBs and benzene," Dr. Nolan instructed him. "And thank you, man. You just helped prevent a lot of future misery."

"Pleasure, Dr. Nolan," the tech said. "We'll be in touch. You going to call the EPA?"

"Soon," Dr. Nolan told him. "I just need a little more data. And I need you to furnish it."

"Should be Monday or Tuesday at the latest. Talk to you then." The call ended.

Dr. Nolan leaned forward with both hands on his desk, trying to slow his breathing. He wanted to shout at the top of his lungs, to release all the pent-up anxiety and anger. But it was too soon, too new. The initial report answered everything, and it answered nothing.

He stood up, selected the giant volume of Harrison's book on internal medicine from his bookcase, and sat down again. He thumbed through the index, searching for PCBs, polychlorinated biphenyl. It was a chemical soup that was fire resistant and an effective insulating material. He read over the list of known carcinogenic associations: liver cancer, melanoma, brain tumors, and breast cancer. By 1977, the lethal mixture had officially been banned.

Next, he looked up benzene. There was a vague memory of using it during college chemistry as a solvent or carrier agent, but always with great precautions. There was no commercial business locally that he knew of that would have any use for it. Also rated as a known cancer-causing compound, it had been linked to leukemia, lymphoma, and lastly, AML.

He remembered that Eileen had said the puzzle pieces did not fit together, that some of them were missing. Now they were beginning to find their place.

"Amanda!" Dr. Nolan shouted, bypassing the intercom.

"Your telephone broken?" she asked from the door, but still able to smile while delivering the mild reprimand.

"No. Sorry. I need to see the afternoon schedule. Anybody we can't move to next week?" Amanda went to her desk and brought back the patient list. He scanned the names and complaints. There was one woman with chronic heart failure that needed her medication adjusted and a blood draw.

"Reschedule everyone except Mrs. Langley. Get her in here now, even if you have to go pick her up. As soon as I see her, only one of you needs to stay until my girls get here from school. Probably Cat. She can bring them down to Eileen's."

Amanda nodded but was almost in shock. Dr. Nolan never took off early, and three-day weekends were nonexistent. He did not believe in holidays or sick time. Patients were always the priority.

"Jeez, who died?" she said.

He closed the book on his desk and put it back in place.

"A lot of people who shouldn't have," he said. He looked at his watch, knowing Eileen would be home from her radiation treatment by two o'clock. "Now, Mrs. Langley please."

Amanda went back to the reception area to begin phoning patients. Dr. Nolan motioned for Cat to join him. The fax machine was just beginning to print out his reports.

"For your ears only," he told her, closing the door. "The test samples show a large area of the Bottoms is contaminated. I need to get more tests back before we go public, but this is a big fucking nightmare. This will be like an atomic bomb going off."

"Jesus, what is it? I have an aunt living there," she said, clearly shaken. She had known for a long time that the pesticide story was not completely true.

"It's actually two poisons," he explained. "And probably responsible for a lot of these cancer cases."

Cat listened, remembering all the colored pins on the map, including the marker for Dr. Nolan's own wife. She sat down and stared at the floor. It was too much to even begin to process.

"What do you think will happen?" she asked.

"If there's enough pressure, first an investigation, and then some kind of a cleanup process," he said. "This isn't tolerable. A lot of people are at risk."

"You think this is why the miniature donkey was killed? Someone afraid of what you were looking for?"

"I do," Dr. Nolan said. "But all that did was piss me off even more."

Cat looked up at him for the first time. "Please be careful," she said. "This is getting scary."

"I'm taking this very seriously," he told her. "Now, can you hang out long enough to bring my daughters down to Eileen's? You still get to go home early."

Cat nodded and smiled. "Of course I will."

"And…" he added.

"Oh shit, I should have known. What else?"

"I need the sheriff on the phone. Try to track him down while I go take care of the last patient. Please." He made a prayer gesture with his hands.

"Okay. You want me to use your office?"

He nodded, grabbing his stethoscope. Quickly reading the printed data from the environmental lab, he folded the papers and tucked them into his pocket.

Mrs. Langley was a little vexed at having been rushed in early, but Dr. Nolan convinced her it was because she was especially important and required his full attention. This smoothed any ruffled feathers, and luckily her condition had improved with an increase in her water pills.

Dr. Nolan had Evie draw her blood sample and was just finishing his notes when Cat called his name.

"Line one. He's upriver," she said.

"Bob, you have a private minute?" Dr. Nolan asked.

"I can make one, Doc," the sheriff answered. "Let me take a little walk. Got a truck wreck out past the dam." There was a slight pause. "Okay, shoot."

"You know Mike and I have been getting test samples along the Bottoms for weeks, that's nothing new," he said. "But not for pesticides. I was looking for something worse, and we may have found it. The first chemical analysis just came back, and it's pretty bad."

"Well, that explains a lot," the sheriff said. "This why that little weasel was following you last week?"

"Probably," Dr. Nolan admitted. "This is just between you, me, and the Carsons for now. I've still got to answer a few questions."

"Jed still on duty? Up at your place?"

"Still there," Dr. Nolan said.

"Good," the sheriff said with authority. "Keep him there. And thanks for the update. You know how much I don't like surprises."

"I'll do a better job of keeping you informed," Dr. Nolan promised. "We're in the same business, trying to keep people safe."

"Tough job sometimes," the sheriff answered. "Call if anything changes."

"Thanks, Bob. I mean it," Dr. Nolan said. He replaced the phone, grabbed his coat, and gave last-minute instructions to Amanda and Cat. The drive down to Eileen's house took only minutes. She had just arrived.

"Sorry about not calling," he said. "Where's Mike?"

"Down at the processing shed. You need him?" Eileen asked.

"Both of you," Dr. Nolan said. "I've got bad news, and I only want to explain this one time."

"I'll give him a call. You eat anything yet today? You're losing more weight than I am, and I've got cancer." She laughed. "Homemade banana bread sound good?"

"God, yes, with coffee please," Dr. Nolan said. "I can't sleep worth shit lately. Too many ghosts."

Eileen put in a call to Mike, then heated up her freshly baked pastry in the microwave. She sat down at the table with him.

"You said bad news? You found something?"

Dr. Nolan took the lab report out of his pocket and gave it to her. She read it but did not understand the implications.

"You've been poisoned," he told her. "Probably for years, maybe your whole life. Megan, too, and everyone else around here. This didn't just happen. This chemical hasn't been legal for decades."

Mike came in and washed his hands in scalding-hot water. "I'm frozen," he said. "What's all the excitement about?"

"Sean got back the report on our farm," Eileen told him. "It's not good news."

They went upstairs to the office. Dr. Nolan pointed out test sites on the map.

"Your old well is here, and that had the highest levels of PCBs. The soil was also poisoned, but not as bad. We should get results back on all the other farms and homes on this end of the dike area next week. Then we'll have an idea how far this reaches."

"And this shit causes cancer?" Mike asked.

"All kinds of cancer," Dr. Nolan said. "And this means your kids were exposed too. The whole time they were growing up."

"But where the hell did it come from?" Mike asked, sickened by what he was hearing.

"That's the problem," Dr. Nolan said. "No one uses this. And then, on the far side of your place, we found another toxic chemical that no one should be using."

"This is all crazy," Mike said. "Someone had to know about this."

"Someone did, and does," Dr. Nolan said. "All of our testing has been on the southern edge of the Bottoms. I need samples from farther north. I was hoping we could do that this weekend."

Mike nodded but was still overwhelmed by the fact that his property had been affected, and that his wife's illness was probably caused by human hands.

"I can start calling people in that area," Eileen said.

"I especially want samples near Lenny Darden's place," Dr. Nolan added. "Then I had another idea. Since we know these chemicals have been here for a long time, we need to look back in time. We need to know what was here in the 1940s and the 1950s. What businesses were located on the Bottoms before the big flood."

"Jesus, you're talking about seventy years ago, Sean," Mike offered. "My dad remembers an old fuel depot somewhere near the rail line, but nothing else."

Dr. Nolan smiled and fixed his eyes on Eileen. "That's where my ace detective comes in," he explained. "City tax records. Woodhaven was incorporated in 1905. There have to be written records of what was here and when. Especially before the flood in '48."

Eileen nodded her head in agreement. "That'll be dusty work, but I can start today," she said. "And Cienna and Aubriel can help me tomorrow when you boys are out in the cold. Whatever was here, we'll find it."

They heard his daughters calling from downstairs. Cat had dropped them off on her way home.

"Only you and Sheriff Dent know all of this so far," Dr. Nolan told them. "You're going to have to come up with some story about why you're looking at old records."

"Historical research," Eileen said, smiling. "It's the truth, and no one's going to call me a liar. At least, not to my face."

Dr. Nolan checked the time. As much as the idea horrified him, having the afternoon free gave him the opportunity to stock up at the local store.

"Okay. Eileen's got records, and, Mike, you and I will start covering the other end of the Bottoms. Anything else?"

Mike was troubled by what Dr. Nolan had said about their grown children. "If our kids were exposed to this, how do we get it out of them?"

Dr. Nolan shook his head. "You can't," he said. "There's no way to just erase it or take medicine to fix it. All they can do is have frequent medical testing to catch any early threat. And all we can do is make certain this doesn't happen to any more kids."

Cienna and Aubriel had tracked them down.

"What's the secret meeting about?" Cienna asked.

"We were doing a family survey to see if you and your sister had been naughty or nice," their father said.

"And?" she asked, smiling.

"Looks like I'll be saving a fortune on Christmas presents this year," he said. "Unless…"

"Unless what!" Cienna asked suspiciously.

"Unless you both graciously volunteer to help your sick aunt do some research tomorrow," Dr. Nolan announced, winking at Eileen.

"Then we get big, expensive presents?" Aubriel asked.

"Let's just say it will be better than a lump of coal." Dr. Nolan laughed. "Is it a deal?"

"Deal," Cienna said.

"I'd hold out for a new car," Mike told her.

"Jesus, she can't even drive yet," Dr. Nolan protested.

"Hmmmm," Cienna thought for moment. "I can take driver's ed next year. That's not a bad idea."

"Thanks a lot, Uncle Mike. I'll see you in the morning," Dr. Nolan said. He hugged his daughters and urged them toward the door.

"That's what families are for," Mike told him.

Dr. Nolan stopped and smiled. He looked at his two girls, then at Mike and Eileen. They were all working now to correct a wrong and to make things better. This is what families are for, he thought to himself. It was a good thought.

23

ON SATURDAY MORNING, MIKE AND DR. Nolan shifted their focus to the northern region of the Bottoms. The temperature was just bearable, but the wind and a constant drizzle made their work miserable. Each had a list of eight target sites, some with wells and some with city water. It was going to be another long day.

Eileen had taken charge of her two nieces. With no radiation treatment scheduled, she made them a hearty breakfast and explained what their role as assistant researchers would entail. They were both eager and engaged. It was an adventure, a treasure hunt, a voyage back in history.

City Hall was only open from ten until three on Saturdays, but the three of them were waiting when the doors were unlocked. Eileen knew everyone in town and was somehow related to half the population.

"Carly, hi," she greeted one of the secretaries on duty. "Kids playing soccer?"

"God, yes, and it's always cold and rainy," the woman complained. "Why can't they play basketball or volleyball in a nice, warm gym?"

"Been there and done that," Eileen acknowledged with a knowing smile. "Hey, we need to look at the old archive ledgers. The city records back to the 1930s. Doing some research on the town's history."

The woman frowned slightly but nodded her head. "Luckily, all those old books were on the second floor when the big flood came. But they're old and musty, and hard to read. Some of the ink just faded away."

"No problem," Eileen told her. "I brought young eyes to help me. You mind if we take a look?"

"It's all public records," the woman said. "If you can stand the dust and cobwebs." She led them over to the stairway that connected to the upper story, unlocking the door.

"Don't go home and forget we're up here," Eileen joked.

"That wouldn't do," Carly said. "Let me know if you need anything."

Eileen and Dr. Nolan's daughters climbed the wooden stairs and searched for a light switch. Only about two-thirds of the overhead fixtures had working bulbs, but it was enough to illuminate the single, large room. There were stacks of old desks, chairs, tables, fans, and outdated office equipment at one end, and the other was lined by eight-foot-high shelves jammed with boxes of files. It was a century of accumulated paperwork.

"It smells like a cat box in here," Aubriel said, wrinkling her nose.

"Probably bats and raccoons," Eileen told her. "Oh, well, we knew this would be a challenge."

Cienna went to the two windows along the far wall and used her coat sleeve to rub away years of dust. The room became less sinister. Eileen rescued one of the old tables and three chairs, then dragged them under a bank of working lights.

"This is our office," she announced. She pulled a small, LED flashlight from her purse. "Shall we, ladies?"

They picked a random aisle, squinting to read the dates and content labels. It was a painfully slow process at first, but after a time, a discernable pattern began to show itself. Private homes had been sequestered from agriculture, logging, and commercial enterprises. And the designated years were usually still readable. Eileen chose to begin in the mid-1930s. One by one, she carried the damp cardboard boxes to their work station, and the search commenced. Only business records were segregated by the girls, then Eileen would match addresses to the old floodplain.

The final step was to compile a list of businesses in the target area over a four-decade time period. Initially, there were only a few, then a notable increase during the post-World War II years, then a drastic fall after the flood of 1948, and then another rising count during the '50s and early sixties.

When they reached 1965, Eileen looked at her watch. She was surprised to see it was two thirty. They had been working steadily since morning, and there had not been a single complaint. There were twenty-seven business names and addresses neatly printed on a single piece of paper. She held it up for Cienna and Aubriel to see.

"Talk about a needle in a haystack," she laughed. "This is it. I hope it's what your dad needed."

"Me, too," Aubriel said. "It's even hard to breathe with all this dust. Are we done?"

"Done," Eileen said. "Let's put this stuff back and go home."

Downstairs, Mayor Tillis had stopped by to collect some files on a zoning request. He heard footsteps above him and the sound of furniture being dragged across the floor. He stuck his head out the door.

"Who the hell's here?" he asked, pointing upward.

"Oh, Eileen and Dr. Nolan's daughters," Carly explained. "Some kind of research." She shrugged.

"Research on what?" he asked.

"Old businesses, I think," she said. "History stuff."

Mayor Tillis closed the door and sat down at his desk. He was already beginning to perspire. The whole town was still talking about what had happened at Dr. Nolan's home. He harbored no doubts about who was involved, but there was a great deal of money at risk, and some of it was his. He picked up the phone and dialed Lenny Darden.

"What is it?" Mr. Darden asked. His caller ID had identified the source.

"Uh, hi, I just thought you should know. Eileen Carson is upstairs going through town records," the mayor informed him.

"Well, that's great fucking news," Mr. Darden answered. "She say anything?"

"No. No. Just told Carly it was research on old businesses."

"Yeah, ancient fucking history," Mr. Darden said, barely above a whisper. "Anything else?"

"No. That's all," the mayor said. "Just a courtesy call." He heard the line go dead. A bead of sweat trickled into his left eye.

Eileen switched off the lights and led the girls back downstairs to the present-tense version of the world. They were all covered with dust and spiderwebs.

"Jeez, you guys look terrible." Carly laughed. "We don't ever clean up there. Too many critters."

"We met some of them," Eileen said. "Thanks for letting us in. Say hi to your family."

"You too." Carly waved them out the door.

They were back at the Carson Farm in just a few minutes. Dr. Nolan and Mike were in the front yard hosing off their boots.

"Holy shit, you look worse than we do." Mike laughed, aiming the garden hose in their direction.

"Don't you dare," Cienna warned, laughing. Aubriel took cover behind the car.

"Oh, you little pansies. A tiny bit of cold, icy water won't hurt you. Right, Doc?"

"I think it would be an improvement," Dr. Nolan agreed. "They're disgusting."

Uncle Mike shot a few test sprays in their direction. The girls screamed and ran for the front door, hiding behind their aunt.

"You spray me, and you don't eat for a month," Eileen said to her husband.

"This sounds serious, Mike," Dr. Nolan said. "You better drop your weapon and surrender. And I need hot coffee." He raced Mike to the entrance, kicking off his boots.

"You're all pansies." Mike laughed, following behind.

Eileen was already making a pot of coffee, then offered the girls pop or juice.

"These guys were troopers," she bragged. "And they made the job fun."

"You find anything?" Mike asked.

"All we could," Eileen answered. "It was like a mausoleum in there. But business later. What do you want to do about dinner? I think we all need a break."

A vote was taken. Dr. Nolan lost four to one. Mike called in an order for pizza, and everyone else took turns trying to make themselves less disgusting. The table was set and waiting when Uncle Mike returned to a round of applause.

"Jesus, I must be hungry," Dr. Nolan admitted. "This isn't bad."

"Can we get that in writing?" Aubriel asked between bites. Their father always equated fast food with a root canal, only embracing it as a last option. The conflict was that his daughters regarded his cooking the same way.

"So, I take them to the store with me last night," Dr. Nolan began, "and the first five items they grab are Captain

Crunch, Ruffles potato chips, Twinkies, frozen burritos, and a case of Top Ramen."

"So, what's wrong with that?" Mike asked, half seriously.

"Because, after that it got worse," Dr. Nolan said. "I'm trying to think about meals, and they just see snacks. It makes me crazy."

"You were already crazy." Cienna laughed. "Maybe I could start to do some of the cooking."

Dr. Nolan dropped the pizza slice from his mouth and let it fall on his plate. His eyes were wide, portraying complete and utter shock. "This must be a dream," he sighed. "I've actually had dreams like this, but then I wake up. Is this real?"

Cienna blushed but did not waiver. "I'm old enough to start helping," she said.

"I'm not," Aubriel informed them, still eating.

Dr. Nolan smiled at his older daughter, then glanced at Eileen. He suspected she was partly behind the dramatic change in attitude.

"Wow," he said. "That would be a gigantic help. Why don't we start with just two days a week? You figure out what you want to do, and I'll do the shopping. Sound okay?"

"Okay," Cienna agreed. "But easy stuff at first. I can get ideas off the computer."

Dr. Nolan looked at her, meeting her eyes. His little girl was changing, evolving into a young woman. It both delighted and frightened him at the same time.

"Okay," Eileen said. "Back to business. Girls, you clean up the kitchen and then you can watch TV. We've got boring paperwork to do."

The girls began clearing the table, and Eileen, Mike, and Dr. Nolan went upstairs to the office. Eileen took out the list containing the names of the old businesses.

"How do you want to do this?" she asked.

Dr. Nolan picked up a red felt pen from the desk and stood in front of the map.

"Let's go through them one at a time," he said. "If they seem like a possible source for the pollution, we mark their position. If they don't, we take them off the list. Who's first?"

"No, who's on second," Mike said. It was an old joke, but still funny.

"Okay, who's number one?" Dr. Nolan shook his head and rephrased the question.

"Ummmm…Alton Logging, '30s and '40s," Eileen said.

"No. Doesn't fit. Cross them off," Dr. Nolan told her. "Next."

"Flying A Fuel Supply. Later sold out to Union 76. Gas, diesel, lubrication. Forty-five to forty-eight."

"Not likely, but where were they located?" Dr. Nolan asked. He drew a small rectangle on the map as Eileen read the address. "Next."

"Thorson Fishing Supplies," Eileen said. "Wiped out in the flood."

"No. Off the list. Next."

"Oh…Ice House, '30s and '40s. Went out of business during the war."

"No. They used ammonia," Dr. Nolan said, more to himself. "Doesn't fit. Next."

"Ummm…PEG, Pacific Electric Generation," Eileen said. "Forty-four to forty-eight, also wiped out in the flood."

Dr. Nolan was suddenly energized. "And where were they?" he asked.

"Just up the road along the rail line," she said. Dr. Nolan drew a rectangle with a star next to it adjacent to the Carson property.

"Good. Good. Next."

"Man, uh, lumber treatment company," Eileen said. "Forty-nine to 1962. Built right after the flood."

Dr. Nolan frowned. He knew green lumber was dried and cured in kilns but did not know if chemicals were involved in the process. "Okay. Where was that?" he made another rectangle on the map. "Next."

"Chainsaw and logging equipment. Gone in '48," Eileen said. "Pruitt or Priest. I couldn't tell."

"No. Next."

"Boatyard. Manufacturing and repair," Eileen read her notes, "1934 to 1954."

"Okay. Possible. Address?" Dr. Nolan drew another marker.

"Let's see. Fugito Nursery. Owners were sent to an internment camp in 1941. Never returned," Eileen said.

"No. But wasn't that a proud moment in our history? Next."

"Uh…Dukayne Chemical Corporation, 1939 to 1948. Gone with the flood," Eileen said.

"Shit, where was that at?" Dr. Nolan asked, anxious for the answer.

"Further north on Goerig Street. Almost to the crossroad," Eileen explained.

Dr. Nolan drew a rectangle with another red star. "Right next to the Darden Farm. The original farm, right?" he asked Mike.

"Yeah. That's where they built the new cold storage plant about six years ago," Mike answered.

Dr. Nolan was thinking. He had heard the name before. He believed they were still in business.

"I know you're tired," he said to Eileen, "but could you look on the computer and see what these guys do?"

Eileen did not hesitate. She typed in the information and initiated a search.

"Here you go," she said. "Pretty big company. Headquarters in Nebraska. Fertilizers. Pest control. Solvents. Paint. Preservatives. They do business all over the world."

"And I wonder what they were doing here in the '40's," Dr. Nolan asked. He did not have a clue how to access that category of information. Any research and development activity would have been highly protected and confidential.

"What are you thinking, Sean?" Mike asked.

"We can't just call these people and ask them what the hell they were doing in Woodhaven half a century ago," Dr. Nolan explained. "Are there any old-timers that worked at these places?"

Mike laughed out loud. "Jesus! They'd be ninety-five or one hundred years old," he noted. "I can ask my dad and some of his friends. Maybe they remember something. Pacific Power and Light took over the dam in early 1950. I know folks that work there. Maybe they know something."

"Good. I don't know where to go next," Dr. Nolan said. He stared at the map. There were seven sites drawn in red.

"Look where most of the pins are," Eileen said. The majority of them were clustered on the southern side of the Bottoms, more toward the lumber mill, the shipyard, and the old electrical company. Only a few were in the area of the old chemical plant.

"We'll get more test samples back early next week," Dr. Nolan said. "We've got tons of new information, but I don't know what it all means. There's no straight line to follow."

"But, it's progress," Eileen said, always the optimist. "You going out again tomorrow?"

"I'm not stopping now," Dr. Nolan said. "But I think my Christmas shopping is going to be limited to gift cards. There's no time."

"The girls will understand, Sean. They know you're doing something important. And they were thrilled to be helping today."

"I'll give them tomorrow off," Dr. Nolan said. "You still in, Mike?"

"Goddamn right! Whenever you show up, I'll be ready," Mike assured him.

"Great job today," Dr. Nolan said, leading the way downstairs. Eileen hugged her nieces and thanked them again for their help, then stood on the porch, waving until they were out of site.

Dr. Nolan turned the heater on full force. He had been cold most of the day, and now the animals still needed to be fed. He could feel the warm air beginning to relax him.

"I'm so proud of you both," he told his daughters. "You're not only helping me, but this is kind of like therapy for your aunt. Keeps her from thinking about other things."

There was no answer. His daughters were sound asleep.

24

LENNY DARDEN DID NOT HAVE THE private cell phone number for Doug Saunders. He called the main office, listened to the recorded message, then patiently waited for the tone.

"This is for Mr. Saunders," he began. "While you're sitting in your fucking office with your thumb up your ass, my life is going to shit! Call me sometime, and we'll do lunch, you useless prick!"

He did not leave a callback number.

25

SUNDAY WAS COLD, DRY, AND VERY productive. Mike and Dr. Nolan managed to sample ten more farms and ranch sites to the north. More of the locals had heard about the supposed pesticide study, and they had become active participants, offering any assistance possible.

By two in the afternoon they had reunited at the Carson Farm. All of the newly acquired soil and water samples were transferred to Dr. Nolan's car.

"Damn, an easy day for once." Dr. Nolan smiled. "And it's still daylight."

"Hey, Sean. I talked to my dad last night," Mike said. "There's an old fart in the nursing home that worked for the power company up until the mid-'90s. Dad says he's half whacky, but that's all he could come up with."

"You have a name?"

"Yeah. Byron Wallace. Guy's like ninety-four or ninety-five," Mike told him.

"I've got a dozen patients in the nursing home, but I don't recognize the name. I've probably seen him."

"He's VA, served at the tail end of World War II. Navy guy, I think," Mike said.

"Well," Dr. Nolan laughed, "I've had a lot of practice talking to whacky people. Who knows?"

They had just finished cleaning up when Eileen came out of the house with a Tupperware container filled with freshly baked chocolate chip cookies.

"For the girls," she smiled.

"There may not be any left by the time I get home," Dr. Nolan said, prying open the lid. For safety reasons, he thought it prudent to sample one, then two of the cookies. Mike was reaching for one when Eileen slapped his hand away.

"You've got your own inside," she warned. "Oh, I almost forgot. My cousin's father worked at that old lumber mill we found. All they had was tar, creosote, and some kind of a clear stain they used to protect the wood. Nothing dangerous."

Dr. Nolan nodded. It was one more potential site they could eliminate from the map.

"Good work, detective," he told her. "Now, on to warmer challenges." He said goodbye and drove to the clinic. He packed the new samples and placed them in manila envelopes.

Finished, he dialed the local nursing home and assisted-living facility. It was just two blocks away.

"Hi, Dr. Nolan. You have a resident named Byron Wallace?" he asked.

"One of our favorites," the nurse said.

"Would it be okay if I came by to visit him? I need to ask him about the old days?" Dr. Nolan explained.

"That's all he talks about anyway," the nurse laughed. "And he'll tell you the same story fifty times a day."

"That's okay with me," Dr. Nolan told her. "Is there anything he likes? Cookies, magazines?"

"Candy," the nurse laughed again. "He's famous for stealing candy from everybody and anybody. But nothing with nuts."

"Perfect," Dr. Nolan said. "I'll be there in half an hour." He drove to Target, purchased a two-pound box of See's Candy, and made it back to the care center as promised. Entering the door, he was immediately ambushed by two of his own patients.

"Hey, Doc, that candy for me?" one elderly woman asked.

"No. You're too sweet already," he answered, squeezing her hand. He spent a few moments talking to both patients, asking about how they and their families were doing. Each visit to the nursing center was as much medical as social. They were all lonely.

After a polite escape, he tracked down the charge nurse, a colleague for many years.

"You working Sundays now?" she asked.

"Seven days a week, just like you," he smiled. "But this is more of a fun visit. I want to speak to a Mr. Byron Wallace."

The nurse nodded toward the west hallway. "Room 32," she said. "You can't miss him. Always wears a red hunting cap."

Dr. Nolan had seen the old fellow a hundred times in passing. He had always greeted him but never knew his name. "You think any family would object if I talked to him?" Dr. Nolan asked her.

"No one visits him anymore," she said. "Even on holidays, he just sits here alone. Kind of breaks your heart."

Dr. Nolan sighed and shook his head. "Okay. Word is he's a little demented? Can he answer questions?"

"He's got good days and bad days," the nurse explained. "He'll just be thrilled to talk to someone."

Dr. Nolan thanked her and headed down the hall. Byron Wallace was in bed, but wide awake, staring out the window. There were a few family photographs on his night table, and a wall filled with old newspaper clippings with stories about his days in the Navy. He was a bit famous in the local community.

Dr. Nolan knocked on the open door. "Mr. Wallace? I was hoping we could talk for a few minutes. I'm Dr. Nolan here from Woodhaven."

"Am I sick?" the old man smiled up at him. "Why do I need a doctor?"

"You don't need me." Dr. Nolan laughed. "I need your help. And I brought a present." He placed the large box of candy on the old man's lap.

"What the hell is this for?" he asked. He even wore his hunters cap when he slept.

"Candy. For you," Dr. Nolan explained. He pulled up a vacant chair and scooted close to the bed. The old man examined his prize and sat it back on his lap.

"Thanks," Mr. Wallace said.

"You're a World War II vet, I heard?" Dr. Nolan asked. He wanted to establish an easy opening to the conversation.

"Last six months of the war," Byron told him. "Escort destroyer. Saw action off Iwo Jima before the Japs surrendered. Lied about my age to get in."

Dr. Nolan nodded and smiled. The list of WWII veterans was evaporating by the day. They were a national treasure that was routinely ignored or forgotten about.

"Long time ago," Dr. Nolan said. "You helped save the world, and then you rebuilt it. I had an uncle who fought in the Pacific. He would never talk about it."

The old man nodded, then picked up the box of See's Candy again. "What the hell is this?" he asked.

"Candy. It's yours." Dr. Nolan laughed. He helped remove the wrapper and opened the top. The old man selected one of the treats.

"Thanks," he said again.

"Then, after the war, you came home and worked for the power company. Is that right?" Dr. Nolan offered, trying to change topics.

"Pacific Power. Up at the dam," Byron said. "Long time ago."

"But before that, you worked at a company out on the Bottoms, isn't that right? Until the flood."

The old man leaned forward. A hazy memory had been dusted off the shelf. "The flood," he said. "Twelve feet of water everywhere. Over the roofs. You could see barns and houses floating away. Dead cattle. And people, too."

Dr. Nolan remembered the pictures he had seen. Nothing in the low-lying areas had escaped damage.

"And your company. It was flooded out?" he asked, pressing for answers.

"All gone," Byron said. "We couldn't get in for weeks. Water ruined everything. Two feet of mud."

Dr. Nolan scooted even closer. "Mr. Wallace. Try to remember. What happened to the company?"

"Went belly up," the old man said. "Drowned in the flood. Dead." He grabbed up another piece of chocolate with gnarled fingers yellowed from years of smoking.

"But the equipment. Do you know what happened to it?"

"You bury dead things," Byron answered. "We dug a hole and buried it all."

Dr. Nolan leaned forward and put his hand on the old man's forearm. "Do you remember where?" he asked, making eye contact.

"Sure," Byron said. "In the ground."

Dr. Nolan leaned back in the chair. The old man was getting tired, and not able to stay focused. He was staring out the window again.

"Thank you, Mr. Wallace. And thank you for your service to your country," Dr. Nolan said. He stood up and moved toward the door.

"What the hell is this?" Byron asked, again holding up the box of candy.

Dr. Nolan smiled and raised his hand to say goodbye. There was no point answering the question.

He went to find the duty nurse again. She was also a lifelong resident of the town. Her father, Walter Bannon, had been owner and founder of a local logging company, one of the largest in Cowlitz County.

"Hey, Pam, I know you're busy, but who would have old photos of the town before the flood? The way it used to look."

Pam thought for a moment. "There's a heritage museum up at the old grist mill," she smiled. "They get tons of old pictures and newspapers from families when someone passes away. What are you looking for?"

He shrugged. "I'm just curious about what was out on the Bottoms before it was washed away. You weren't even born yet."

"Five years later," Pam admitted, giving away her age. "But that's your best bet."

"How long you going to keep working?" Dr. Nolan asked, smiling.

Pam laughed and looked around her. "Until they reserve me a room," she said. "I love these old people. If I wasn't here, I'd just worry about them anyway."

"Thank God for people like you," Dr. Nolan told her. "And thanks for the advice. If Mr. Wallace develops diabetes in the near future, you can blame me." He headed for the exit.

"We will." Pam laughed again. "We will."

Dr. Nolan managed to avoid any additional stops on his way outside. He drove home and helped Cienna in the kitchen, both of them trying to follow a recipe for beef stroganoff. To equal levels of surprise, it turned out quite well. Even Aubriel was impressed.

When the dishes were cleared, he phoned Eileen.

"Now that you've raided the city records, you must have a lot of spare time on your hands," he began. He filled her in on what he had learned from Byron Wallace.

"So, what do you need?" she asked.

"The museum at the old mill house. Pam Bannon said they had boxes of old pictures. We need to try and locate where the old electric company was built. If they buried something, it has to be near where the building was."

"I'll find out their hours and see what I can do," Eileen said. "I've got a cousin who volunteers there."

"Of course you do." Dr. Nolan laughed. "You have any relatives in the boat building business?"

"Sorry, all farmers and loggers," she said.

"There are two or three shipyards on Swan Island in Portland," Dr. Nolan said. "I'll call tomorrow and find out what chemicals were used in the '40s to build boats. Hell, I don't even know when fiberglass replaced wood."

"Okay," Eileen said. "I'll call if I find something. I've still got a week of radiation treatments. Thank God, no chemo till after the holidays."

"Thank you, again and again," Dr. Nolan said. "I can't even imagine how hard this is."

There was a long hesitation before she answered. "I think of all the people who live here, my kids. I don't want this happening to anyone else," she said.

"We're almost there," Dr. Nolan said.

"I hope so. Call you tomorrow."

Dr. Nolan hung up the phone. It would be a challenge, but he wanted one normal evening with his daughters. After homework and baths, they watched *60 Minutes* together and discussed the mounting dangers of global warming, and the dire consequences of inaction.

"Then why do we have a government that denies it's a problem?" Aubriel asked.

Their father sighed. There was never a day he did not fear the challenges they would be faced with as a result of his generation's failure.

"For all the greatness this country produces, we never have a shortage of stupid people," he explained. "And in the words of one of our most famous philosophers, Forrest Gump, 'Stupid is as stupid does.'"

26

Dr. Nolan was deep in a REM cycle when the phone began ringing just before 3:00 a.m. It took multiple repetitions before his conscious mind could make sense of it, but his hand finally fumbled for the receiver. Night calls were an ugly reality. He hated them all, but it was just another part of his job.

"Dr. Nolan," he whispered, still trying to clear his thoughts.

"Sean? Sorry to wake you. It's Bob Dent. You better come down. Your clinic is on fire."

"Shit! What! What do you mean?" Now he was fully awake.

"Your clinic," the sheriff repeated. "Someone set it on fire."

Dr. Nolan looked at the clock. He dropped the phone on the bed, went to the bathroom, and splashed ice-cold water over his face and neck. He quickly dressed in jeans and a sweatshirt, grabbed his coat, stepped into his ankle-high winter boots, and half ran down the stairs.

Jed was in the living room. He had heard the phone.

"My clinic is on fire," Dr. Nolan explained. "Can you get my girls to school? Don't say anything about this until I see how bad it is."

"Sure, Doc, just go," Jed told him. "I've got this covered."

"Thanks. Thanks. Got to go," Dr. Nolan said, rushing past him. The drive to work that normally took fifteen minutes was accomplished in ten. When he arrived, every street was barricaded by police cars and fire equipment. He parked as close as possible and jogged the rest of the way. He spotted Sheriff Dent at one of the driveways leading to the parking lot.

There was still heavy, black smoke coming from the building. The front brick facing was charred, the windows all shattered, and part of the roof was gone. Two of the volunteer fire department responders were still spraying water into the waiting room area. With the fire station only a block away, they were able to stop the flames from devouring more of the structure. But the reception area and business offices, including his records, had been destroyed.

"Jesus fucking Christ! This can't be real!" Dr. Nolan almost shouted.

Sheriff Dent had his hands shoved into the pockets of his coat, just staring at the building. There were so many floodlights trained on the scene it was almost like daylight.

"Sorry, Sean," he said. "The first fireman said he smelled gasoline. This wasn't an accident. Started inside. Probably a Molotov cocktail."

"Goddamn it! Anybody see anything?" Dr. Nolan asked.

"Nothing reported yet," the sheriff said. "We'll talk to folks in the morning, but not many people up this late. Tow truck driver heard the smoke alarms."

"Oh shit, shit, shit," Dr. Nolan repeated. He was pacing back and forth along the street.

"Let's take a walk," the sheriff suggested. He led Dr. Nolan up to the corner to the main road running through town. He surveyed the avenue to the east and west. It was the older part of the city, and none of the businesses had outdoor security cameras. He turned to face his friend.

"First your farm, and now this," he said. "I don't have enough men to protect you. And I had to call ATF. This is a bombing. This is federal now. I'm going to be pushed to the sidelines in about an hour. Where is this going, Sean?"

"We're close to figuring this out, Bob," Dr. Nolan said. "And a lot of people are at risk, not just me. This is bigger than I thought at first, and it might be more than one thing. I just need a few more days."

"Why not tell the Feds what you know and let them handle it?" the sheriff asked.

"Because it could all just disappear. Get covered up," Dr. Nolan explained. "I'm no hero, but if we don't know the truth up front, we may never get the whole story."

Sheriff Dent looked down at his boots, twisting the heels against the pavement. "They'll want to interview you," he said. "You gonna mention any names?"

"Not yet," Dr. Nolan answered. "If they find any evidence, then everything changes. But what can I say, that he wouldn't let me take test samples from his farm? That won't carry much weight."

"It's my town, too, Sean," the sheriff told him. "I can't abide this. It's already gone too far. You really think two days will make a difference?"

"I do," Dr. Nolan assured him. "We've got dozens of test results coming today or tomorrow. Then I'll know how big this is."

Sheriff Dent sighed heavily. The radio on his coat lapel announced that ATF had arrived. "Two days," he said. "That's it. I can act like a small-town hick for two days, then I'll tell them what we know. Fair enough?"

"Fair enough," Dr. Nolan said. "I really have to talk to these guys?"

"It's your clinic," Sheriff Dent reminded him. "And whatever you do, don't lie to them. That could get your ass in trouble."

They walked back slowly. There were three ATF agents waiting by the sheriff's cruiser.

"Good morning," Sheriff Dent said, shaking hands with them. "Sorry about the early morning call. This is Dr. Nolan."

"Sheriff. Doctor. I'm Daryl Abrams. I'll be on lead here. We've barely been inside, but there's broken green glass on the floor just inside the window, and it's clear there was an accelerant. Not very sophisticated, but still effective."

"Sounds right," Sheriff Dent commented. "First fireman in smelled gas."

Agent Abrams shined his flashlight in Dr. Nolan's face for a moment.

"Sorry," he smiled. "You look pretty standard issue, so a racial motive is probably unlikely. Any recent problems with a patient or family member?"

"No. None that I can think of," Dr. Nolan answered. "You never please everyone, but no patients have expressed any anger."

"Any phone or written threats?"

"No. None," Dr. Nolan answered.

"Do you know of any reason someone would do this?" Agent Abrams asked.

Dr. Nolan hesitated. He sculpted his words to chisel a finely crafted response. "I can't think of anything that would make a normal person behave this way," he told the agent. "People around here aren't like that."

"And how long have you been here?" Agent Abrams asked, taking notes.

"Eighteen years," Dr. Nolan told him. "And I've never missed a day of work."

Agent Abrams turned to look at the damaged building and shook his head. "I'm afraid you won't be working for a while," he said. "This is a crime scene now. No one in or out until we finish our investigation. Luckily, this looks pretty straightforward."

"So, how long before we can start cleaning up and try to rebuild?" Dr. Nolan inquired.

"Just a few days," Agent Abrams said. "And I need your contact information. We may have more questions."

"Whatever you need," Dr. Nolan said. He thanked them and watched as they headed back to the door of the clinic. A fairly large crowd had formed at the corner. Dr. Nolan recognized Mayor Tillis and a number of his patients. The first news van out of Portland had also arrived on the scene, already busy setting up their satellite dish.

"Big show," Sheriff Dent commented, looking around. "You doing any interviews?"

"Fuck no," said Dr. Nolan. "Not without makeup on. I rushed out this morning without getting dolled up."

Sheriff Dent smiled. "That's more like it," he said. "Still a smart ass. I'll deal with the media. Why don't you get out of here and figure out how you're using those two days I gave you?"

Dr. Nolan nodded. It was only four thirty and brutally cold. "Thanks, Bob," he said. "And I will keep you up to date." He made his way through the maze of emergency vehicles back to his parked car. One old man he had cared for over the years, was at the curb waiting.

"Dr. Nolan? That you?" he asked, squinting in the darkness.

"Oh, Mr. Lowry, yes, yes, it's me," Dr. Nolan said. He took the man's hand.

"What are we going to do?" Mr. Lowry asked, clearly shaken. The clinic was the only local resource. It was home base.

"I'm working on that already," Dr. Nolan answered him. "We'll fix it. Promise."

The old man nodded, but was not smiling. He could see how badly the clinic had been damaged.

Dr. Nolan got in his car, then checked his watch for the second time in five minutes. There were not many places open at such an early hour. He turned around and headed to the Safeway east of town. There was a twenty-four-hour Starbucks there.

There were no other customers in the seating area, and that meant no one to ask him questions. He went to the school supply aisle and purchased a legal pad and two Pilot gel pens. Back at Starbucks, he ordered a large coffee, a bagel with cream cheese, took over the corner table, and began working.

27

DOUG SAUNDERS HEARD THE FIRST NEWS reports over his car radio on the way to work. Arriving at 6:30, he switched the television on his office wall to local coverage. The segment was short, but came with film of the burned clinic in Woodhaven. There were no suspects, no apparent motive, and no onsite interviews. ATF was in charge of the scene, and it appeared to be an intentional act. Updates would follow.

His secretary brought coffee and a copy of the Wall Street Journal. She reminded him about an early meeting.

"Oh, and there was a potty mouth message on the recorder from a Mr. Darden. You want to hear it?" she asked.

"No. I can use my imagination," Mr. Saunders smiled. "Mr. Darden has a rather limited vocabulary. Just erase it."

"No response?" she asked.

"Not necessary," he sighed. "We have nothing to discuss. Thank you." He waited until the door closed behind her. After a sip of coffee he made a call on his cell phone.

"Good morning," the woman said.

"I hope you're well rested," Mr. Saunders began. "You're working tonight."

"That was fast," she said. "You originally sent two options. Is there clarification?"

"Watch the news later," Mr. Saunders told her. "I've got a white knight crusader that the whole town adores, and an old, red neck asshole who nobody likes. Both of them are going to cost us a lot of money, but that's manageable. What's not is all the publicity."

"Your call," the woman said.

Doug Saunders thought over all the potential ramifications of his decision.

"I think Mr. Darden should retire," he finally said. The woman hung up.

28

DR. NOLAN MADE OUT THREE LISTS; one for Amanda, one for Evie, and the last one for himself. He had waited until 7:00 a.m., but could not delay any longer. He texted each member of his staff and asked them to be at the clinic early, and to wear work clothes. He made no mention of the fire.

He then borrowed a phonebook from the barista, searching for the home number for one of his patients. Thankfully, the man was already awake and getting ready for work.

"Todd. Dr. Nolan. You hear?"

"Shit, yes, it's all over the news," the man answered, his voice animated. "What the hell is this about?"

"Not certain," Dr. Nolan said. "But I need a goddamn giant favor from you, and I need it fast. How soon can you get to your office?"

"Fifteen minutes, Doc," he said. "What do you need?"

"If I tell you over the phone, you'll have a heart attack." Dr. Nolan laughed. "Just meet me."

"Okay, Doc. On my way," the man said.

Dr. Nolan crossed the first line out on his register. He finished his second cup of coffee and headed out, the sky just beginning to lighten in the east. He pulled into Todd Blackwood's sales lot just as the other man arrived. After a quick review of the options, Dr. Nolan begged, pleaded, and cajoled the other man into submission, finally reaching a deal.

"And when again?" Todd Blackwood asked.

"One fucking hour," Dr. Nolan repeated. "We're burning daylight, man!"

"Okay. I'll try. Get out of here before you come up with some other crazy idea. I've got calls to make."

"Thank you, Todd. This is important for the whole town," Dr. Nolan told him.

"Yeah, yeah, go away." Todd laughed, already dialing the phone.

Dr. Nolan reached his clinic before his staff. There was yellow crime scene ribbon running along the entire perimeter of the building. He stepped as close to the gaping front window as he could. Everything was black and smelled of rancid smoke. It was not a grand or fancy office, but it had been his second home for nearly two decades. And in that time, it had offered care to tens of thousands of patients.

"Thanks for the warning," Cat said from behind him. "My mom heard on the Kalama Fire radio and called me around five. How long you been here?"

"Oh, three thirty, I think," Dr. Nolan said. "But I forgot marshmallows."

"Very funny," Cat said. "What the hell do we do now?"

"The best we can," Dr. Nolan almost whispered the words. Amanda and Evie had also arrived, both surveying the carnage with looks of disbelief. It was their second home as well.

"This is a nightmare," Amanda said, tears in her eyes.

"Minor setback," Dr. Nolan informed them. He had been given enough time to process the severity of the situation.

"You're still on the payroll, and we have a lot of work to do," Dr. Nolan said, being as positive as possible. He handed his list of immediate duties to Amanda and Evie. They stared at them in outright amazement, slowly reading each numbered line.

"You serious?" Amanda asked, half smiling.

Cat peered over her shoulder. Number 1: Call phone company for emergency hookup of phone and fax lines. Number 2: Power company, emergency hookup of power. Number 3: Two honey buckets, one large enough for handicapped patients. Number 4: Notify billing company there would be no computer link for now. All billing would be paper only.

Evie's list was even longer. Dr. Nolan smiled and handed her his Visa card. It covered an entire page. Sanitary hand wipes—all you can buy. Typing and copy paper. Bottled water. Plastic cups. File folders. Lined notepaper. Toilet paper. Envelopes. Kleenex. Pens, Scotch tape. Paper clips.

Stapler with staples. Notepads. Clipboards. Coffee maker. Coffee, cream, and sugar. Plastic spoons. Coffee cups.

"Jesus, I need a truck," she said.

"And what about me?" Cat asked, feeling left out as a member of the team.

"You're with me," Dr. Nolan said. "We're going to salvage what we can."

He looked at them each in turn and smiled, confronting their skeptic looks.

"And why are we doing all this?" Amanda was the first to voice the question. "There's no clinic."

Todd Blackwood drove into the parking lot honking his car horn. Close behind him was a semitruck towing a twelve-by-thirty-six-foot modular home.

"Where you want this, Doc?" he smiled. It was 8:45 a.m.

"God bless you!" Dr. Nolan shouted. "Back it in directly across from the clinic, close to the power pole."

Todd Blackwood went to give directions to his crew.

"Are you kidding?" Cat squealed. "This is too funny. A trailer?"

"No, a manufactured home," Dr. Nolan corrected her. "And our new clinic until Serv Pro can get in here and fix things up. Which reminds me. Amanda, you need to call the insurance company and tell them we burned down. They need to get going on this."

"I'll add it to my list." Amanda laughed. "I still don't believe this. None of it."

"I'm calling my husband," Cat said. "He'll want to help too." She dialed her phone.

They watched as the mobile unit was maneuvered slowly into position. Finally unhooked from the truck, the crew balanced it with corner jacks. Todd Blackwood was beaming. He came over and handed two keys to Dr. Nolan.

"World record," he bragged. "Ordered, delivered, and set up in less than two hours. Not bad."

"You're a miracle man," Dr. Nolan said. "None of this would have been possible without you. I don't know if I can ever repay this favor."

"Nothing owed," Mr. Blackwood said. "You've kept this town alive for eighteen years. I think we owe you. Let me know if you need anything else." He gathered up his crew and headed back to work.

"Shall we?" Dr. Nolan asked. He walked over and unlocked the door. Without electricity, the only light was from the windows. There was a one-foot step from the parking lot to the entrance.

"Shit, we need a ramp," Amanda noted.

"On your list," Dr. Nolan said. Inside to the right was a small living space.

"Waiting room?" Cat asked. It was only large enough for four or five chairs.

"Yep. And this lovely kitchen area with the foldout table is Amanda's new reception desk. The kitchen will do for a lab. And the two bedrooms will hold exam tables. The bathroom is off-limits for now. No sewer or water."

"Let me guess. On my list," Amanda said.

"That might not be doable," Dr. Nolan said. "But for now we make it work. So, let's get power and phones. And

Evie, you head to Target. Oh, a fax machine! See if they have one. If not, we'll call Office Max."

They went back outside. It was now 9:20. Amanda went home to make phone calls, and Evie left on her shopping spree. Dr. Nolan was just about to commit a crime, with Cat as his accomplice, when an old pickup truck pulled in, barely any paint left showing that the years and weather had not eaten away. It came to a stop in the far corner of the parking lot.

An elderly man got out slowly. From the open bed, he took out a canvass tent chair and unfolded it. From the front seat, he retrieved a thermos and a portable radio. His last chore was to pull a shotgun from the rack behind the driver's seat. He sat down, facing the road, laying the old rifle across his lap.

Dr. Nolan and Cat walked over to where he had stationed himself. It was Ed Freeland, a patient since Dr. Nolan's earliest days in the community. He was in his early '80s, but still fit, working his cattle ranch seven days a week.

"Ed. What are you doing here?" Dr. Nolan asked. He knelt down and placed his hands on the old man's forearm.

"Just keeping watch, that's all," he smiled. "More people coming. Word's out. We won't have this."

Dr. Nolan leaned his head against the old man's shoulder for a moment. He pushed back against a wave of emotion.

"Okay," he said. "Thank you. Just don't shoot your own foot off. We're not open yet."

"I knew a guy that did that climbing over a fence." The old man laughed. "He still limps around like a three-legged dog."

"One story like that is enough," Dr. Nolan said. "And don't catch pneumonia out here."

"Don't worry, Doc. Like I said, plenty more people coming. We're taking shifts."

Dr. Nolan and Cat went back to the front of the building.

"That has to make you feel good," Cat said. "They're standing up for you."

"It does," Dr. Nolan admitted. "I just don't want this to be a geriatric version of the O.K. Corral. You ready for a little covert activity?"

"Why not," Cat shrugged. "What could possibly go wrong?"

He led her around to the rear of the building, pulled off the security tape, and unlocked the door. The back rooms had been spared from the flames, but the walls and ceiling were coated with soot, and a two-inch-deep layer of murky water covered the floor. Dr. Nolan made his way to the supply room to get the emergency lanterns. The contents of the room were dry.

"Okay. We need two exam tables, any workable phones, the microscope, all the medical and surgical supplies we can find, and these billing forms. We've got cardboard boxes. Load up whatever you can."

They split up, two ghostly figures working by battery-powered lights. One box filled with necessary equipment after another, they transported their treasure from the clinic to their new quarters. Dr. Nolan was delighted that the phones in his office and the nurses' station were undamaged. He even found his stethoscope.

On one commute out the back door, carrying the small refrigerator from the breakroom, Sheriff Dent was waiting for him. He was sitting in his patrol car with the window down.

"Goddamn it, did you break into a sealed-off crime scene?" he asked.

"Of course not," Dr. Nolan said. "That would be illegal."

"Where'd you get that refrigerator?" the sheriff asked.

Dr. Nolan was struggling to keep hold of it. The weight seemed to be increasing by the second. "Found it," Dr. Nolan said.

"You need to find more stuff?" Sheriff Dent asked, somewhat amused.

"That would be helpful," Dr. Nolan said. His arms were beginning to shake.

"How long will it take you to find things?"

"About half an hour," Dr. Nolan said. Now he was beginning to bend over, regripping the bulky appliance.

"Well, I'm going to get some breakfast," the sheriff said. "I'll be back in an hour. I sure hope that tape is back over the door."

"Should be," Dr. Nolan said. "I think the wind blew it off."

The sheriff nodded. "Probably so," he said. "That refrigerator you found looks kind of heavy. You should go put that down somewhere."

Dr. Nolan just nodded. He went waddling off toward the front. He did not see the smile on Sheriff Dent's face as he drove away.

"Jesus, my arms feel like jelly," he told Cat, barely making it to their temporary office.

"My husband's here with a friend. They can get the exam tables. Anything else?"

"The medicine in the cupboards and the big refrigerator. You got that?"

"Yep. And all the surgical instruments. And the sterilizer. You look up front?"

"No. Too painful," Dr. Nolan said.

"The copy machine just melted into a lump. Nothing left," she told him.

He nodded. It would take months to fully recover.

The power company had just arrived. One man was already working the junction box on the nearby pole. Mike and Eileen drove in behind them.

"You've been busy," Eileen noted. "Pretty impressive. You need help?"

"No. Besides, I need you to try and pinpoint the site of that old building. We've got this under control. Kind of," Dr. Nolan said, looking around and smiling.

"Three cousins are up at the museum as we speak," Eileen told him. "They'll find something if it's there to be found."

"What's with the posse?" Mike asked. Now there were three elderly patients on guard duty in the parking lot.

"Volunteer militia." Dr. Nolan laughed. "I actually feel better with them around. I just wish they didn't have bullets."

Mike rolled his eyes and nodded.

"Okay, I'll check back after my treatment," Eileen said. "Good luck."

It was 10:50. Evie returned with her SUV overflowing with supplies. They helped her unload, then started the process of trying to organize the small, cramped space available. They kept running into each other.

"We have to cover those windows in the bedrooms. I mean, exam rooms," Cat said. "And there's not supposed to be carpet. The Health Department won't like this."

"If they call, don't answer the phone," Dr. Nolan joked. "Speaking of phones, where's the damn phone company?"

Evie looked out the window. "Parked right next to the electrical guys," she informed them. "Amanda's been busy."

The lights flickered off and on, then stayed on. Cat raced to turn the electric room heaters to seventy. They had worked all morning in near-freezing conditions.

"That will help," she said, rubbing her hands together.

Dr. Nolan was stacking up empty files on the counter, placing a few sheets of lined paper in each one.

"Back to handwritten chart notes," he announced. "This will make the privacy patrol happy. No one can read my writing anyway. It's perfect."

"That will certainly make our jobs easier," Cat remarked sarcastically. "We'll probably have to hire a cryptologist."

Dr. Nolan gasped. "I don't know what those big words mean, but I don't like the sound of them. Was that something dirty?"

Cat just shook her head, but Amanda and Evie laughed. They were a much more receptive audience for his banter. Cat had heard it all before.

"You know, you used to be funny," she told him. "But you're not anymore."

Dr. Nolan was about to launch into his deeply wounded routine to invoke sympathy but was interrupted by a knock on the door. Cat's mother had dropped by with homemade cinnamon rolls.

"Just to help keep you going," she said. "Sorry about the trouble."

"Thank you very much." Dr. Nolan smiled, accepting her gift. "At least someone in your family has a warm and caring heart. It gives me renewed hope for mankind."

Cat pushed him aside and gave her Mom a hug.

"You smell like smoke," her mother said.

"We had to recover some equipment from the clinic," Cat explained.

"Okay. Enjoy. And be safe," the woman said. As she was leaving, one of the local hairstylists came to the door with oatmeal cookies, still warm from the oven. Behind her was another patient with a plate of brownies, and another with a chocolate cake. The counter space was quickly covered with offerings from the community.

"Jesus, we could open a bakery," Dr. Nolan said. "This is great." He had a brownie in one hand and a cookie in the other.

"You don't have to worry about your figure," Cat informed him. "This is torture." She helped herself to a piece of cake balanced on a paper towel, using her fingers as utensils.

There was another knock on the door. It was Ned Thomas, a local contractor. Behind him was a pickup half filled with two by fours and plywood.

"Hi, Doc. Heard you needed a ramp for wheelchairs. You got a place I can plug in my saw?" he asked, a wide grin on his face.

"God, yes, thank you." Dr. Nolan shook his hand. "We've got tons of fresh pastry. Take your pick."

"Thanks. Maybe after I'm done. Should only take an hour," Mr. Thomas said. "We all feel terrible about this."

"It's getting better by the minute," Dr. Nolan said, mentally taking note of all the positive events in the past few hours. Mr. Thomas, aided by Cat's husband, began unloading the lumber and construction tools.

"Who's the boss here?" one of the telephone workers asked. Dr. Nolan, still eating, pointed to Cat.

"Where do you want these lines?" he asked.

"Uh, one at the kitchen table, one in the kitchen… where the hell do we put the fax machine?"

Dr. Nolan swallowed hard. It was an essential tool. With everything in turmoil at the clinic, it was still critically important he be able to receive the reports from the lab. He looked around the room.

"Set it up on the toilet," he said. "There's no other place for it. Just make sure it's working."

The man looked puzzled, but nodded and began stringing wires. They drilled through the metal siding, fixed connecting plugs, and sealed the damage with caulking compound. It was not pretty, but it was functional.

Just as the phone at Amanda's desk area was plugged in, it was already ringing.

"Woodhaven Medical Clinic," she answered, just as she had thousands of times before. She listened, nodding her head, then covered the speaker.

"Tilson logging," she whispered. "One of their guys cut his leg with a chainsaw. Are we open?"

Dr. Nolan smiled at her question.

"We will be," he said. "How far out are they?"

Amanda relayed the question.

"About twenty minutes," she said.

"Tell them to come in," he said. Now he had a cinnamon roll in his hand. He held it in his teeth as he pulled on his coat. "I'll be back in a few minutes."

Dr. Nolan walked briskly up the main street and turned left. There was an ACE Hardware store one block east. He knew everyone there.

"Doc, sorry about your trouble," the clerk at the counter said as he came through the door. "What can I do you for?"

"Red paint and a brush," Dr. Nolan said. "I don't need much."

"Oil or water base?" the man asked.

"Something we can take off later," Dr. Nolan shrugged. He knew nothing about paint.

"This should do you," the clerk said, handing him a pint-sized can and a flat-edged brush. They went back to the counter.

"What do I owe you?" Dr. Nolan asked.

"Nothing," a voice answered from behind him. It was the store owner. "Your money is no good here. Anything else you need, just come and get it."

Dr. Nolan met his eyes and smiled. "Thank you," he said.

"That's how we do business," the owner said. "I was on that fire last night. Broke my heart." He had been an unpaid volunteer at the fire department for thirty years.

"You guys did a great job," Dr. Nolan told him. "You saved most of the building."

"Shouldn't have happened," the man said. "Anything. Anything at all. If you need it, we'll try to get it."

"Thank you all," Dr. Nolan said. He nodded to both men and went out, retracing his path back to the temporary clinic. The men from the phone company had finished, and the two portable sanitary units were being placed at the far end of the building.

"You got a screwdriver?" Dr. Nolan asked them. "One with a flat head?"

Dr. Nolan shook the can of paint, then pried off the lid. To the left of the entry door, in thick, broad strokes, he fashioned a red cross with an arm span of nearly four feet. There was so much excess paint that tears of flaming color dripped down from every branch. He stepped back, smiling, to admire his work.

It was a symbol with universal recognition. Wherever it stood, medical care was available.

Cat, Evie, and Amanda came outside. It was 12:08 p.m.

"Now," Dr. Nolan smiled at them. "Now we're open for business."

29

SHERIFF DENT HAD GONE TO ANNIE'S Café for breakfast. He sat in the far corner booth with his back to the door. The fatigue and emotional strain of the long night had worn away the edges of his easygoing personality. He was liked and respected in the town as a compassionate and fair man, and had won reelection easily four terms in a row. But today there was a darkness on his face, his eyes focusing somewhere else.

"Bad business," the waitress said when he first came in, but he had only nodded. He was in no mood for conversation. When he had finished eating, he continued to sit there, holding his forehead in his left hand, just staring at the table.

He loved the town and the people in it, and it had always been a safe and open community, a good place to live and raise a family. But now he couldn't remember exactly when that had changed. There had been so much turmoil and disorder in the past weeks, he could not recall when it was last tranquil, quiet.

It gnawed at him. His mandate was to be a peace officer, not to manage chaos. In some respects, he and Dr. Nolan shared the same duties. While they sometimes had to deal with emergency situations, their primary goals were to prevent trouble, to stop events from getting out of control.

But they were now. For the first time as sheriff, he felt like a failure, an imposter, incapable of controlling his surroundings.

"More coffee, Sheriff?" the waitress asked.

"One more," he nodded. Checking his watch and surprised by the time, he called the dispatch office.

"Who's on swing shift tonight?" he asked.

"Ummm. Jim Cochran. Three till eleven."

"Good. I want you to call Lenny Darden and have him come to my office for a chat," the sheriff said. "Say, ten o'clock. And I want Deputy Cochran to come in just in case. Lenny can be a hothead."

"Why so late?" the dispatcher asked.

"Too much going on," Sheriff Dent explained. "I'm staying out to keep tabs on things until later. And I might need a nap."

"Okay, Sheriff. I'll make the calls. See you later."

Sheriff Dent picked up his white Stetson hat and set it in place. He still wasn't certain what he was going to do, but it wasn't going to be nothing.

30

AFTER SEWING UP THE INJURED LOGGER, a slow but steady stream of patients began to flow through their makeshift clinic. The phone rang almost continuously, a mix of people amazed they were open, and an equal number of patients scheduling care. Amanda was struggling to stay afloat but doing her best transitioning back to appointments on paper only.

In midafternoon, over one hundred pages of lab data chattered through the fax machine. It was a massive volume of information, and Dr. Nolan did not have time to review it. Stacked on a counter in the new lab area, he glanced at it between patients, but could not even begin to sort through the numbers.

He had called Eileen earlier, and she once again came to his rescue. She picked up his girls from school and took them to her house. There was nowhere else for them to go. In the smaller clinic, he did not even have an office. Finally finished, he picked up Chinese food, collected all the lab tests, and kicked at the front door.

"I need more hands," he protested, setting the food down on the kitchen table. "We got back most of the test samples, but I need help going through them."

"Eat first," Eileen commanded. He hugged his daughters and sat down.

"What an amazing day," he said. "My clinic burns down, and in eight hours we're back in business. Half the town was helping."

"What happened?" Cienna asked. She had heard rumors at school.

"Someone started the fire on purpose." Dr. Nolan told her. "We don't know who for sure, and we don't exactly know why."

They took turns filling their plates, with Mike trying to push everyone else out of his way.

"You think it's the same people that hurt the donkey?" Aubriel asked.

"Probably," their father admitted. "At any rate, I want you girls to stay here for a few days. It's safer. I can bring down clean clothes in the morning."

They both protested, but it had been decided.

"It will be fun," Eileen assured them.

"Two days at most," their father said. "Now, finish eating and start homework. The grown-ups have work to do upstairs. Okay?"

There were moans and groans and twisted faces, then acceptance. They knew their father was exhausted, and worried. It was not time to argue or bargain.

Mike, Eileen, and Dr. Nolan went to the office.

"Oh, we found two pictures, kind of," Eileen announced. "The old electric building is in the background, but at least you can tell where it was along the road."

Dr. Nolan studied the faded, black-and-white images. The building had been fairly large, two stories tall, and to the side of it was an equally large lot filled with line trucks and flatbed trailers stacked with telephone poles.

"You have a good idea where this stood, Mike?" he asked.

"I can guess pretty close," Mike said. "See the old Catholic church steeple in the distance? That's still there. Kind of like a compass."

Dr. Nolan nodded. "What's here now?" he asked.

"Nothing. Just a big empty lot with cottonwood trees," Mike said. "Some corporation owns the land now."

"Let me guess," Dr. Nolan sighed. "We don't know who that is, right?"

Eileen laughed. "Don't worry," she said. "I'll find out first thing in the morning. I'm getting good at researching tax records."

"Okay. Good. Good job," Dr. Nolan said. He held up the small book of lab reports. "This is what we spent weeks getting, and now we have it. But this is going to be a pain in the ass."

There were over eighty test sites from the south side of the Bottoms and just over twenty from the northern area.

He separated the two groups. His greatest concern was the land west of the Carson Farm.

"I'll give you the address," he said to Eileen, "and you write in blue on the map where it is, and the PCB levels. Let's see how big a footprint we have."

It took nearly an hour to complete the task, and with each notation, the scope of contamination became more alarmingly obvious. The toxic levels of PCBs spread out in the shape of a fan, with the central point directly in line with the old electric company. The well at the Carson Farm had the highest levels of pollution, but every other property sampled was also showing dangerous levels of the chemical, but with lower readings as they moved westward. And worse, the last farm tested was nearly at the river.

"Jesus, this shit has moved over two miles," Mike calculated. "And it's a mile wide. What happens if it gets to the Columbia?"

"Then it poisons every fish, animal, and human from here to the Pacific Ocean," Dr. Nolan told him. "And look at the cancer patients. They're all inside that zone except for five cases."

"Including me and my sister," Eileen reminded them.

"It's no wonder someone didn't want this to come out. But who?" Dr. Nolan said. "This company went out of business seventy goddamn years ago. All of those people are dead. Who's left to care?"

There were no answers. All three of them sat in silence.

"What about the other tests?" Eileen asked finally. "You said that there was something else, right?"

"Correct. A small amount of PCBs at the Darden Farm, but mostly benzene," Dr. Nolan explained. He started sifting through the results from the north side of the Bottoms. He again read off addresses and toxin levels, this time noted in yellow pen. The benzene had only been at critical levels in well water from the Darden site and the two nearest farms. The soil samples were all normal, and water taken from a mile west of that area was free of contamination.

"Now, I'm confused," Mike admitted. "What the hell does this prove?"

Dr. Nolan was standing close to the map. "It tells us the exposure was confined to a small area," he said. "And it doesn't seem to be spreading. And, since it's not in the ground, the only people affected were exposed through their own water supply."

"Didn't you say Darden had a daughter die from cancer?" Mike asked.

"That's right. A baby girl in the early '60s. And it was a rare cancer that typically affects older people," Dr. Nolan explained.

"How many pins are in that zone?" Eileen asked.

Dr. Nolan counted them, still acutely aware that they represented people, victims. "Thirteen," he answered. "Fourteen, if you add the Darden girl. Maybe more. We didn't look back this far." He went to the desk and sat down heavily. He felt sick.

"So, what now?" Mike asked him. His anger over his wife's illness, and the risk to his own children had been steadily growing.

"Well, we've got over a hundred unofficial test results, the eyewitness testimony of an old fart with Alzheimer's disease, and a shitload of speculation," Dr. Nolan summarized. "We need one last thing."

"What? A confession from dead people?" Mike asked.

"Proof," Dr. Nolan said. "You've got a backhoe, right?"

"You bet," Mike answered. "And I know how to use it." He was smiling now.

"Okay. Eileen, you find out who the legal owner of the property is now. I'll call them and explain that we need samples from their land. Then we dig a hole. The odds are, they used the old truck yard."

Mike was re-energized, and probably would have been willing to start immediately. "Finally," he said. "At least I'll feel like we're close to an answer."

"I can't even think anymore," Dr. Nolan admitted. "Tomorrow is my deadline with Sheriff Dent. We better find something."

He thanked them for their help, kissed his daughters good night, and drove home.

Jed Marcus was waiting when he arrived.

"I saw the news on TV," he said. "Sorry, Doc. We should have watched your clinic too."

"Not your fault." Dr. Nolan smiled. "You kept my family safe. That was much more important."

"I fed the animals for you," Jed told him. "And the dog. You look like you need some sleep."

Dr. Nolan was genuinely surprised, and deeply grateful.

"Jesus, thank you, kid," he said. "This may be your last night of guard duty. We may finally have an answer."

"Whatever you need, Doc," Jed told him. "Get some sleep."

Dr. Nolan nodded and went upstairs. For the first time in his life, he unplugged the phone. He kicked off his shoes, let Callie up on the bed next to him, gave her a pet behind her right ear, and was asleep in less than a minute.

31

LENNY DARDEN'S SULLIED DEMEANOR HAD DETERIORATED even further. The call from the sheriff's department had been an irritant, but the late night appointment time was an added abuse. His normal schedule was to be in bed by eight, then up before sunrise. Any deviation from that custom was a rare event.

But the call intrigued him, and with it there was a growing concern. Given his recent activities, had there been a witness? Had someone seen him or his truck near Dr. Nolan's farm or his clinic? He had taken extraordinary precautions, but in such a small community, he was easily recognized.

The call itself had been cordial and businesslike. There had been no hint of any unusual intent. The sheriff's secretary simply relayed a request for a meeting without emotion, explaining the late hour on the need for added patrols. It was all routine.

So what did Sheriff Dent know, or think, or suspect? Why not just come by the house for a talk? Why was it necessary to meet in the sheriff's office? His annoyance growing by the minute, at nine forty-five he grabbed his coat and went outside. He did not speak to his wife or tell her he was leaving the house. They rarely communicated at all anymore.

The old dog on the porch barely looked up as Lenny went past. There was no wagging tail or effort to greet him. She had bargained her tolerance of him for food and shelter, but there was no affection. Depending on his mood, he could offer a random pet or the toe of his boot. It was more prudent to keep a safe distance between them.

Lenny pulled the zipper on his coat up to his chin. The temperature had fallen below zero, and a glistening frost was already reflecting back a ghostly shimmer from the light on the barn. He quickly walked to his crew cab truck and got in, fishing for his keys.

Looking down, he did not see the shadowed figure move silently behind him. A gloved hand reached forward, holding a single-action .22-caliber Ruger pistol. A rubber nipple from a baby bottle had been fitted over the barrel. When the trigger was pulled, the muffled sound was like fingers snapping. The bullet entered Lenny's right temple, and exited through the driver's side window. The hole in the glass was highlighted by a halo of scalp tissue and hair particles.

Lenny slumped forward and to the left, his head bowed. Most of his brain had been liquefied by the shock wave from the projectile. He took two long irregular breaths, moaning ever so slightly as he exhaled, then he was still.

The shadow in the back seat leaned forward. Taking Lenny's right hand, the shooter molded it around the handle of the pistol, weaving Lenny's index finger through the trigger guard. The passenger window was rolled down, and a second baby nipple was placed over the muzzle. The next shot was aimed at the stars, with barely a sound.

The shooter rolled the window back up, then removed the extra spent cartridge from the cylinder, replacing it with a live round. The gun was rechecked one last time to make certain the remaining used bullet was positioned beneath the firing pin. Then it was placed next to Lenny on the front seat.

The shadow exited the truck on the passenger side. Wearing plastic shopping bags as foot coverings, the shooter walked to the tree line, crossed the fence, a waiting car parked nearby. The entire sequence of events had taken four minutes.

32

SHERIFF DENT RETURNED TO POLICE HEADQUARTERS in City Hall just before 10:00 p.m. Deputy Cochran had arrived just before him.

"Man, you look beat," he told his boss. "I just made coffee. You want some?"

Sheriff Dent tossed his hat on the desk, sat down, unzipped his coat, and propped his feet up.

"I don't usually indulge this late," he said. "But nothing's going to keep me awake tonight. I'm bone tired."

The deputy brought back two cups of coffee and a carton of creamer, then took the chair on the other side of the desk.

"Jesus, what a day," he remarked. "You believe Doc was up again and seeing patients by noon? It doesn't seem possible."

Sheriff Dent allowed himself to smile. The vision of Dr. Nolan clutching the ill-gotten refrigerator crossed his thoughts.

"It wasn't possible," the sheriff said. "He's a smart ass sometimes, but there's no quit in him. He's a good man."

Deputy Cochran nodded. "Any progress on figuring out who did this?" he asked.

Sheriff Dent gave a short laugh, but it was not from amusement. "ATF sent in a forensics team this afternoon," he said. "Found a few bottle fragments on the waiting room floor. But with the fire and all the water, there won't be any prints. Unless someone saw something, this will just stay an unsolved case."

Deputy Cochran sipped his coffee.

"Still, makes you wonder. Who's pissed off at Dr. Nolan enough to do this?" he asked. "This have anything to do with you bringing in Mr. Darden?"

The sheriff looked up at the clock. It was ten after.

"Just following up on a rumor I heard," the sheriff said. "Where the hell is that bastard?"

Deputy Cochran stood up, moving back toward the main dispatch office. "You want me to call his house? Or I could go get him for you," he offered.

"No. No, let it be," Sherriff Dent sighed deeply. "I'll give him a few more minutes. If he doesn't show, it can wait till tomorrow."

"He's probably sound asleep," the deputy said.

Sheriff Dent finished his coffee, then sat staring into the empty cup. "Probably so," he said.

33

IT WAS JUST PAST 6:00 A.M. when Sheriff Dent was paged by the dispatch office. He had managed to get seven hours of sleep, but felt the worse for it. A full minute passed before he could identify the harsh buzzing sound or what it meant. Twice he had slammed his hand down on the alarm clock snooze button with no response.

Finally awake, he dialed his office.

"Oh, Sheriff, sorry," the voice said. "They just found Lenny Darden. He's dead."

"What? Where?" the sheriff asked, throwing back the covers and sitting up.

"At his farm," the woman said. "He might have been shot. I've got Deputy Ingram on the way. You want to meet him there?"

"Sure. I need a quick shower. About half an hour. Anyone call the coroner?"

"Not yet. We just got the notice. You want him rolling now?"

"Might as well," Sheriff Dent told her. "I'll be there soon." He could feel his heart racing. A cool shower urged him to be quick. He skipped shaving, put on a clean uniform, and was out the door in twenty minutes. The occasion even permitted him to use his lights and siren through town. He pulled into the Darden Farm just at sunrise.

Sheriff Dent waved to his deputy, signaling a brief delay. He went up the steps of the house and knocked. The old dog came to him, tail wagging. He bent down and gave her a good rub behind her ears and around her neck. From his inside coat pocket he pulled out a Milk Bone and gave it to her. She trotted back to the bed at the far end of the porch to savor her newfound treasure.

Sheriff Dent knocked a second time, then a third. Mrs. Darden finally opened the door just enough to frame her face. She stared down at the floor. He noticed her eyes were not red.

"I'm sorry for your loss, ma'am," Sheriff Dent told her. "I'm afraid there's going to be a lot of activity here for a while. We'll try to be respectful as best we can. Did anything unusual happen that you are aware of?"

"Didn't know he was gone," Mrs. Darden said without emotion.

"So, no strange noises? Dog didn't bark? Anything at all?" Sheriff Dent asked.

"No, nothing. Good day," Mrs. Darden answered, closing the door. It was not the reaction he had expected. He tossed the old dog a second treat, went down the stairs, and over to the truck. Deputy Ingram, Zeke, was half inside the front seat on the passenger side.

"What've you got?" the sheriff asked. He could see Lenny's body now, and a large pool of blackish blood on the floormat.

"Looks like he blew his brains out," Zeke answered, backing out to face him. "Single shot to the right side of his head. Pistol is right next to him. I don't see any other marks or bruises on him."

Sheriff Dent nodded. He leaned his head in the door and surveyed the immediate scene. It all looked typical for a suicide by gunshot, but a lot more tidy than what remained after a rifle blast. He sometimes had nightmares from things he had witnessed. This was clean and neat.

Sheriff Dent then walked around the perimeter of the truck. There were the expected boot and shoe prints, a few smeared, flat areas by one rear door, but nothing that indicated a disturbance or a struggle.

"Who found him?" Sheriff Dent asked.

Zeke checked his notepad. "Diesel mechanic," he said, nodding toward the barn area where another pickup truck was parked. "Came early to work on a tractor. At first he thought he was sleeping. Then he saw the bullet hole in the glass and called 911."

The sheriff nodded again. "What kind of gun?" he asked.

"A .22 Ruger," Deputy Ingram answered. "One shot fired."

The coroner pulled in and parked his black van near the sheriff's car. They gave him an update on everything they knew so far.

"Goddamn, I'm freezing," the medical examiner said.

"You're not as cold as he is," Sheriff Dent told him, tilting his head toward Lenny Darden's body. "Stick a probe in him and tell me how long he's been dead."

The coroner laughed. He opened his medical supply kit and took out a pointed thermometer. Inside the truck, he made a puncture wound and shoved it into Lenny Darden's liver.

"I'll have to do some calculations," he said, "and even then, it's an estimate. He would have cooled off fast in this weather." He waited five minutes, used a scale balanced by ambient temperature, then shrugged. "Probably last night."

"Well, that explains why he never showed up at our meeting," the sheriff said. "Zeke. Go ask Mrs. Darden if Lenny had a .22 pistol. She's not much of a talker."

Deputy Ingram went to the house while the coroner looked over the front seat of the truck. It only took a few minutes.

"I'll check for powder residue on his hand," he said, "but it sure looks like suicide. I don't see any reason for an autopsy. He can just be released to the mortuary. You going to help me get him out of here?"

"Hell, no," the sheriff laughed. "He's stiff as a board. That's what young deputies are for. Zeke can help pry him lose."

The deputy was coming back, shaking his head. "That was enlightening," he said. "She told me he had lots of guns, and she didn't know one from the other, then slammed the door. Doesn't seem too broken up about this."

"I don't think anyone around here will miss old Lenny," the sheriff remarked. "Anything else? I'm satisfied, if you are."

The coroner shook his hand. "I'm done here," he said. "I'll get the stretcher and see if we can straighten him out. Sure you don't want to stay?"

Sheriff Dent smiled and headed back to his car. He made a quick stop for coffee at a convenience store, radioed in to his office, then drove to Dr. Nolan's clinic. He kept the engine running and the heater on full. At eight thirty Dr. Nolan arrived, and Sheriff Dent waved him over and had him get in.

"What's up, copper?" Dr. Nolan smiled.

"Good news for once," the sheriff said. "We found Lenny Darden with a hole through his head. Looks like suicide."

"What do you mean, looks like?"

"Just kind of convenient, is all," the sheriff noted. "Solves a lot of problems. I think you can rest easy now. I don't think there's going to be any more trouble."

"You think something's fishy?" Dr. Nolan asked.

"Coroner says suicide," the sheriff said. "That's all that matters. Just thought you'd like to know."

"I appreciate it," Dr. Nolan said. "Now my daughters can come home, and Jed can look for a new job. It'll be like the good old days."

Sheriff Dent looked over at the burned clinic. "Sure hope so," he said. "Where you at on this other thing?"

"Close, Bob. I'll know more later today," Dr. Nolan explained. "And I won't do anything until I let you know."

"Used to be a nice, quiet town," Sheriff Dent said.

"Will be again," Dr. Nolan told him. "But I'm afraid not for a while. Thanks again for telling me about Darden. If I was a drinking man, I'd buy a bottle of champagne."

"I feel the same way," Sheriff Dent told him.

34

Doug Saunders was on a conference call when his cell phone rang. He glanced at the number and let it go to voice mail. He knew there would be no message. It was half an hour later when he could safely call back.

"Do we have closure?" he asked.

"We do," the woman said.

"Good work," he complimented her efficiency. "Payment will be finalized within the hour."

"More good news," the woman said. "It's a half price sale."

Doug Saunders frowned. He had no idea what she was talking about. "I don't follow," he said.

"The problem was already solved when I got there," she informed him. "You might say that your friend took matters into his own hands."

Doug Saunders sat back in his chair and laughed. "You're kidding," he said.

"I don't kid about work," the woman said.

"How timely," Mr. Saunders commented. "So, you're good with half?"

"Perfectly," the woman answered. "I didn't earn the other half."

"Well, as always, it's been a pleasure doing business with you. I've got your number," Mr. Saunders said.

"Any time," the woman answered, then hung up.

Doug Saunders was still smiling. The day was off to an auspicious beginning. He rang his secretary.

"I need to meet with the regency board. Tomorrow is probably too much of a time squeeze. See if we can get a consensus by Thursday. Tell them it's urgent."

"Is that all?" she asked.

"No. Get a message to Mr. Dukayne. Have him call when it's convenient. And let them know it's not urgent. Just a social call."

35

EILEEN CALLED THE CLINIC JUST AFTER 10:00 a.m. The tax records had led to a holding company registered in Delaware as the landowners. Following a series of three phone calls, Dr. Nolan was finally directed to a management company in California. After a lengthy explanation, he was routed to the legal department.

"This is Arthur Sheldon," the man said. "How may I assist you?"

"Thank God, a human being. This is Dr. Sean Nolan in Woodhaven, Washington. Thank you for taking my call. This is a lot to throw at you over the phone, but we have a toxic pollution situation here, and we're hoping we could take some samples from your property?"

There was dead silence for a moment. "And who do you represent, Dr. Nolan? Is this an official inquiry?" the man asked.

"I guess I represent the people of the town," Dr. Nolan explained. "People are getting sick here."

"That's unfortunate, of course, but we're only an investment agency. We have nothing to do with the actual land. There would be complex legal matters at play here and complicated liability issues."

"I'm not accusing your company of any wrongdoing," Dr. Nolan tried to explain. "But we're trying to find the source of this. It can't be allowed to continue. The risks are too great."

"I understand your concern, Dr. Nolan, but I have a duty to protect the legal rights of my clients. Now, if you would like to submit a written request for us to review, I would be happy to set up an email resource to try and sort this out."

Dr. Nolan took a deep breath and struggled to curb his growing frustration. "Okay. Let's try this again," he said. "I have evidence of a lethal toxic dump site that poses an immediate health risk to living people, and you want me to fill out paperwork? Do you hear how crazy that sounds?"

The attorney cleared his throat. "Unless you have a court order, Dr. Nolan, you do not have permission to set foot on that property. If need be, we'll file an injunction preventing you from even discussing this matter. It must be handled through proper channels."

"And how many more cancer cases come to my clinic while you're agonizing over paperwork?" Dr. Nolan asked him. "What if one of those patients was your brother, or sister, or one of your children?"

"Again, I applaud your passion," the attorney said, "but there is no room to negotiate here. Send us a request. The matter will be reviewed in a timely manner, and we'll get back to you. But as of now, you are barred from any type of testing. Are we clear?"

Dr. Nolan closed his eyes and sighed heavily. "Nothing has been clear about this from day one," he said. "You're just another roadblock trying to stop what's coming. But you know what. Nothing has stopped us yet, and the truth of this is going to come out. So, I guess you need to ask your corporate board if they want to be part of the problem or help with the solution."

"Submit the request, Dr. Nolan," the attorney said again. "That's where we start."

Dr. Nolan slammed the phone back in its carriage. The small modular unit they were working in did not come equipped with privacy. Cat and Evie had heard most of his conversation.

"Temper, temper," Cat said. "Sounds like you hit a brick wall. And what was that comment about a lethal dump site? Did you guys find something?"

Up until now, Dr. Nolan had not shared with them what the environmental testing had indicated. With all the threats directed against him, he still wanted to minimize the risk of a panic in the area based on gossip. He wanted facts.

"We found toxic levels of a chemical, but not the source," he admitted. "So, please, please don't talk about this yet. We only need one more answer."

Cat and Evie were worried, but understood the urgency in his voice.

"Didn't sound like the answer was going to be easy to get," Cat said, referring to his phone call.

"Minor detail," Dr. Nolan said. But he was worried, too. This was not like having Jed sneak in at night to collect water samples. This was much bigger. He went into the small bathroom and sat on the edge of the tub. If there were potential legal ramifications involved with moving ahead, he really didn't care. As overly dramatic as it sounded, it really had become a matter of life and death. When all the other arguments were exhausted, it was actually that simple.

He called Mike on his cell phone and made an effort to keep his voice low. After a detailed review of his call to the holding company, Mike's anger was much quicker to the surface.

"That's bullshit!" he shouted. "Those bastards don't live here! They couldn't care less. Their wife isn't fighting cancer!"

"It is bullshit," Dr. Nolan agreed. "But they really have no power. What are they going to do? Burn down my clinic?"

Mike actually laughed. "How about we go in there with metal detectors and find this shit?" Mike suggested eagerly.

Dr. Nolan considered the idea. "No good," he answered finally. "They would have buried the evidence too deep. You know anybody around here that uses ground radar?"

Mike had an immediate answer. "Jesus, the city has one," he said. "They use it to locate old pipe systems. And Eileen's got a cousin who works the maintenance yard."

"No," Dr. Nolan laughed. "Why doesn't that surprise me? Have Eileen talk to him and see if he can help us out with a little night job?"

"He will, I guarantee it," Mike assured him. "What time were you thinking?"

"Ten. You think Eileen can keep my girls again? It's a school night."

"All for the cause," Mike said. "What's the name of this goddamn company that doesn't want us on their property?"

Dr. Nolan pulled the crumpled paper from his pocket that held the name and number. "Eastern Seaboard Fidelity Trust," he told Mike. "That's almost an oxymoron."

"Yeah, they're morons, all right," Mike said. "We'll check back with you about tonight, but I don't think it'll be a problem."

"Okay. Thanks, Mike. Dress warm," Dr. Nolan said.

It was going to be another late night. He had promised Sheriff Dent to keep him informed, but there really wasn't any new information to report. Nothing had changed yet. He came out of the bathroom.

"Is the militia still on duty?" he asked Cat.

She looked out the window and nodded, a smile on her face. "Four right now. There's been as many as seven," she informed him.

Dr. Nolan grabbed his coat. Old Ed Freeland was at his corner post, shotgun ready.

"Ed, how you doing?" Dr. Nolan greeted him.

"Still upright," the old man answered. "At least most of the time."

"Good. Keep it that way." Dr. Nolan laughed. He knelt down close to him. "I'm grateful for all the security, but I don't think there's any more danger. But I was wondering if you, and a few of your friends, might help out with something else?"

"Just name it, Doc, and it's done," the old man answered.

"You know Jed Marcus?"

"Know his mother," the old man said. "That the boy in the service?"

"Yes," Dr. Nolan said. "He helps me with special projects now and then. We might need some extra guards later tonight. It will be late, but you interested?"

"Hell yes. I don't sleep much anyway. Have to pee every hour," Mr. Freeland told him.

Dr. Nolan nodded his understanding. "It will probably be a few hours. I'll have Jed call you at home," he explained. He mentally counted the main roads and side streets bordering the vacant property site. "And we need three other volunteers."

"I can get thirty," the old man said.

"No. Just three, and keep this quiet," Dr. Nolan said. "This is a secret mission."

"Got it, Doc," he promised. "I'll be waiting for the call." He got up, stretched, and began to collect his belongings.

"This is a big help, Ed. It's important," Dr. Nolan said, shaking his hand.

Before returning to the temporary clinic, he called Jed from the parking lot. "You free tonight?"

Jed laughed.

"I got more time off in Afghanistan," he said. "What's up now?"

Dr. Nolan explained the plan, the players, and the time frame.

"No digging? Just eyes?" Jed asked.

"Call it an early warning system," Dr. Nolan said.

"You got it, Doc," he said. "Just give me Ed's phone contact. Anything else?"

"Oh yeah. Pick up some more two-way radios and fresh batteries. Eyes won't do much good if we can't communicate. I'm sorry to keep bothering you like this," Dr. Nolan added.

"Not a problem, Doc. I just hope you find what you're looking for."

Dr. Nolan just nodded in response. "Me too," he said.

36

"MEDICAL EXAMINER CALLED," THE DISPATCHER TOLD Sheriff Dent. He had just returned from a domestic dispute call.

"Thanks. Try to get him back," he said, closing the door of his office. Dealing with drunks before noon had not brightened his mood. For the past twenty-four hours, he had been distant and distracted.

"Line two, Sheriff."

"Bob Dent here," he answered.

"Sheriff? Good. I wanted to update you on the Darden case," the coroner said. "There was gunpowder residue on the back of his right hand and on his sleeve. He definitely fired the weapon. And when we got him thawed out and cleaned up, there were no signs of any other trauma."

"That's good," Sheriff Dent remarked.

"There was one odd thing, though," the coroner added. "Around the entry wound, we found some traces of a brown sticky substance. Not sure what it is."

Sheriff Dent thought for a moment. "Old guns. They sit around and you get oil, dirt, sometimes even bugs down the barrel. Doesn't sound too interesting."

"No. Pretty clear cut," the coroner said. "We're signing it off as suicide. Body can be released at any time."

"That's good with us," Sheriff Dent replied. "Thanks for the speedy work."

"Hopefully, we don't do any more business until the weather warms up a little," the coroner said.

The sheriff gave a brief laugh. "Speaking of weather," he said. "That's the one thing about old Lenny. He ended up in a much warmer climate than the one he left. Thanks again."

37

Doug Saunders was unusually animated. All but two members of the board of regents were in attendance, and the news was fairly positive.

"We're off record today," he began, "but it was necessary we all be in agreement. Our main concern over exposure has been eliminated. Mr. Lenny Darden committed suicide Monday night. While tragic, it does lend itself to the old adage that dead men don't tell tales."

He smiled while delivering the news.

"So, that gets us back to deniability," he went on. "The event was seventy years ago, and was set in motion by the floodwaters. There's no one alive that worked there, and as I explained before, if this does come out, we end up with a fine and a cleanup bill."

There was some discussion in the group.

"What about Mrs. Darden?" someone asked.

"She signed the same nondisclosure agreement as her husband. She won't talk, and the law firm involved can't say anything. This is the best possible outcome. Minimal damage."

There was consensus.

38

JED MARCUS WAS NOW IN CHARGE of a four-man army unit, the youngest recruit seventy-six, and the oldest eighty-three. They were ready and eager to serve. He made certain the short-wave radios were on the same channel and gave one to each of his soldiers.

He assigned guard stations to each member of the team. One man would be at each end of the main road, about half a mile from the property site. The other two would monitor the pair of crossroads. Any warning they issued would give the search team about thirty seconds to conceal their activities.

"I only want two messages over the radio," Jed told them. "Either 'car coming' or 'all clear.' No fishing stories. No weather report. No nothing. Okay?"

They all nodded. It was 9:50 p.m. Jed thanked them and ushered them to their vehicles. He had Ed Freeland drop him off at the search area. Mike, Dr. Nolan, and Eileen's cousin had already unloaded the wheeled radar sled and pushed it up into the tree line. Eileen's cousin, Bill Kinney, was making last-minute connections to the computer screen.

In the dark, they had paced off an approximate location for the old equipment yard based on the photographs. The terrain was flat, but in seventy years, it had been repopulated with cottonwood trees and blackberry bushes.

"We'll be weaving around like drunk drivers," Bill told them. "But if there's anything big here, we'll find it."

The sled sat on four small pneumatic tires, but it was not designed for jungle warfare. There was a front control handle like a lawn mower, but it took two men to propel it through the undergrowth. Guided by LED flashlights, each pass up and down the old yard took ten minutes.

"Car coming," the radio warned. Jed relayed the message. Lights out, they crouched down and waited.

"All clear," came the call.

Back and forth, over and over, tripping over roots and cussing, sometimes laughing, ninety minutes later they had only recorded random signals. Wet with sweat, but warmed by the physical exertion, they were all dealing with frustration.

Mike farted so loud and forcibly that leaves on nearby trees shivered.

"That's a goddamn security breach," Dr. Nolan yelled out. "Jed! Shoot the bastard!"

Now they were all laughing. The methane release had also broken the tension they were feeling. As each wave of laughter would begin to ebb, another would begin. It was infantile and infectious. No one could speak for minutes.

Mike had tears in his eyes. "So now what?" he managed to ask.

"I think we're in the wrong place," Dr. Nolan suddenly replied. "They didn't want anyone to see what they were doing, so they buried it under the floor. We've got to move south."

"Worth a shot," Bill said. He turned the sled, and, with help from Mike, maneuvered it some forty yards in a new direction. On the third pass there was a long, high pitched tone. It would fade and then grow louder, but it never disappeared.

"Car coming."

Lights out, they lay flat on the frozen ground for a moment.

"All clear."

Circuit after circuit, they expanded the pattern until the tone finally dissipated into silence. Dr. Nolan had brought a can of orange spray paint. He made a mark at each border. In another hour, they had etched out a skeleton nearly fifty by one hundred feet in size.

Bill Kinney was reviewing the collected data on the memory card.

"I don't know what you guys are looking for," he said, "but this is pretty uniform, and about ten feet down. That help?"

"Man, you have no idea," Mike answered. Dr. Nolan illuminated him with his flashlight, his smile stretching from ear to ear.

"Good work, gentlemen," Dr. Nolan said. "What do you say we call it a night."

They pushed the radar device back to Bill's truck. It took all four of them to lift it into the bed. They were all exhausted.

"Son of a bitch. Under the floor," Mike said. "Now we've got them."

"Not quite yet," Dr. Nolan reminded him. "One final nail. Then we're done."

Bill Kenney drove them back to the clinic and dropped them off, receiving their deep appreciation. Jed put a call out to his team.

"We're done. You all did great. Now head home and warm up." He handed the radio to Dr. Nolan. "Until next time, Doc. Always a pleasure." He drove out of sight, leaving Dr. Nolan and Mike alone.

"Almost finished, Mike. You ready for this?" Dr. Nolan asked.

"Sometimes, I just want to kill someone with my bare hands," Mike said. "For what they did. But it's not people, it's a thing. I want to kill this thing."

"We're going to," Dr. Nolan assured him. "What time do you want to start?"

"Noon. I'll meet you here. Eileen has to get some kind of scan tomorrow morning. See where we're at."

"Noon it is," Dr. Nolan nodded. "And if everything goes as planned, we're just about to unleash the hounds of hell."

39

MAYOR TILLIS HUNG UP THE PHONE in his office, his face flaming red. It had not been a good week. There had been the clinic fire, the suicide of Lenny Darden, and now an angry call from a California law firm. Their conversation had been decidedly one-sided. The city had been threatened with an injunction and a potential lawsuit if Dr. Nolan set foot on their property.

The mayor did not have the slightest idea what was going on, but the intended intimidation had been successful. He was sweating heavily when he made his way through the building to the sheriff's office. He wanted nothing to do with lawyers.

"Sheriff in?" he asked, not waiting for an answer. He opened the door without invitation.

Sheriff Dent did not like the mayor on a personal level. He only tolerated the man on the basis of political necessity, and could only suffer him in small doses.

"Mayor, you seem excited. Have a seat," the sheriff said.

"What the hell is Dr. Nolan doing!?" he demanded.

Sheriff Dent looked at his watch. Anything that annoyed the mayor gave him great pleasure. "Probably taking care of patients," the sheriff answered dryly. "Kind of goes with the title of town doctor."

"I just got off the phone with some law firm threatening to sue my ass off if Dr. Nolan trespassed on their land. What's he up to?"

Sheriff Dent showed no emotion, and calculated his response to be as vague as possible. "Oh, he's been doing some testing around the Bottoms for bug spray, or something. I haven't heard all the details," he answered.

"Well, these guys are serious. And mad. They don't want any publicity. They said Nolan called them asking permission, and they turned him down. He's got no business on their property. You've got to talk to him."

Sheriff Dent nodded his head. He was enjoying the fact that he was much more informed about the recent events than the mayor.

"I can talk to him, but, you know, when he gets revved up about something, it's hard to rope him in. He feels like he's doing what's best for the town."

"He should just keep to his own business," the mayor said.

"Kind of is his business, keeping folks safe," Sheriff Dent offered, trying not to smile. "But I'll have a word with him. Helps that he's only two blocks away."

"And tell him he'll be arrested if he sets one foot on that land. It's officially off-limits. We can't afford a lawsuit."

Sheriff Dent leaned forward and folded his hands together on the desk. "You seriously want me to arrest Dr. Nolan if he trespasses on some vacant lot? Then he'll probably sue you."

"Well, it's the law, isn't it? You have to do your job," the mayor said.

"Lots of ways to do a job," the sheriff pointed out to him. "Let's just start with a good, old-fashioned chat. That okay with you?"

The mayor stood up, aware that Sheriff Dent was losing his patience. He was still sweating. "Okay. Just don't let this go any further," he said, backing toward the door. "There's already been too much trouble around here this week." He went back down the hall to his own office, not feeling at all reassured.

Sheriff Dent slowly stood and went outside. It was a clear, cold day, but the sun actually felt good against his face. Instead of driving, he walked to the clinic and took a seat in the waiting area.

"Business or pleasure?" Amanda asked from her office-kitchen.

"Just a brief social visit," the sheriff said, looking around. "I love what you've done with the place."

Amanda laughed. "It's a challenge, but we're still seeing patients," she said. "And they're starting to work on the clinic next week."

"Good. Good," the sheriff said. "Doc in a better mood?"

Amanda peeked behind her shoulder and lowered her voice. "He's just dead tired, is all. I think we're all worn down right now."

Sheriff Dent nodded. He knew exactly what she meant.

Dr. Nolan came out of the exam room and handed Amanda a chart.

"Have a minute?" Sheriff Dent asked, tipping his head toward the exit.

"I never turn down people carrying guns." Dr. Nolan laughed. They went outside and walked a few feet away from the building.

"You should change your name to Shit-storm Nolan," the sheriff suggested. "Mayor was just in my office. He wants you arrested if you keep stirring things up. He got a call from some lawyer about you."

Dr. Nolan was smiling. "That didn't take long," he said. "I called them about testing the empty lot just east of Mike's and Eileen's place. They weren't very accommodating."

"Well, now they warned the mayor to keep you away, or there'll be legal action. He's scared to death."

Dr. Nolan turned to face the other man and met his eyes. "We know where to look now," he told the sheriff. "I'm meeting Mike there at noon. This is what we've been looking for."

"Goddamn it, Sean. I'm getting squeezed from all sides here. Every day you keep asking for more time. I don't know if there is any more."

"I know. I know. You've been great. But I can't let this go. Not now."

The sheriff looked at him for a long minute. "Noon? That gives me an hour to think things over. I sure as hell don't want to put handcuffs on you," he said.

"It won't stop anything if you do, but I understand," Dr. Nolan said. "All it can do is slow things down and put more people at risk. I don't think either of us wants that."

"Dr. Sean 'Shit-storm' Nolan," the sheriff repeated, then shook his head. "I think I'll get you a name tag with that on it for Christmas."

"Be an honor to wear it," Dr. Nolan said. "I guess I'll see you in about two hours?"

"Guess so," the sheriff said. "You might have an attorney on standby to bail you out."

"Thanks for the advice, Bob. See you soon," Dr. Nolan said. He shook Sheriff Dent's hand and gave him a smile, then went back to the clinic.

"What was that about?" Amanda asked, feeling left out.

"Just guy talk," Dr. Nolan answered. "See if you can get Mike or Eileen on the phone. Sooner is better."

He saw one patient before Amanda could get Mike on the line. Dr. Nolan retreated to the bathroom again. He explained his talk with the sheriff, the mayor's involvement, and the threat from the landlord group.

"Screw them all." Mike laughed. "And get this! There's no cancer on Eileen's scan! It's gone! They said they can do an easier kind of chemo. Just to be safe."

"Jesus, that's great news," Dr. Nolan told him. He did not want any more pins on his map. "Tell her congratulations from me."

"We're going to celebrate tonight," Mike said. "Maybe two things. You're not quitting, are you?"

"No," Dr. Nolan said.

"Good. Then we're still on," Mike promised. "I'll see you there."

Dr. Nolan hung up. He looked in the mirror, noting the dark circles under his eyes, then checked his hair. If he was going to have mugshots taken, he wanted to look presentable.

There were five more patients to be seen in the morning schedule. With no walk-in emergencies, Dr. Nolan finished with ten minutes to spare. At the last second, he gave in to common sense. He looked up the number for a local attorney, wrote the number down, and placed it in his wallet.

"I'll be on my cell phone if you need me," he told Cat. She nodded, but said nothing. Even she seemed to be acting oddly. Out at his car, he took a deep breath, then drove down to the Bottoms. He parked in front of the property they had visited the night before. The sheriff and one of his patrol officers were already there.

"What a coincidence," Dr. Nolan told Sheriff Dent. "Imagine running into you twice in one day."

"Sean, nice to see you," the sheriff remarked. "You have business here?"

"I believe I do," Dr. Nolan said. "If I remember correctly, something to do with a toxic waste site that's killing people."

"What the hell?" the deputy said. He knew nothing other than the request he had received for backup duty.

"You remember our talk? The mayor doesn't want you on this property. You plan on going on this property?" the sheriff asked.

"I thought I might." Dr. Nolan smiled. "It seems like a lovely place to dig a hole."

Before the sheriff could respond, a car horn began honking from down the road. It was Eileen in the farm truck. Mike was close behind her on a large, orange Kubota digging machine. He pulled up onto the edge of the property and stopped, letting the diesel engine idle. He sat in the seat, looking down, his smile growing.

Now there were more trucks and cars pulling in along the road. Old Ed Freeland arrived, got out, set up his canvass chair, pulled out his shotgun, and sat down right next to Dr. Nolan.

"Ed, nice to see you," the sheriff said. "Is that cannon loaded?"

"Bird shot and rock salt," Mr. Freeland answered.

Four more of the old patients that had guarded the clinic walked up. They were armed as well. Jed Marcus showed up with a friend, then Bill Tillis, then more and more cars until there was no longer any room to park. Slowly, a single-file line of people formed along the border of the property. Cat, Cat's husband, Evie, and Amanda were among them.

Dr. Nolan fought back tears. He looked up at Mike.

"Made a few phone calls," he explained, still smiling.

Dr. Nolan could not speak.

"What do you want to do, Sheriff?" the deputy asked.

Sheriff Dent looked right, and then left. He knew almost everyone there by their first name.

"Well, my orders were to keep Dr. Nolan off this land," he said slowly. "The mayor didn't mention any other names. And I don't see any 'No Trespassing' signs. So, I guess I'll just follow orders and keep my eye on the doc here. You got other things to do, Mike?"

"A little digging," he said. "If you'll excuse me." He drove onto the property, located the painted markers etched on the ground, leveled his base pads, and began shoveling dirt.

"You can supervise from here, right, Doc?" The sheriff smiled.

"And obey the law at the same time," Dr. Nolan noted. Some of the women who had shown up were passing out coffee.

"Turned out to be quite a party," the sheriff said. "And here I thought you didn't have any friends. It just goes to show."

Dr. Nolan nodded, looking out over the scene. There were over a hundred people now in line.

"I didn't know about his," he admitted. "I thought I was going to spend the afternoon in the big house. Mike and Eileen did this."

"They're good people," the sheriff said. "Looks like we have a bunch of good people."

"Oh, shit," the deputy said. "Don't look, but here comes the mayor."

Mayor Tillis had to park his car out on the roadway. He headed directly for Sheriff Dent.

"Goddamn it, Bob! Arrest him!" he demanded, pointing a finger at Dr. Nolan.

"He's standing on a county road, mayor. What would you like me to charge him with?" the sheriff asked.

Mayor Tillis stood blinking. He noticed one of his office staff in the crowd.

"Then arrest him!" he shouted, pointing out Mike.

"He's busy right now," Sheriff Dent informed him.

"Goddamn it! I'll have your job! You can't just ignore orders!" the mayor threatened.

"Only the city council can fire me," the sheriff explained. "And most of them are here helping. Why don't you go take a vote, you little asshole?"

Even the deputy laughed, then thought better of it.

Mayor Tillis, though it seemed impossible, became even redder in the face. He turned, pushed through the line of people, and retreated to his car. He drove back to City Hall and just sat in his office, waiting. He wasn't sure for what.

After an hour, the sound made by the digging machine suddenly changed dramatically. There was a screeching noise, almost like a woman screaming. Mike repositioned his machine, then carefully removed two, three, four more buckets of earth. He climbed down, examined the deep trench, then waved to the sheriff and Dr. Nolan.

"Is this legal?" Dr. Nolan asked.

"You're in my custody," Sheriff Dent explained. "Let's take a look."

They walked up to where Mike was waiting.

"All that work," he said. "Does this answer your question?"

Dr. Nolan and Sheriff Dent examined what Mike had uncovered. There were rows and rows of rusted transformer casings visible in just the small area that had been exposed. The radar images had indicated a target zone of five thousand square feet. It was possible that hundreds of the PCB-containing electrical units had been buried.

It was the end of their search, but there was no elation, no relief, no feeling of triumph. Dr. Nolan just felt sad, and tired, and ashamed that people had died because of greed. This was what had killed his own wife.

"Good job, Mike," he said. "This is ground zero. No need to dig anymore. Our part in this is over."

Mike nodded. He left his machine in place and walked back to Eileen, giving her a big hug. They could finally answer the questions being directed from people in the crowd. Word spread like a windblown flame that they were living in the center of a toxic waste site.

Not knowing or understanding the health implications was the quickest way to invite panic. Dr. Nolan went toward the center of the group and spoke in a loud voice.

"This southern part of the Bottoms is contaminated with PCBs, a cancer-causing agent that was banned years ago. If you have city or river water, there is no immediate risk. If you have wells, stop using them for drinking or cooking. Only use bottled water for now. Tomorrow we'll get the government involved and try to sort this out."

"Did this kill my husband?" a woman shouted out.

"It's possible," Dr. Nolan told her. "It probably caused my wife's cancer. But at least now we can stop it. That's what matters the most right now. The past we deal with later. So, please go home and wait till tomorrow. We'll find a way to address all your questions. And thank you for helping us end this."

The crowd did not disperse quickly. Fear, anger, and uncertainty held small groups together for a time, but slowly, one by one, they began to move back to their cars and go home. It was the ending point of the mystery, but only the start of crafting a solution. The disaster had been set in motion in just hours. The remedy would probably take years.

Dr. Nolan tracked down Amanda and Cat.

"Thank you for being here," he said. "But we're not finished. I need you to call the EPA, the Army Corp of Engineers, and the Shoreline Management Agency. I want them all here at noon tomorrow. We can use the board-room at City Hall."

It was 4:30 p.m. With no time margin to spare, Cat and Amanda headed back to the clinic to make phone calls.

"So, now the real work begins," Sheriff Dent said. "This is what you meant when you said it would be like a bomb going off?"

Dr. Nolan sighed. He just wanted to hug his daughters and go home.

"We just saved a lot of lives," he told the sheriff. "But we may have just killed the town."

40

EILEEN HAD COMPLETED HER RADIATION THERAPY, and would not begin chemo for a few weeks. With the sudden gift of free time, she collected all the maps and lab data, setting up a display easel in the boardroom at City Hall for Dr. Nolan to use. Mike was at her side to help, and by noon everything was in place.

Word of the waste site had worked its way through the community, and when Dr. Nolan arrived, a small crowd of thirty to forty people had assembled on the sidewalk. Luckily, to this point there had been no media involvement or press coverage, but he knew that would soon change. People were scared.

His intention had been to brief the various government agencies with local authority first, but the townspeople deserved to know what they had discovered. It was their home, their lives, and their children that were affected.

"Let them all in," he told Sheriff Dent. "I want the agency people up front, but anyone else that wishes to hear this is welcome. No more secrets."

"You sure about this, Sean? I don't have enough officers for any kind of disturbance."

"The quickest way to get people mad is to lie to them," Dr. Nolan explained. "They deserve the truth."

"Okay. It's your show," the sheriff said. He went out and began to direct people into the hall.

The EPA, Army Corp of Engineers, and the Shoreline Management Agency had all sent representatives as requested, but knew nothing of the subject.

Dr. Nolan introduced himself, thanked them, and placed them in the front row of chairs. The room was now filled, with the back area and aisles crowded as well. Sheriff Dent and the mayor were standing near the entrance door.

"This is a sad day for our town," Dr. Nolan began, "but it also marks the beginning of how we rebuild and move forward. This is not the first tragedy that Woodhaven has faced, and the history of this community has proven it to be resilient and unbreakable. Those qualities will be tested again over the next months and years, because what we're facing now is an enormous challenge."

He directed his attention to the men in the front row.

"It recently became apparent that the cancer rate was excessively high in this area. With help from a lot of local people, we were able to identify a toxin in the water and soil, in part of the Bottoms, and yesterday, we finally identified the source. After the flood in 1948, one of the companies that had been wiped out decided to bury their problem, and now we've inherited it. A large area has been contaminated with PCBs. And worse, it's slowly working its way to the river."

He paused a moment for the information to be processed. Everyone remained silent.

"We have with us today members of the three local agencies that will have to guide us through the proper response to this. Until now, none of them knew the reason they were invited. Now they do. And we are all aware how slowly government moves at times, how bureaucratic red tape can lead to one delay after another. In this case, that will not be acceptable. I do not know these men, but I trust that their intentions will be honorable."

The three men nodded in response.

"The map provided shows the area affected," Dr. Nolan went on, "and the test results show the levels of contamination we've found so far. Yesterday afternoon we uncovered the dump site. If something does not start to happen here within the next twenty-four hours, I personally will call the governor, the local papers, the local TV stations, the local radio stations, and every national news agency that will speak to me."

The townspeople erupted into spontaneous applause, with whistles and shouts. Dr. Nolan waited for the celebration to fade away.

"I apologize for framing this as a threat," he said, again looking at the visitors. "But that's just what it is. We've had people die here, and more people are at risk. So figure it out, and do it fast. No delay will be acceptable."

The audience applauded again.

Dr. Nolan stood aside and motioned an offer to speak to the EPA emissary. His name was Arthur Campbell, and he did not look pleased. He was well aware that they were victims of a squeeze play.

"Good day to you all," he said, trying to make sweeping eye contact with the crowd. "This is all brand-new to us. I can promise we will review this information and go to the dump site today. There will be no delays. Between the three agencies, a plan will be put together to address this, and the response will be immediate. I give you my word on that, and I have a feeling Dr. Nolan will make certain I keep it."

Again there was clapping, but the enthusiasm was tempered by skepticism. Mr. Campbell had exhausted his available platitudes. He walked over to study the map, and was quickly joined by his two associates. They were foreigners in the room, and clearly uncomfortable.

Dr. Nolan was satisfied for the moment.

"Everyone, please," he said. "Now that we have their promise to step in, let's give them a chance to get started. We will get information out in the local paper, and I'm sure the mayor's office will help keep everyone up to date on what's happening. Thank you all."

The room began to empty. The three government envoys were now reviewing the volumes of lab reports, relieved the public event was over.

"Nice speech," Sheriff Dent told him with a faint smile. "I had a high school football coach that used to give talks like that. You think it will do any good?"

Dr. Nolan shrugged. "We'll know soon enough," he said. "It would be pretty dangerous for them to sit on their hands now. We just turned up the temperature a little."

"I guess," Sheriff Dent agreed. "They want me to take them out to the dig site. You want to ride along?"

Dr. Nolan sat down on a vacant chair. "Not really, Bob. My part in all this is pretty much done," he said. "I'm tired. I've short-changed my practice, and according to my staff, I'm ill-tempered and almost unbearable. I've got to step away."

"But, you're the lead on this," the sheriff argued. "You're the only one who understands all this."

"You can handle this," Dr. Nolan told him. "This is going to become a logistical nightmare and a feeding frenzy for the press. I'm not doing interviews or commentary. I don't even want my name mentioned. This isn't in my job description."

"Wasn't in mine either," the sheriff sighed. "These guys better step up. I'd like to get my town back."

Arthur Campbell politely interrupted, holding six pages of analytical data.

"Thanks for setting us up like that," he said, almost allowing himself to smile. "What's this second spill site? The benzene contamination?"

"Good question," Dr. Nolan told him. "It's small, local-ized, and in an area where a chemical plant had a building in the '40s. We've shown a cancer link there, too, but nothing in comparison to the PCB exposure."

"You did a lot of good work here, Doctor," Mr. Campbell said. "This was a lot of time and money."

"And a whole bunch of good people helped me," Dr. Nolan told him. "It was a community effort."

"Well, I'm impressed. But why didn't you notify us sooner? Give us a heads-up."

"No offense," Dr. Nolan said. "But we did this a lot faster than you would have. Our incentive was personal. And until all the dots were connected, we weren't too confident there would be an expeditious response."

"We'll prioritize the PCB site," he assured Dr. Nolan and Sheriff Dent, "but down the line, we need to find out more about this other spill zone. You said there was a chemical company there? You recall the name?"

"Dukayne," Dr. Nolan answered. "They're still in business."

"And always in our active file," Mr. Campbell told him. "This wouldn't be the first time we've had an issue with some of their business practices. You have any contact with them?"

"No. We just tracked them down through old tax records. See that blond lady over there? She's my number one detective. And she did all this while fighting a cancer probably caused by the PCBs."

"I see what you mean about this being personal," he commented. "Well, Sheriff, you feel like taking us out to the site? I think it's best if we can show the locals that we're serious about this."

"Whenever you're ready," Sheriff Dent told him. "We'll even turn on the flashing lights for you. Add to the excitement."

Mr. Campbell shook hands with Dr. Nolan and headed out with the other two agency officials.

"You think this will get them moving?" Eileen asked, coming over to where Dr. Nolan was sitting.

"I actually do," he answered. "I think Campbell from EPA is a good guy."

"I believe what I see," Eileen said. "What do you want to do with the map and the lab reports?"

"They can have the lab stuff," Dr. Nolan said. "But the map belongs to us. That's what started all this."

"I can keep it in the office," Eileen offered. "I kind of got used to it on the wall. Made me feel good that we weren't forgetting all those people."

"And Megan," Dr. Nolan added.

"Most of all, Megan," Eileen said.

Dr. Nolan smiled at his sister-in-law. It was the strongest bond between them.

"You and Mike kept me going," he told her. "Helping with the girls. All the research. The cold, rainy weekends."

"And you kept us going," she said. "And now we've got to keep these other guys going. It's never-ending."

"Well, that's a depressing note to end on," Dr. Nolan said. He stood up and hugged Eileen. "I've got patients to see. And then I'm going home with my daughters, with no armed guards on duty."

"And I'm going to go see what the government boys think of the hole I put them in." Mike laughed. "I think it's deep enough now that they can't get out of it."

"Let's hope so, Mike," Dr. Nolan said. "Let's hope you're right."

41

AT TEN THE NEXT MORNING, FOUR trucks from Clark County Fencing drove through town and headed for the transformer burial site. By noon, a six-foot-tall cyclone barrier had been set in place to isolate the area. Triangular yellow hazardous material signs were fixed along the barricade every few feet.

In the early afternoon, a half dozen sealable container trucks arrived. Plastic sheeting was then spread out to prevent additional spills, and a much larger excavator began to remove the leaking metal cylinders. There were hundreds of them, and as each one was placed in the HazMat trucks, the source of future pollution diminished. That was the easy part.

While the immediate removal of the toxic waste eased tensions in the town, Dr. Nolan knew that eliminating it from the soil and water was next to impossible. The greatest challenge would be to minimize the exposure risk to those in the target zone, and to slow, or stop it from reaching the Columbia River. The problems facing the government agencies were massively complex, and he was glad not to be involved.

The EPA had assumed the primary role in the cleanup program, and had issued a press release that mentioned the town doctor had been pivotal in identifying and exposing the dump site. And that was the beginning of a tidal wave, a tsunami of phone calls to Dr. Nolan's office from media outlets both local and national. Patients had difficulty reaching the clinic, and Amanda was forced to wear a Bluetooth headset. She even answered calls when using the outdoor bathroom facilities.

It quickly became a comedy routine. As he came out of every exam room, she would update the growing list of requests.

"How about the *Seattle Times*?" she asked.

"No."

"Now I've got ABC, CBS, and NBC?" she said.

"No, no, and no," he answered.

"How about AP or CNN?"

"No. Not now. Not ever," he answered.

"How about the high school paper?" she asked on one occasion.

He considered it for a moment. "No. Have them talk to Sheriff Dent. He's my publicity agent."

Dr. Nolan knew that the typical hot news cycle was a forty-eight-hour phenomenon, and on schedule, the calls began to stop after the second day. He had even been ambushed in the parking lot by local television reporters, one wanting to know if the firebombing of his clinic was a related issue. He would smile and wave but had vowed not to say one word to anyone.

Sheriff Dent had called daily to thank him for all the referrals, but his tone was disingenuous at best. On one occasion he made a veiled threat of bodily harm if Dr. Nolan persisted. In full chivalrous form, Dr. Nolan blamed Amanda and hung up on him.

"You could be famous," Amanda informed him.

"I'm already famous," he answered. "Just ask my patients. They think I walk on water."

"And we think you walk in water," Cat corrected him. "Remember?" She was referring to the morning of the fire when they liberated their equipment from the flooded building.

"Which reminds me," he asked. "When do we get our clinic back? This downsizing is a pain in the ass."

"Next week," Amanda announced. "New flooring, paint, and we move in. Kind of a late Christmas present."

"That's worth celebrating," Dr. Nolan told his staff. The holidays had come and gone, and for most of the people in town, the prevailing atmosphere had been somber. The celebration of family and friends managed to prevail, but the ambiguity over the town's future hung over them like an angry sky. Property values had dropped precipitously in the wake of the news coverage. People could not sell their homes, and, without that equity, could not afford to move elsewhere. Even planned business expansion in the area had come to a grinding halt. No one knew what to expect.

Dr. Nolan and his daughters had spent Christmas Day with the Carson family. The sum total of his shopping had indeed been limited to gift cards, but they were a welcome relief to his girls. They not only understood and accepted the time constraint he had been under, but were more than thankful he had not picked out clothes or jewelry for them. Their esthetic inclinations had long since diverged.

The overall tenor of their Christmas had been quite different. While the monetary foundation of the Carson Farm and business had been damaged, they were much more focused on the better, safer future, and rightfully proud of how they had helped unravel the cause and identify the source of the toxic spill. They had not been passive observers, and they did not feel like victims any longer. They had regained control of their lives.

As for the cleanup process, a staggering amount of progress had taken place in just weeks. After removal of the leaking PCB transformers, the EPA had excavated the entire property to a depth of twenty-five feet and exchanged the contaminated soil with ash residue left over from the Mt. St. Helens volcanic eruption. All existing wells in the southern Bottoms had been capped and welded shut, and freshwater supplies were being trucked in twice a week for the local residents. They had even assisted with a federal grant to help the city expand existing underground water systems to every home and farm.

The EPA had also repeated test data on every parcel of land in the floodplain. Their results duplicated Dr. Nolan's studies, but now they were official, and could be used as evidence. They finally completed and defined the severity of the toxin levels. And, as Dr. Nolan had feared, there was no way to remove it from the environment. Like DDT, only time would erase its effects.

Since the health risks were an exposure-level variable, the only realistic advice was to inform the local population that frequent medical exams and early reporting of any unusual symptoms was recommended policy. There was really nothing else to do. And since the owners of the defunct electrical company were long dead, there was no one to pursue legally. There would be no lawsuits, no settlement, and no compensation for damages. People had died, and had been made ill, had been financially harmed, and there was no recourse.

As for the Army Corp of Engineers and the Shoreline Management Agency, they were still arguing over exactly what to do. The closest consensus had been to dig a thirty-foot trench along the far western border of the dike, and to pour a cement barrier with a catch basin. Contaminated water would be captured, pumped out through a purification filtering system, and only then be released into the drainage culverts. It was still a work in progress, but the paramount mandate of their involvement was to protect the river. They would ultimately be forced into action.

Two weeks into January, Arthur Campbell from the EPA requested a meeting with Dr. Nolan. Finally back in their home clinic, he once again had a private office that did not feature a toilet and bathtub. Dr. Nolan was grateful for the swift response and decisive actions taken by the agency, and gave a genuine, warm welcome to his visitor.

"I'm truly impressed," Dr. Nolan told him. "This almost restores my faith in the government being able to get anything done in a timely fashion."

"Well, I wouldn't get used to it just yet," Mr. Campbell warned him. "Our budget to deal with these types of issues is getting cut to ribbons. Makes me glad I'm close to retirement. Pretty soon we'll just hand out Band-Aids."

Dr. Nolan nodded. He was painfully aware that nearly every bureau dealing with environment concerns had been stripped of power and resources.

"Well, at least here, you're a superhero," Dr. Nolan said. "How many other toxic dump sites do you think are out there somewhere?"

"Hundreds," Mr. Campbell answered. "Thousands. Mining, dredging, coal, petroleum, chemicals. No one will ever know. Just like no one knew about this until you came along. Has to make you proud."

"Just relieved," Dr. Nolan said. "I don't know what I feel right now. Did you find anything about that other pollution site?"

Mr. Campbell gave a constrained laugh. "Absolutely nothing," he admitted. "But you were right again. It's a small area, and only water sources were contaminated to three or four farms. All of them stopped using well water years ago. We interviewed who we could, and called Dukayne Chemical, but no one knows anything. It's a dead end."

"Except for the fact there were seven or eight cancer cases concentrated there that could have been caused by benzene," Dr. Nolan reminded him. "There's no risk from soil exposure?"

"Not now," Mr. Campbell said. "Pretty much degraded to safe levels. I'm sorry, but we don't have the manpower to keep looking."

"I understand," Dr. Nolan said. "So, you're about done with your part of this?"

"Yep. Came to say goodbye," Mr. Campbell said. He stood up and offered Dr. Nolan his hand. "You ever think about changing professions, give me a call. You're a pretty fair investigator."

Dr. Nolan smiled, then shook his head. "I think I'll give this town another twenty years or so," he said. "No other doctor would be dumb enough to take over."

"I think they're damn lucky they have you," Mr. Campbell said. "You take care."

Dr. Nolan watched the older man leave. The PCB site had been cleaned up, and now there was nothing to do but wait and watch over the local population. It was at least a partial sense of closure. But the other site was still an unanswered question, an open riddle.

He dialed Sheriff Dent. "You busy tonight, Bob?"

"You asking me out?" the sheriff responded.

"Kind of," Dr. Nolan explained. "I'll buy dinner if you drive me out to see Mrs. Darden. She may be a little more social if you're along."

"What's this about?" Sheriff Dent asked.

"Oh, just unfinished business," Dr. Nolan said. "It's driving me crazy about this other chemical spill. I keep thinking about what Lenny did, and I don't know the why of it! It makes no sense. What pushed him that far?"

There was a long pause before the sheriff answered. "It bothers me too," he said at last. "I haven't had a good night's sleep since this all started. I just want things to settle."

"I do too," Dr. Nolan said. "But I've got to try and talk to her. If she won't, then at least I tried."

"Okay, but I want a steak, and no goddamn lectures on plugging up my arteries," the sheriff laughed.

"No lectures," Dr. Nolan promised. "Swing by about five thirty and I should be done."

"It's a date, Doc. I just hope it doesn't start any rumors."

42

DR. NOLAN ASKED EILEEN TO SUPERVISE his daughters for a few hours after work. Sheriff Dent picked him up at the clinic, then drove north on the freeway to the new restaurant along the Columbia River in Kalama. He ordered a New York steak with a baked potato and sour cream, and there were no lectures. Dr. Nolan settled for halibut fish and chips, with only a small serving of guilt.

They did not speak much during dinner, each of them isolated in their own thoughts. They had become closer on a professional level, but a social friendship was still at an awkward infancy. Most of the meal was spent watching large cargo ships navigate past them on the river.

"You want me to pay half?" Sheriff Dent asked when the bill came.

"Not this time." Dr. Nolan smiled. "This is for all the hell I put you through in the last two months. Kind of a thank-you dinner."

"Then I should have ordered dessert," Sheriff Dent remarked. "Or a bottle of champagne."

"No way. You're the driver, and we're in a police car," Dr. Nolan pointed out. "I don't want you weaving all over the road. I feel conspicuous enough already. Everyone we pass looks at me like I'm some kind of criminal."

"Well," Sheriff Dent laughed, "if the shoe fits..."

"Okay. Okay. I deserve that." Dr. Nolan laughed. "We'll keep tonight low-key. Just a nice, friendly conversation."

"We'll see," the sheriff said. "Getting a sentence out of Mrs. Darden is a hard pull."

It was dark now. They drove back to Woodhaven, crossed the railroad tracks, and found their way to the Darden Farm. There were only a few lights on in the old house.

Sheriff Dent took the lead. He knocked softly, then louder, and then the locking chain rattled in response. Mrs. Darden opened the door slightly, glanced up at him, then looked down.

"It's late," she said.

"We only need a moment, ma'am," Sheriff Dent explained. "Just a few questions. Won't take more than a minute."

Mrs. Darden was already trying to close the door, but the old farm dog, back indoors after Lenny's death, pushed its head into the opening and blocked her efforts. The sheriff knelt down. He petted the dog, gave her a treat, and used his left shoulder to gently create a wider opening. Mrs. Darden lost ground and backed up a step.

"Please, ma'am. Dr. Nolan and I only need a few moments of your time."

"All right, then," she acquiesced. Backing up a few more steps, she turned, went into the living room, and sat on the edge of the sofa, staring at the floor, her hands in her lap.

Sheriff Dent closed the door, then settled into an armchair across from her. Dr. Nolan joined her on the couch, but kept a space between them. He was studying her in the dim light. It had been years since he had seen her as a patient, and she was much smaller now, almost tiny. She avoided their eyes, only looking down. There was an accentuated curve of her upper spine, the beginning of a hunch back, and her hands were bony and gnarled at the joints.

"Thank you for seeing us, Frances," Dr. Nolan said, using her first name to put her at ease. "I don't know if you remember me, but I used to take care of you and your husband."

She nodded her head. "I remember," she said. "Farm switched insurance."

Sheriff Dent stayed occupied with petting the old dog and did not enter the conversation. He was just an observer.

"I think it's been close to twenty years," Dr. Nolan reminded her. He wanted her moving toward the past, to gently direct her memories back in time.

"Twenty years," she repeated, almost a whisper.

"I was sorry to hear about Lenny," Dr. Nolan continued. "How long had you been married?"

"Fifty-four years," Mrs. Darden answered. There was no emotion when she spoke, and no expression on her face. She reminded Dr. Nolan of patients with Parkinson's disease, but she had no tremor. She was merely a prisoner of a deep and profound depression, long withdrawn to another place.

"That's a lifetime," Dr. Nolan said. "I know this must be a hard time for you, but something very important has happened in the town. You probably heard about it, but a dangerous chemical was found in some areas around here. And when your old well was tested, the results were positive. One of the toxins was in your water."

Mrs. Darden nodded, but she clasped her hands more tightly. "The water was bad. Long time ago," she said.

"When I talked to Lenny, he seemed angry at me for asking about it," Dr. Nolan told her. "Do you know why he was upset?"

Mrs. Darden glanced up at him for a moment. "He was always angry," she said. "At everything."

"But people only get angry when they feel they've been wronged, or if they're frightened," Dr. Nolan explained. "Was Lenny afraid of something? Of someone finding out about the chemicals?"

Mrs. Darden scooted up further on the sofa, averting her eyes again. "He should have been ashamed," Mrs. Darden said, her voice barely perceptible. It was the beginning of an open bridge, an invitation to travel further. Dr. Nolan turned toward her and leaned forward, closing the distance between them ever so slightly.

"I know about Amy," he told her. "And I think I know what happened to her." He kept his words soft and consoling. It was a risk, but there was no other viable option.

"Amy? She was my angel," Mrs. Darden said. She sat frozen, without making a sound, and then the tears began to flow down her cheeks. The pain it released had not diminished in the five decades since the death of her daughter. The anguish, the burning depth of it had never eased.

Dr. Nolan reached out and gently took her right hand, but waited until the tears slowed. There was nothing to be gained by pushing her beyond tolerance.

"The type of cancer that caused Amy's illness was because of the chemicals in the water," he told her. "It usually doesn't happen to young children, but in Amy, it acted like poison."

Mrs. Darden gave a single nod of her head, then pointed toward an old framed photograph of her baby daughter on the bookshelf. Dr. Nolan stood, brought the picture to her, and placed it in the old woman's lap. This time he sat down closer to her.

Mrs. Darden drew her fingers over the outer border of the image, then touched her daughter's face as if the likeness was real, a mother caressing her child.

"Lenny knew," she said finally. "When Amy got sick, he knew. He tested the well and proved they did it."

Dr. Nolan shared a look with Sheriff Dent. It was as close to an explanation as they had ever come. "Who poisoned Amy?" Dr. Nolan asked. "Who was to blame for making her sick?"

For the first time, Mrs. Darden raised her eyes and held his gaze. When she spoke, there was no anger, no malice, just a statement of fact.

"The chemical company," she said. "One of their big tanks collapsed during the flood, and all of it washed onto the farm. Lenny knew. He warned them, and they said not to worry. Then Amy got sick."

"Did Lenny tell them about Amy?" Dr. Nolan asked.

"Oh, they knew, all right," Mrs. Darden went on, now almost eager to tell the story, to lift the burden of it from her shoulders. "But then they offered Lenny money. A lot of it. And that's all he could see. He traded my angel for money."

She hugged the photograph against her chest and closed her eyes, trying to shut out the memories, to bring her daughter closer to her.

"I have two daughters," Dr. Nolan reminded her. "They were just little the last time you saw them. I can't begin to imagine the pain of losing one of them, what you've suffered all these years. I'm truly sorry."

Mrs. Darden nodded and managed the faintest trace of a smile, but it faded quickly. "It was just for money," she repeated. "To buy more land, other farms. Just business. We signed a paper not to tell anyone."

"And the other nearby farms. Did they get money too?" Dr. Nolan asked her.

She shook her head. "They never knew. Lenny didn't tell them. As long as he got the money, he didn't care about anyone else," she answered.

"Lenny understood that other people were at risk? That they could get sick?" Dr. Nolan asked.

"Didn't care," Mrs. Darden said, clearly ashamed of what her confession implied. "When we signed the legal forms, he said it was done, finished. Like Amy was never here. But it wasn't the end of anything. First the poison killed my baby, and then the money killed us. Just a different kind of poison. Slower."

Dr. Nolan squeezed her hand. In his career, he had rarely encountered a patient more subjugated by agony.

"Mrs. Darden. Frances. Would you be willing to tell your story to someone else.? To the authorities? There's still danger here. Other people could still be harmed by this."

"I will now that Lenny's gone," she told him. "I don't care about the farm or the money. If it can help someone, then yes, I'll tell what happened."

Dr. Nolan sighed. It was finally done. There were no more questions. He stood, helped Mrs. Darden to her feet, then he hugged her for a long moment.

"This will matter," he assured her. "It may even save other children. Thank you for telling us the truth. And if we can help with anything, all you have to do is ask. If good comes out of this, it's because of you." He knew the words were an inadequate show of gratitude, but wanted her to know her offer had value, that she still mattered.

She walked them to the door, the old dog at her side.

"I'll stop by tomorrow, ma'am, just to check on you," Sheriff Dent said. "And thank you for clearing this up. Dr. Nolan is right. It matters to a whole lotta folks. Good night."

He and Dr. Nolan walked back to his patrol car. They were halfway to the clinic before either of them spoke.

"Wow, that was a pretty good job of interrogating a witness," the sheriff said. "You are one hell of a detective. I can't believe they kept this a secret for all these years."

"And Mrs. Darden was right," Dr. Nolan said. "It killed them both. She's so depressed. I'm afraid she might hurt herself."

"I'll keep watch on her," Sheriff Dent promised. "I think this might be a good thing for her. A new start."

"Let's hope," Dr. Nolan said. "I might try to find out who her Kaiser doctor is. She could use a little medical help right now."

Sheriff Dent laughed. "You just can't stop, can you? Don't you have enough to do minding your own business?"

Dr. Nolan smiled and shrugged his shoulders. "The town is my business," he said. "Just like you. Everyone matters."

"I'll call the district attorney's office tomorrow morning and see if they want to have a chat with Dukayne Chemicals. Sounds like they've got some explaining to do. The locals won't be happy about being poisoned and lied to. Might get interesting. Old Lenny turned out to be a bigger piece of shit than I thought," the sheriff remarked.

"Money can do that to people. Or worse," Dr. Nolan said. He wondered how many people had been harmed over the years, and if it was truly over.

Sheriff Dent pulled into the parking lot next to Dr. Nolan's car. He shifted into park, but kept the engine running, the heater on full. The pine-scented air freshener hanging from the mirror was starting to bother Dr. Nolan's nose and eyes.

"Something I've been meaning to ask you," Sheriff Dent began, then hesitated, searching for words. He was staring straight ahead into the darkness.

"Jesus, what? Spit it out before this deodorizer suffocates me," Dr. Nolan complained.

The sheriff yanked it off the mirror, rolled down his window, and threw it out.

"I forgive you for littering," Dr. Nolan said. "Now, what's your question?"

Sheriff Dent was still struggling to frame his thoughts. "I ran into Jim Belson this morning," he finally began. "Says his brother came to see you and asked if you'd kill him. Put him out of his misery."

Dr. Nolan sighed heavily. Talking about patients violated their privacy and was strictly unethical. But, in this case, a family member had opened the door. Ed Belson was the patient he had diagnosed with the brain tumor, and his treatment was failing. He did not wish to suffer the indignity of losing command of his mind. Last week he had asked Dr. Nolan to help end his life.

"Ed Belson did ask for my help," Dr. Nolan admitted. "This comes up a lot more often than people realize. It's something we don't talk about much."

Sheriff Dent nodded his understanding. "So, did you help him?" he asked.

"Not as an active participant," Dr. Nolan said. "But I did offer hospice care with an aggressive tone, and I also wrote two prescriptions, that if taken together in large doses with alcohol, would probably put him to sleep. I gave him the power to make a decision."

"So, what's the difference?" the sheriff asked. "It's still you setting things in motion. How do you get comfortable with it?"

"I don't," Dr. Nolan admitted. "But sometimes, a patient is suffering so much, is in so much pain, that they've already moved beyond their humanity. The greater sin would be to prolong their death."

"So, you look at it as mercy. To end the torment?" Sheriff Dent asked.

"I suppose," Dr. Nolan answered. "I decided years ago that I couldn't be the hand that ended a life, but I could be the will behind it. The difference is just semantics. But it was the one way I could offer the last, final kindness to a patient and keep my own sanity. For the greater good."

Sheriff Dent sat thinking. "For the greater good," he repeated the words. "That I can understand. And I can see why it's not an easy thing."

Dr. Nolan sneezed once, then twice, then a third time. "Why so philosophical?" Dr. Nolan asked him.

"Oh, hell, I don't know," the sheriff answered. "I've known the Belson brothers my whole life. Good people die too soon, and bad people not soon enough. Doesn't make sense."

Dr. Nolan sneezed again. "If you want any of this to make sense, you're talking to the wrong person." Dr. Nolan laughed. Now his nose was running. "Goddamn it! You have any tissues?"

"Glove box. Help yourself," the sheriff said.

Dr. Nolan opened the compartment and found a travel-sized package of Kleenex. Next to it was a cardboard carton that originally held four baby bottle nipples. Only two remained.

"What the hell are these for?" Dr. Nolan asked. "Something you want to tell me?"

Sheriff Dent smiled momentarily, a long pause before he replied.

"Oh, those," he explained. "Once in a while I get a calf the mom won't take to. I have to step in. You know. For the greater good."

Dr. Nolan nodded. "So, we good?" he asked.

"Getting better every day," the sheriff said. "You're a good man, Sean. Thanks for answering my question."

"You want to kiss me good night?" Dr. Nolan laughed, opening the door.

"Not on the first date," Sheriff Dent answered. "Now get the hell out of my car."

43

DURING THE NEXT WEEK, MRS. DARDEN gave a deposition to the district attorney, and subpoenas were issued to company directors of Dukayne Chemical Corporation. Their public response was a total denial of any involvement in the matter, and a pledge to be fully transparent. Behind the scenes, there had been no threats to prosecute Mrs. Darden for violating her confidentiality agreement, but it remained a possibility.

The Army Corps of Engineers and the Shoreline Management Agency were still relegated to paper remedies, but were in civil discourse. A solution was promised by spring. And the town, slowly, day by day, was getting back to the business of living. There was less talk of the past, and much more debate about the future. There was no easy or immediate cure for the ailment, but the patient was expected to survive.

With his clinic fully restored, Dr. Nolan had completed a week of just dealing with medical issues. There had been no extracurricular activities, and his life was as normal as possible. It was Friday afternoon, the last patient had been evaluated, and his daughters were waiting to go home.

Just as he finished the last of his paperwork, the fax machine printed out five documents. He read them, nodded, and placed them into a manila envelope. Cienna and Aubriel were in his office. He dialed Eileen on his phone.

"Thank goodness you're home," he said, his tone implying urgency. "Something has happened. I've got papers you need to see right away. I'm sorry, but this can't wait."

She would be home waiting, mildly annoyed that he would not tell her anything in advance.

"Five minutes," Dr. Nolan said. "This is big."

He rushed his daughters into the car and drove straight to the Carson Farm. His expression was dark as he went into the house. He handed the envelope to Eileen without a word. Uncle Mike was also waiting. He stood leaning against the kitchen counter as Eileen sat down at the table.

She removed the papers, studying the pages carefully, a smile brightening her face. "Is this for real?" she asked.

"I told you it was big," Dr. Nolan said.

Mike was laughing. He had been a coconspirator from the beginning, but Cienna and Aubriel were totally confused.

"Tell me this is real," Eileen said again.

"It is," Dr. Nolan assured her. "Your chemo is on hold for a while. Mike has someone to watch the farm. I've got a substitute doctor covering the clinic. My neighbor is taking care of our place. And we're all going to Maui for two weeks."

"Oh, when, when?" Cienna and Aubriel were both asking together.

"Tomorrow morning," their father said. "I rented a beach house in Lahaina. It's time to rest and recuperate. The only medicine I could think of to make things better was to leave for a while."

Eileen turned to Mike. "And you knew about this? You can't ever keep a secret," she said.

"I've gotten better at covert operations," he laughed. He gave her a big hug.

"Sean, this is incredible," Eileen said, still in disbelief. "Thank you so much."

"No, thank you. Both of you," he said. "Now, go pack. I've got to get my girls organized. We'll see you in the morning."

Dr. Nolan and his daughters headed home. At the upper road, he turned the car and slowed as they drove past the security fence protecting the toxic waste site.

"Is that where it is?" Cienna asked. "Why does it look like that?"

The entire property was a light-gray rectangle of volcanic ash, in sharp contrast to the surrounding land.

"That's the wound it left," Dr. Nolan explained. "Now it will heal, and in time it will just be a tiny scar."

"And how long will that take?" she asked.

He sped up and drove toward the freeway.

"A lifetime," he told her. "Scars always last a lifetime."

End

About the Author

THE AUTHOR BEGAN HIS LITERARY PURSUITS at age four, focusing on inane, vapid rhyming poetry. With no job prospects and a crushing rejection from the Hallmark greeting card company, he then opted for public education. His writing shifted to free-verse prose and short stories and a first inept novel at fifteen. Penniless and chastised, the poet bowed to the sciences.

Entering medical training in 1980, E.W Johnson M.D., a board-certified internist, served as the town physician for a rural community in Southwest Washington until 2018. When he moved to Hawaii, part-time writing finally became a full-time obsession, with four novels completed within the first six months.

Unraveling is the first to reach print, with a sequel already waiting in the wings.

CPSIA information can be obtained
at www.ICGtesting.com
Printed in the USA
LVHW090409020620
657199LV00001B/96